THE HOUSE AT BLACK HEAD RIDGE

The Adam Barrie

Paranormal Investigations Book 1

First Published in the UK 2024 by Mirador Publishing

First edition: 2024

Any reference to real names and places are purely fictional and are constructs of the author. Any offence the references produce is unintentional and in no way reflects the reality of any locations or people involved.

ISBN: 978-1-915953-87-2

THE HOUSE AT BLACK HEAD RIDGE

BY

ELIZABETH REVILL

~ PROLOGUE ~

GULLS MEWLED AND CIRCLED ABOVE the rugged cliffs where the salty sea foamed and crashed against the rocks below. As the storm clouds rolled nearer, becoming blacker and heavier with their burden, the seabirds stopped their plaintive cries, and retreated to their perches on the side of the cliff. Colonies of black-legged kittiwakes had already returned to their ledges and their calls became subdued as the first flash of lightning streaked across the sky followed shortly by a growling rumble of thunder, resulting in a torrential downpour, where the rain attacked the land and the surface of the sea like daggers. The oppressive leaden sky seemed to close in as more clouds massed together as if in an attempt to attack and crush the earth.

The once golden sand, now sodden, was pitted with the marks of the dart-like driving rain and in the middle of the beach stood the lonely figure of a young woman. Her corn blonde hair streamed behind her in the aggressive wind, which plastered her fringe to her forehead. She was wearing a diaphanous white dress, tied in the middle with a blue sash. She raised her arms in supplication as if to embrace the storm and cried out. Tears streamed down her face, mingling with the raindrops and her dress stuck to her body revealing her womanly curves. She began to wade out into the angry water but stopped as a name was shrieked on the wind. The woman turned, waded back to shore and then ran back across the sand towards a cave, her footprints vanishing as soon as she lifted her feet. As she disappeared inside the cavernous gloom, it was as if she had never been there.

ADAM BARRIE STRETCHED LUXURIOUSLY AS the warm sunlight filtered through the gap in the curtains and spread its glowing fingers of light across the floor. He smiled, threw back the covers and stepped out towards his bedroom window. He opened the drapes and gazed out at the rooftops that stood between him and beautiful Smugglers' Cove, a favourite spot for holidaymakers and, as Adam confessed, for himself. Whenever he had time off from the boarding house, Smugglers' Cove was his choice place of escape. Today was a day to enjoy and enjoy it he would. He loved the sea and all it had to offer, determining that one day he would live right beside a beach, somewhere.

He heard the clatter of crockery downstairs and his mother's voice; she was singing in that carefree way that she had. Her voice was sweet and pure and gave Adam chills, she was so good that he had to stop what he was doing and listen to her sing. He often wondered why she had never performed professionally, she was that talented.

Once the song ended and he could only hear her hum, he ambled into the en suite and studied himself in the mirror. He needed a shave, this fad for designer stubble and beards just didn't suit him. Adam had thick dark hair, which he kept well-groomed, although this morning, his bedroom hair stuck up in tufts as if rebelling against his taming hand and his dark stubble just made him look dirty. He stepped in the shower and allowed the full force of the spray to hit his body and he gasped as the cold water shocked him fully awake.

As the water warmed he enjoyed lathering on the shampoo and scrubbed his scalp until it tingled before rinsing and conditioning his hair. He soaped his taut muscular body and delighted in the sound of the water as it rained and splashed over him. He wasn't certain but he thought he heard a woman's cry, a name that he couldn't quite make out as it was almost obliterated by a rumble of thunder. He switched off the shower and began to towel himself dry and again heard a voice, which sounded like "Help me," accompanied by silver tinkling bells. He stared out of his window again. He must have imagined it. There was no storm brewing, no thunder. The day promised to be warm and sunny. The sort of day he loved. Adam shrugged off the strange feeling and began to dress, then stopped. Once more he puzzled over his experience in the shower.

This was crazy, was he sleepwalking? Or had he carried remnants of a dream into the shower with him? He shook his head, no, that was impossible. In his twenty-two years of life he had experienced some strange things, things that couldn't be explained, things he had ignored and turned his back on; he supposed this must have been another such incident. He had, had premonitions before that had proved to be correct. Was this another? If so, he didn't immediately recognise the beach or the woman, so he dismissed it from his mind.

Ah well, no matter; he had to get downstairs and quickly, as some of the guests were leaving today, regular guests who came twice a year and who had fallen in love with the house and the area. Adam recalled the number of times these visitors and many others had offered to buy the guesthouse; Smugglers' Cove just down the road, was a popular destination for many and the guesthouse was well placed being only five minutes from the beach and sea.

With a spring in his step he dashed down the stairs, where his mother, Martha had finished cooking breakfast. She had set a place for him at the kitchen table and there she laid his full English before taking a large tray with four more piping hot meals into the dining room.

He could hear the chatter filtering through, the odd word here and there and his mother's girlish laughter, and he grinned between mouthfuls. He knew he was lucky. Lucky to be alive and to have been born in such a beautiful place with loving parents, but a part of him longed for adventure, independence and a change of direction or would he always be working in the house as part of the family business? He hoped not. Still, he could always dream.

Adam rinsed his plate and placed it in the dishwasher as his mother returned. "Adam, darling. Can you pop up and help the Underwoods down with their luggage, please?"

"Of course." Adam trooped up the stairs and knocked politely on room four. The door opened.

"Ah, Adam. Thank you. Can you manage this one?" Brent Underwood pointed at a stout looking heavy leather case that was a little battered but still very sturdy. Adam picked it up and grunted as he lifted it. It was indeed heavy. The thought of how Mr Underwood had carried it up here in the first place was a puzzle, he wasn't a tall man and must have been almost the same age as his parents.

"No problem," he replied and carried the case down the stairs to the hall and waited until Mr and Mrs Underwood appeared, with the rest of their luggage.

"I'll just get the car," said Brent Underwood and he fished in his pocket for the car keys as Mrs Rhonda Underwood handed over her room and door key to Adam's mother.

"Oh, Martha, it's been lovely, as always, and we were so lucky to have the weather. I managed to swim almost every day. Two weeks is just not enough."

Adam's father, James, came down to see the guests off and Adam opened the front door. Brent's car was ready and waiting. The baggage was collected and taken outside and stowed safely away in the boot.

Adam received a flash of something he didn't quite understand. The image of a 'For Sale' sign outside the house and of himself shaking hands with Brent Underwood. He shook his head quickly. That was crazy, just him and his wishful thinking. His dreams of getting away were only wild imaginings and so he buried the thought and continued to smile.

The Underwoods shook hands with Martha and James, and ever the gentleman, Brent opened the passenger door for his wife. He turned to James, "Remember, if you ever decide to sell, please give us first refusal."

James laughed. "You say that every year."

"And I mean it."

James chuckled, "If I had a pound for every time I was asked that, we'd be rich."

Martha broke in, "Until then, will we see you next year?"

Rhonda chuckled, "Has a mouse got a tail? You can bet on it." She got in the car and Brent closed the door. They set off down the drive with James, Martha and Adam waving them goodbye.

Martha left James and Adam clearing up in the dining room and she went upstairs to clean the room and change the bed. As she was upstairs she heard the plop of a letter pushed through the letter box. She stopped what she was doing and dashed downstairs to see what had arrived. Recognising her father's writing she popped it in her apron pocket to read later and returned to her chores.

*

The gentle sun beat down on the lighthouse standing tall on the cruel rocks at the bottom of the neighbouring cliff of Black Head Ridge. Further inland a cloud hovered over a majestic looking house and a small cottage annexed to it. On the far side was another impressive house, which had rocky hewn steps leading down to a small inlet adjacent to the main beach.

Twenty-two-year-old Caroline Mitchell gazed at the sea and magnificent views around her. This place was a great find. She moved back from the cliff edge and settled on the field grass with thrift, and wild flowers, growing in abundance along the path, and returned to the landscape she had been sketching with pastels, before two squabbling gulls had disturbed her, and she had ventured to look and see what was going on. Before she realised it, two hours had already raced by.

Walking along the cliff path towards her was a fit looking elderly gentleman in his late eighties or nineties. A gentle breeze blew, ruffling the man's silver hair, worn longer than most men of a similar age. He was accompanied by a much younger man in his thirties. They stopped on the path and the younger man asked, "It's quite a spread. Is all this land yours?"

The older man, Victor Channing, gestured towards his surroundings. "Here, on this side of the cliff, from the fields behind the house down to the beach. That manor house across the way is nothing to do with me."

The two men strolled on until they saw the young woman. Blake Simmons, the younger man frowned as he saw Caroline on the grass. "This isn't on…"

He marched up to her and said officiously, "Do you know, you're on private land?"

Caroline flushed. "Oh, I'm sorry I had no idea. She closed her sketch book and picked up her pastels before scrambling to her feet. A white lace hankie dropped from her sleeve as she began to walk away.

Victor who was approaching, picked up her handkerchief and called out, "Wait! Don't go… I've seen you here before, haven't I?" He handed her, her hankie, which she took.

"Thanks. I walk here almost every day and on a glorious day like today, I come here to sketch."

Victor stilled Blake who was about to speak. "Then please continue to do so. I have no objection to you coming here."

"Why, thank you."

"You are welcome to come as often as you like."

"But, Mr Channing, sir," Blake interjected.

"No buts. This view is meant to be enjoyed by more than just me. You are…?"

"Caroline, Caroline Mitchell."

Victor took her hand and kissed it in an old fashioned manner with a little bow as he introduced himself, "I am Victor Channing, and this is my estate agent and friend Blake Simmons." He paused. "If I may be so bold, I have but one request… Will you do a picture for me?"

Caroline beamed in delight, "I would love to. Thank you." She settled back down on the grass and continued to sketch as the men walked on.

The lighthouse keeper, Ted Johnson, in his fifties, dressed in a tatty duffle coat, walked out on the catwalk around the light and looked out to sea. He turned back and studied the cliffs. He saw Victor and Blake entering the house and then spotted Caroline sitting sketching and smiled fondly as he took in the wonderful views just as he did every morning.

It looked as though Caroline had finished her sketch, and was packing her things away. She took another long look at the spectacular vista and spotted the lighthouse keeper. She gave him a friendly wave, Ted smiled and waved back.

It was their regular exchange when he was working, that is, if she happened to be there.

Caroline waved again and proceeded to walk back across the cliffs, her long corn blonde hair blew in the wind behind her and as she walked she trailed her free hand through the tall grasses, that rippled like water as the breeze whispered through. Caroline felt curiously at ease; this was a wonderful place.

Ted took his binoculars from around his neck and swept them across the landscape, noting the seabirds, and the door opening on the manor house opposite Black Head Ridge. A man emerged with another person carrying a 'For Sale' sign, which he hammered into the ground. He swept his field glasses back around and eventually saw Caroline again as she disappeared over a stile. He sighed, happily. 'What a glorious day,' he thought, as he set to, polishing the reflective glass of the light.

*

Martha was, as usual, busy in the kitchen, making lasagnes and portions of chilli and bolognaise that she could freeze, as well as providing morning coffee for her husband and son. On the table was the open envelope from the letter she'd received, and James was engrossed in reading the letter. He finished it and sighed before passing it across to Adam who eagerly devoured its contents. He looked up hopefully, "Lovely letter from Granddad. He wants me to visit, can I?"

James pursed his lips, "I'm sorry, son. You know the business can't manage without you, especially at the height of the season. Maybe next year."

Adam's face filled with disappointment, which Martha noticed and added, "Maybe later this year, when we have our family break. We can all go and see him."

*

Victor and Blake were enjoying a brandy after a light lunch and discussing the future of his property. Victor elaborated on their discussion, "Honestly, Blake, I feel it will soon be the right time to let the cottage."

"Of course, you must miss Elaine dreadfully."

"It's been ten years since her death. I still feel her presence around me. She often gives me little signs that she's watching."

Blake raised his eyebrows. "Are you saying the place is haunted?"

"Not really. I prefer to think she is with me, in spirit. But now…" he sighed wearily. "I rattle around this place on my own. And with my daughter and family living so much farther away up the coast it would be good to have a neighbour. I just need to renovate and decorate the cottage before it will be ready, a new kitchen and bathroom, you understand. The place needs a good clean and airing. I want it to be the best it can be."

Blake nodded. "No worries. I'll arrange everything. Let me know what you want doing."

"In fact," he paused, "when the time is right, young Caroline Mitchell would be a perfect tenant."

"I'll see to it, sir."

"Come, Blake. We're friends. Victor, please."

Blake felt himself smiling with pride, "Very well… Victor."

"I also need to prepare."

"Prepare?" he asked puzzled.

"I am in the winter of my life. I'm leaving all this to my grandson, Adam. I want the house to be ready for him."

"You're talking like you want to die…" said Blake concerned.

Victor laughed wryly, "I'm not afraid of dying, but I'm in no hurry to die."

2

Time passed.

Life in the boarding house had not changed. It was still hectic and busy, and Adam hadn't yet managed to stay with his granddad apart from a hasty weekend with his family that was over all too soon and off season when he couldn't enjoy all that the house and sea had to offer. He was in his room, playing his music and reading the seafaring stories that he loved. He knew his father was settled in their living room playing against the computer in a game of chess.

Martha was in the kitchen and in the middle of cleaning down the table with an anti-bacterial spray. She wiped a weary hand over her brow and swayed. She tried to steady herself and feeling the need to sit she dropped into a kitchen chair. Her head was spinning. She felt giddy and almost not there. Her left arm fell and dropped down, as her face began to droop on the same side. Panicked, she tried to call out for help, but no matter how she struggled to speak, she couldn't. No words would come. All that came out was a strangled gurgle before she slid off the chair and onto the floor.

After James finished his game he wandered into the kitchen whistling cheerily and stopped abruptly in shock as he saw his wife collapsed on the floor. "Oh my God, Martha!" He ran to her and shouted urgently, "Adam, quickly come here, now. ADAM!"

Adam heard the shout impinge on his concentration, was that his father? He heard his name again, this time there was fear mingled with the urgency and he jumped up, raced downstairs into the kitchen and looked on in disbelief at his mother on the floor. "Oh, no! What's happened?"

"Quick, help me to get her up we have to get her to hospital. I think it's a stroke. We have to act fast. Hurry!" His voice was filled with urgency.

In the hospital, Adam and his father sat bleakly at Martha's side. Her face was pale, and her eyes closed. She was unconscious, wired up to a machine with various monitors that bleeped. James was watching the doctor's face, trying to gauge his expression as the doctor checked Martha's chart. He grunted, looked up, adjusted his owl-like spectacles and caught James' eye and signalled with a jerk of his head to follow him out of the room.

The doctor spoke quietly and confidentially to him, "I'm afraid it's much more serious than we thought. The bleed was too great, and I don't think she'll ever recover her speech or movement on her left side."

"What? … Can nothing be done?"

"It's doubtful. There are research programmes available for those who qualify and have the money, that's if you want to travel to the States, and one holistic, experimental treatment in Brazil, but both would be very expensive and there's no guarantee that either would work. I'm afraid the damage sustained to the Broca's area…"

"Broca's area?"

"Broca's area, is located in the left hemisphere, and associated with speech production and articulation. Our ability to articulate ideas, as well as use words accurately in spoken and written language, has been attributed to this crucial area. I'm afraid that it will be impossible for her to recover from that."

"She will never sing again?"

The doctor shook his head. "I'm sorry…"

"What about movement? Will she be able to walk again?"

"That's harder to answer. It's doubtful but not impossible. You see, her motor cortex is also damaged. I wouldn't want to hazard a guess and I don't want to fill you with false hope, but I think it might be possible. It will require a lot of hard work on your behalf. However, we'll know more after she has her second scan. The danger, of course, is that she could have another stroke."

James looked grief-stricken and trying hard not to sob, he murmured, "I don't want to think about that. Martha always said, 'that words have power'.

Superstitious or not, I won't bring anything else, down on her. Tell me what we need to do."

*

Blake Simmons sat behind his desk facing Caroline Mitchell. He was somewhat distracted by her wild beauty, there was a natural glow to her skin and her hair flowed like seaweed with the tide, which carelessly tumbled over her shoulders, and her intelligent grey eyes that seemed to know so much, appeared to pierce his soul. He was broken from his moment of reverie as she spoke.

"You were saying, Mr Simmons?"

Blake cleared his throat and struggled to continue with what he was saying. "So you see, Mr Channing is keen that whoever rents his annexe loves Black Head Ridge, the land, beach and house. He remembered everything you said and wanted to give you first refusal and is offering you a reduced rent, as an incentive, that's if you are interested?"

Caroline gasped in delight, "Interested? You betcha. That's wonderful news." She smiled radiantly and her face shone with hope and gratitude. Her phone rang. She glanced at the screen and frowned declining the call and it promptly rang again.

"I think you might as well get that. We are done here for the moment. There is a lot of work to be done on the cottage, it could take a while. As soon as the cottage is ready and Mr Channing has completed his preparations in the house, I will be in touch. He just wanted to know if you were interested before he proceeded. I'll have the papers drawn up in readiness and be in touch."

Caroline smiled brightly and left the estate agent's office clicking, 'accept' on the persistent caller. She moved down the street, her shimmery summer dress floating as she walked. "Hello? ... Philip? ... No, I've already told you, I'm not prepared to do that. I don't do copies, not any more... I've given you my answer, now leave me alone." Caroline curtailed the call and turned off her phone as she strode angrily down the street.

Caroline needed to calm down, she marched into The Dog and Duck and stormed to the counter and ordered a large G and T. She took a big gulp and made her way to a vacant table. There were a few people in there grabbing a lunch time snack and a pint. She drew many admiring glances from the men in the bar but was seemingly unaware of their interest in her. She took another mouthful of her drink, which seemed to calm her.

Steve one of the barmen strolled across and smiled. "Caroline?" she looked up. "Are you okay?"

"Fine!" she exclaimed abruptly and then relented. "Sorry, just dealing with a difficult and persistent person."

"Anything I can do to help?"

She shook her head, "No, but thanks for asking. It's nothing I can't handle. Just infuriating. I came in here to cool off before doing my shopping."

"If you're sure?"

"I am. Thank you," and she smiled. Caroline looked more settled now and requested, "Although, I could murder a pasty, if you've got any left?" The aroma from other people's plates of food was tantalising. Caroline could feel her mouth beginning to water.

"Sure thing. Coming right up," said Steve with a wink and he strolled back to the bar. The pasty was served, and Steve glanced across at her as she enjoyed her snack. Occasionally he caught Caroline's eye. He blushed and looked away embarrassed. He was almost glad when Lisa Devereaux, the barmaid came to relieve him of his duty. He logged out of the till and Lisa entered her own details. She gave Steve a quick smile as he nodded to those standing by the bar, murmured goodbye and skulked out of the back to return home. He just had a few errands to do first.

Lisa turned to her customers and smiled broadly as John Grey, the local gallery owner walked in, "What can I get you, John? Usual?" John nodded and Lisa went ahead and began pouring him a pint of Guinness. The chatter rose in the bar and was soon alive with laughter as Lisa joined in the banter.

Caroline struggled through the street carrying a large bag of shopping. She appeared more composed, and her anger seemed to have dissipated. She took a deep breath, ran up the stone steps and put down her shopping as she hunted for her keys the moment she arrived at the top of the flight, which led to an apartment building.

Steve the barman from The Dog and Duck walked past the bottom of the stone steps in his scruffy duffle coat, which had seen better days. He grinned broadly when he saw Caroline and called out, "Hey, Caroline."

Caroline looked up and smiled, "Steve."

"Can I help you with that?"

"Thanks, Steve. I've got this." She laughed and continued, "I should have met you two blocks away, when I was flagging. It's a bit of a trek from the High Street."

"I'll arrange my schedule better next time," he said jokingly.

"Promise?" said Caroline with a flirty giggle.

"Promise." Steve carried on walking as Caroline fiddled with her key and opened the main outer door.

Steve stopped, turned and watched Caroline as she entered the building. He sighed almost longingly with a small smile on his lips.

Caroline moved up the stone staircase, her footsteps echoed hollowly as she reached the third floor and her flat. She dropped her shopping outside her door with a sigh and murmured, "Bloody hell, that was hard. Should have accepted Steve's help. I'm pooped." She selected her key and stopped. Her front door wasn't closed properly. She pushed it with her finger and called out, "Hello? Anybody there?" There was no answering call, so she picked up her shopping and entered tentatively.

She placed her groceries on the table and noticed the drapes blowing in the open window. Puzzled, she crossed to the window and looked out before she scanned the room around her and walked back to the front door and closed it. It popped open again. The catch was faulty. "Damn. I must get that fixed."

A hand lightly touched her shoulder, and she spun around in fright to see Philip Chapman standing there and gasped in shock.

"Yes, you should. I was able to just walk in."

"Philip! What are you doing here?"

"We need to talk. You've been declining my calls, refusing to speak to me," he said accusingly.

Caroline groaned inwardly as Philip steered her to the sofa and sat her down, firmly. He began to talk, and Caroline's mind raced away, a thousand thoughts tumbling through her mind. She didn't hear half of what he said, but his tone was menacing, and she sat there in a daze. Eventually, she realised he had asked her something. She didn't know what. She was looking more and more uncomfortable as he stood behind her on the sofa looking threatening. He continued in his oily tones as he leaned over her, "You can't refuse me, Caroline. You're in this right up to your neck." He stroked the side of her neck and gently squeezed it with one hand as she flinched and he added, "Such a pretty little neck… it would be a pity if…"

Suddenly, Caroline snapped. She jumped up and turned to face him, "You promised me. Five and I was done."

"I lied."

"I can't. I don't want to do any more."

"There are more players involved in this than just me." His tone became more vicious. "If you refuse you had just better watch your back."

Caroline looked defeated and sat back down with a thump. She dropped her eyes before putting her head in her hands feeling trapped. Philip sensed victory and added, "Besides, if we are to get your career off the ground these are the people that can help you. You need to do this. Instructions will follow and there are two old canvases propped up against your fridge in the kitchen. We have a deal?" Reluctantly and sadly she nodded, not trusting herself to speak. "Good. I'll be in touch. I'll see myself out." A satisfied smirk spread across his face as Caroline began to weep.

*

Martha Barrie, laid in her bed, apparently sleeping, as her eyes were closed. A plump middle-aged nurse sat in attendance and watched sadly as Adam continued to read aloud to his mother. He finished the chapter, closed the book and set it on the bedside table. His face was creased with hopelessness, and he lowered his head and laid his forehead on the bedside, despondently.

His father, James came in and rested his hand sympathetically on his son's shoulder and said quietly, "Adam, we really need to talk."

Adam rose, his shoulders drooped in despair, and he meekly followed his father from the room. They moved downstairs to the kitchen where his father gestured Adam to sit and he poured out his fears elaborating on the practicalities of trying to look after his mother. Adam listened to all that was being said, occasionally nodding or shaking his head. Finally, James spoke in a small voice, "So, with all the extra costs it's more and more difficult to manage and I am sad to say, with all the time taken up for both of us, it's impossible to continue with the business."

Adam paused as he tried to digest all his father had told him. He looked up and offered, "Will it help if I get another job?"

"We can't survive financially unless you do. The nurse will only be here at weekends. One of us will have to be here with her, at all times, especially now Martha's beginning to walk again."

Adam's eyes followed his father as he left the room and Adam was overcome with a feeling of loss. His mother's voice echoed in his head. "Look after your father, Adam. For me. I won't be there. He will need you." He had a flashing image, in his head, of his father sobbing. It confused him, his mother wasn't dead, but did this mean she would be?

*

Blake was as good as his word to Victor and contacted Caroline, again by phone, and asked her to come to his estate agent's office as soon as she could. Knowing what was proposed she was ecstatic and promised to get to his agency right away.

Caroline replaced the receiver and did a little jig around the room with a whoop of joy crying out, "Yes, yes, **yes!**" She grabbed her jacket, keys and bag and raced out of her flat and down the stairs almost tumbling down them in her haste to get out. Her hair streamed behind her as she ran. She passed a surprised Jake, the postman, caught hold of his hands and whizzed him around as if in a country dance and giggled deliciously before she ran on, waving wildly at a bemused Steve who was just going into The Dog and Duck. She almost collided with the lighthouse keeper, Ted and apologised profusely. He smiled and shook his head, "No problem, Miss Mitchell." He watched her as she skipped and danced down the road towards the estate agents. He was still watching, an amused look on his face, as she dived inside the office.

Caroline sat in the seat indicated by Blake and listened as he launched into his 'pitch' to get her to move into the cottage at Black Head Ridge as quickly as possible, finishing with, "I know you have agreed in principle but now I need it confirmed. Mr Channing is keen that whoever rents his annexed cottage loves Black Head Ridge as much as he does. He remembered you and wanted to give you first refusal. As I said, before, now all the work has been completed on the cottage, he's offering you a reduced rent as an incentive, if you're still interested?"

"I don't even have to think about it. It will be like a dream come true. Of course my answer is, yes."

"In that case, I have already taken the liberty of drawing up all the papers and letting forms. I just need to print them off, if you'd care to wait? Did I say, he'd like you to move in as soon as possible, now that the cottage is ready?"

Caroline nodded and as Blake moved across to the printer her phone rang. She called across to Blake, "Just going to take this outside. I won't be a mo." Blake nodded his acknowledgement as she stepped outside the door. "Hello?... Philip? ... No, listen. I'm not prepared to do that. I've given you my answer and kept my part of the bargain since your last blackmailing threats. Now leave me alone." She ended the call looking unhappy but changed her expression and returned inside with a bright smile on her face. She refused to be upset by the man, especially today.

Caroline was really excited as she sat, pen in hand, opposite Blake in his office. She studied the papers put before her, and could not stop smiling. She duly signed in all the places marked with a cross and took out her debit card to pay her deposit and rent. She passed him her debit card, which he placed in the card reader and waited for her to insert her pin number. She collected her receipt and removed her card.

"It might be easier if you set up a standing order or direct debit regards to the rent," Blake suggested.

"I will, as soon as my account can manage it."

"In that case, I'll give you the keys, now. Enjoy your time there."

"I can't wait."

Blake took a set of keys from his drawer and passed them to her, which she took, and her smile grew wider, if that was possible. The two rose and shook hands and Caroline stepped towards the door, but Blake stopped her.

"Miss Mitchell?"

"Caroline, please."

"Very well, Caroline... I just wondered, now all the legal stuff is completed would you like to join me for a drink sometime?"

"Why not? You have my number. Give me a call... But, let me finish packing up and then settle in first, I have masses to do. First of all, I need to buy a bicycle."

"Of course." Blake nodded. And with that, she left the office still beaming, leaving Blake looking absolutely delighted. As the door closed, Blake's face creased in utter pleasure and he murmured, "Yes!" He afforded himself a little punch in the air accompanied by another resounding 'Yes!' as he raised his clenched fist in a victory move.

*

The next few weeks saw Adam wandering along the quayside approaching the skippers of fishing trawlers that came in to unload their catch. Every day it seemed to be the same, one after the other would shake their heads apologetically and say that there were no jobs available.

Adam walked along the pier looking miserable at receiving yet another rejection. He stared up at the sky where the gulls were circling, crying greedily for the scraps that the fishermen threw for them that they couldn't sell. He said a silent prayer pleading for someone to take him on before returning home to help his dad. He picked up the local Advertiser with its vacant job section.

That afternoon he decided to have one last shot at getting some sort of job related to the sea, before rethinking his future. As he walked further down the quay he bumped into the Harbour Master who was just leaving his office and thought he'd ask just once more.

"Good morning, Mr Sugden."

"Morning, Adam; what brings you here again? I've seen you wandering up and down here the past few weeks. Is there anything I can do to help?"

Adam explained his situation and finally said, "So, I am in desperate need of a job. Do you know of anything? Anything at all, sir? I would be very grateful."

Mr Sugden scratched his head as he thought, "… Yes, maybe I do. Captain Bill Leighton on the 'Saucy Jane' has just had one of his men retire. I believe he's looking for some fresh blood to join the crew. He's been at sea, came in this morning, moored right at the top end of the pier. Give him a try. And, Adam?"

"Yes?"

"Good luck! Tell him, I sent you."

"Yes, sir. Thank you, sir."

Adam moved off at a pace with hope and eagerness in his stride. He looked at all the names of the trawlers and other fishing boats until he found the 'Saucy Jane'. A fisherman in his fifties was standing on deck coiling up a thick chandler's rope.

"Excuse me, are you the skipper? Bill Leighton?"

"That'd be me. What can I do for you?"

"The Harbour Master, Fred Sugden, recommended I come and see you."

"Why's that then?"

"He said there might be a job going here, on the boat. I really need the work and I've helped out on boats in the past."

"Really? Where?"

Adam went on to explain which trawlers he'd helped out on, in his school holidays and about his need for the work.

Bill Leighton dropped the rope, and jumped down onto the pier. "I was just thinking about advertising for help now one of my men has retired."

"Don't know how I've missed your boat."

"Probably because I'm often away longer than a day. Anyway, you're here now. What say I give you a trial?"

Adam couldn't stop the smile that stretched across his face as Bill stated his terms. He was so excited he'd have agreed to anything, but he knew he'd have to be sensible. After a bit of wrangling they finally came to an agreement and shook hands. Adam grinned from ear to ear, assuring Bill that he wouldn't let him down and that he'd be back the next day at five a.m.

Adam strode back the way he came with renewed vigour, gave a little jump, and punched the air in victory. Bill Leighton watched him go with an amused smile. He had a good feeling about this young man. He didn't think he'd regret giving him the job.

3

VICTOR STOOD IN THE EXPANSIVE Victorian hallway of Black Head Ridge House. He studied the large portrait of his wife, Elaine, which was surrounded by many other family photographs. He gazed at her face with her knowing eyes and said quietly, "It's time. Surely, it's time. What do you say, my love?"

A white feather fluttered down from the central light and landed at Victor's feet. He picked it up and put it in his pocket with a smile, whispering, "Is that you, my love?" As if in response the lights flickered, and Victor smiled again. He walked around his house with its nautical themed furniture and artwork. His library had a complete section devoted to the sea with sea-faring yarns. Many changes had been made to the property, making it look like a boat without sails in its design. Some windows resembled portholes, the colour scheme favoured both sky and navy blue, and white. His grandson's bedroom was shaped to look like a forecastle. The taps in the en suite were modelled like porpoises and the tiles in the shower had embossed seahorses, shells and mermaids. He wondered if it was a step too far, Adam was now a grown man, would he still be as crazy about the sea as he had been as a child? Victor thought, he would. Anyway, it wasn't the whole house given over to the sea but just one wing, where he was sure Adam would choose to sleep when he inherited it.

Satisfied he had done what he could, even down to using a ship's wheel to electronically draw and close blinds in the bedroom, he retreated to the drawing room to play his music and enjoy a small port before bed, but first he would call Blake.

"Victor here. Tell me, have you heard anymore from Miss Mitchell?"

"It's all done. She's signed the papers, paid the deposit and first month's rent. She's busy packing up her things as we speak. You will soon have her as your neighbour."

"Splendid."

"Was there anything else?"

"No. I am just looking forward to her moving in." Victor sighed contentedly as his music began to play. "That's all, Blake. Speak soon. Ciao." As he lay back in his chair listening to the voice of Andrea Bocelli, he heard a faint fluttering against his window. He opened his eyes and saw a beautiful, brightly coloured butterfly flapping at the glass desperate to get out. Victor rose and opened the window and let the red admiral escape to the wild flower meadows. He closed the window and felt a soft breath of wind blow through his hair, and he could swear he felt Elaine's hand on his cheek, which she stroked gently. He smiled, satisfied that all was well.

The cottage that was annexed to Black Head Ridge House was busy that day. A brand new bicycle with a basket, containing all kinds of oddments, was propped up against a wall. Some knick-knacks were nestled on top of a folded throw. There were two large suitcases plonked on the ground outside the front door, an easel leaning against the wall and Caroline stood on the step, fishing for her key. On her shoulder was a large art folder case on a strap, together with her handbag, which she was forced to put down as she tried to get the key in the front door lock. She jiggled and fiddled with it but couldn't get it to work and swore just as Victor emerged from his house and walked around to her.

"Caroline!" Caroline stopped and turned. "Let me help you with that." She passed him the key as he explained, "It goes in upside down. Once inserted, push against the door, and turn the key to the left and voila!" The door opened, but Victor closed it again. "Now you try."

Caroline did as instructed and the door popped open. She turned and smiled at him, "Thank you."

"Don't worry, you'll soon get the hang of it. Here," he indicated the heavy luggage. "Let me help you in with those." He took the cases and entered the cottage, and as he passed her on the step, a pleasurable expression crossed his face. "Tell me, what is the perfume you are wearing?"

"Patchouli oil. I can't wear ordinary perfumes. Many fragrances contain chemicals to which I am allergic."

"It's lovely. Reminds me of my travels in India."

Victor set down the cases in the quaint hall as Caroline gazed around her. She beamed at him. "I can't thank you enough for this. I was stuck in a poky little flat-come-bedsit in town, and I hated it. This is just heaven, and I can paint."

"Paint, sketch, draw. Don't forget my next picture."

"I haven't." She stooped down and picked up her art folder and opened it and removed a pastel sketch of the view from the cliffs showing the lighthouse and passed it to him.

He sighed appreciatively as he studied it. "It's beautiful. Thank you. I'll get it framed. It will have pride of place on my wall."

"I plan to do another and, if you would let me, I'd love to do a portrait of you."

"With pleasure," the delight was apparent in his voice. "I can see I'll need a whole wall to devote to your work."

A white feather came fluttering down from nowhere and landed at Caroline's feet. She picked it up. "What on earth? What does this mean?"

"It means," said Victor with a grin, "that my wife approves. But now, I'll leave you to settle in... By the way, you're not afraid of ghosts, are you?"

*

Further down the coast, Adam was on board the 'Saucy Jane' as they steamed out to sea. The water was choppy, spray flew up and soaked him, but he just laughed. He felt free. Freer than he had in a long while. How he wished he could have done this years ago. Coming out on the boat gave him some respite from things at home, which were difficult to say the least. His mother had begun to walk a little but was still unsteady on her feet. She was reliant on gestures to make herself understood as she had no speech at all. His father was finding it hard and the effort of looking after her drained him. Most of all, Adam missed his mother's singing. He missed her voice and the songs she would sing, but out here, on the water, he could forget. Forget his problems, forget everything but the job in hand.

Bill Leighton, the captain, interrupted his thoughts, "Over there… yonder. Look!"

Adam peered across the water to where the skipper pointed and saw a pod of dolphins. Above them the gulls circled and cried, and cormorants dived. That was a sign that the fish were there. The boat changed direction and headed for the marine activity to drop their nets. They hoped they would be the only fishing vessel to spot them. They didn't have the up to the minute fish finder detectors that most of the fishermen used. Bill was reluctant to fit his boat up with the latest technology. A part of him believed it wasn't sporting, but he knew he would be forced to do something at some point, or go out of business.

Adam stepped up to the prow to help gather the nets and as the boat dipped and dived he had an image of Elaine, his grandmother, stretching out her arms to him, in welcome, and smiling. She mouthed the word, "Soon."

Adam shook his head as if to clear it. Where had that come from? Why was he seeing his grandma? She'd been gone for ten years or more. Still, Adam took it as a good sign, something to look forward to, something good was coming and he pursued his work with greater vigour, a feeling of love and warmth spreading through him.

*

Caroline felt happier than she had in a long time. She was loving the cottage and really enjoyed putting her own stamp upon the place to make it seem like her home. She hummed as she put the finishing touches to her sanctuary, the throw was draped over the sofa, she plumped up the cushions on the settee and she placed some trinkets around the room. It already looked lived in, as if it belonged to her.

She opened the cottage door and hung a set of wind chimes, which tinkled gently in the warm southerly breeze. Happy with the result she moved back inside to the sitting room and twirled around ecstatically, this was her home, her beautiful home thanks to the kindness of the old man.

Caroline looked through her CD collection and selected one. "Perfect," she murmured and put it on her player. Portishead's Glory Box, 'Give me a reason to love you' began to play and she pirouetted around the room, swaying and twirling, lost in the music. She moved to the front window, gazed out at the spectacular view and smiled in delight. She picked up her sketch pad and flicked through the pages of her artwork. She paused at an impressive portrait of Victor Channing, and studied it critically, appraising her own work and a look of satisfaction crossed her face; she had captured the man's personality, perfectly, or so she hoped. She took it out and placed it on the table. A robin trilled outside and watched her cheekily through the window and a white feather spiralled down and landed on the painting. She raised her arms and shimmied with a giggle at the heavenly affirmation and picked up the mystical feather.

Outside the cottage, partially hidden by bushes, someone was watching. A camera was raised, and several photos were taken in quick succession. A long drawn out sigh mingled with the whispering wind. Caroline was dreamily waltzing away from the window holding the small feather as if it was very precious, when there was a sudden rap on the door startling her. Her heart pounded and she laughed nervously for jumping at the sound, and moved to the hallway and opened the front door.

The young postman, Jake, stood holding some letters and two small packages, which he passed to her. "I really must get a proper mailbox," she said almost chidingly.

Jake smiled back at her. "Or tell me a safe place to leave it."

"If I'm not in, you can always leave it in the greenhouse at the back. But, I promise you I will buy a letter box next time I am in town."

"No worries if you do or you don't. I love coming out here as part of my round. It's always a pleasure to see you."

"Why thank you, kind sir," said Caroline teasingly, with a small curtsey.

"You're welcome," said Jake with a laugh. "It's really beautiful here."

"Yes, it is. I'm very lucky." She turned to go, and Jake gave her a mock salute.

"Until the next time," he said with a chuckle.

Caroline went back into the cottage and looked at her mail. Some were from utility companies welcoming her to their services. There was a letter from her sister bemoaning the fact she hadn't set up an internet service provider yet, as email made it much quicker and easier to communicate and ordered her to 'sort it'. Caroline resolved to have a word with Mr Channing to see what she could do about that. She would ask him which companies were best suited to their location for her needs.

There was also a letter from Philip Chapman that was less than pleasant and instructed her to complete her assignments. He was careful not to admit to anything incriminating, but Caroline, picked up her journal and placed the letter inside, determined to report every meeting, request and project she was required to do. She had had some earlier communications, which were far more damning, until she foolishly let it slip that she was documenting all of their business deals. Chapman was not amused and had insisted she destroy any messages and hand over her journal. She had managed to placate him, cursing herself for being so stupid as to let him know what she was doing. She assured him all text and WhatsApp messages were deleted, and that she would burn her evidence. But, in fact, all exchanges were being stored in her journal as a form of insurance. Caroline also had the perfect hiding place for this important book.

In one package were some artists' materials: brushes, pastels and paint that she had ordered locally from John Grey at the gallery in Brinkworth and the other contained an amount of various crystals and gem stones from Philip.

She groaned. But, she decided, nothing was going to detract from her excellent mood. She picked up her journal and ran upstairs to secrete it in its hiding place then returned downstairs. She lifted the packets of gems and crystals, and popped them in the table drawer, gathered up her sketch pad and pencils, her new pastels, and stepped outside. The day was too good to be blighted by Philip Chapman's wants and needs.

The sun was warm on her face and the sky a beautiful deep blue. The water was calm today with barely a ripple as there was hardly a breath of wind. On the horizon a few boats bobbed about. She strolled to the headland, a serene smile on her face, as she breathed in the fresh salty air and sighed happily, as she settled on the meadow grass.

She studied the scenery and taking inspiration from nature she did something she hadn't done before, using her mind and imagination, she conjured up a scene of a tall dark young man at the stern of a boat lowering fishing nets into the sea. Wind ruffled his hair, and she could almost hear him sing a sea shanty. She added gulls circling the boat until she had a complete picture of the young sailor. It was no one she had ever seen but was pleased with what her imaginings had created. "Why, I almost feel I know him," she murmured and continued to fill in many more details.

As she sat there lost in time, she was surprised to see a young woman walking along the cliff path with someone she did recognise. It was Steve, the barman from The Dog and Duck. He smiled brightly when he saw Caroline and waved. Caroline acknowledged him with a grin.

"Well, well, well, Caroline Mitchell. I didn't expect to see you here."

"Nor I you," she said. "This is my usual haunt. I only live over there." She pointed to the annexe.

"I see. Oh, excuse me, this is Lisa Devereaux, she works with me at the pub and we both thought a walk along the coast would be perfect today, while we have time off. Our shifts don't start until this evening."

"Hi, Lisa, pleased to meet you."

Lisa returned Caroline's smile. "It is absolutely stunning here." She looked down at Caroline's work. "I so wish I had your talent. I'd love to be able to paint." She studied the picture Caroline had been engrossed in. "Whoever is that? Don't think I've seen him around here."

"Oh, you haven't. It's a creation of my mind. Don't really know where he came from."

"Well, he looks pretty fit to me."

Caroline laughed. "I suppose he does. Amazing what the mind can conjure up, isn't it?"

They chatted a while longer before Lisa and Steve turned to walk back the way they had come. Caroline was watching them go when she felt an inexplicable urge to warn Lisa. Of what she didn't know, and she suppressed the feeling finally shrugging it off as part of her wild imaginings. But the feeling that had come upon her dampened her mood, so she picked up her things, scrambled off the grass and returned to the annexe.

Caroline made her way into the town the next day and walked to the hardware store. She emerged gaily from the shop clutching a new letter box. She popped it into the basket on her bike and began cycling up the street passing lots of people that she knew and recognised, either waving or acknowledging them with an 'hello'. It seemed the small town of Brinkworth had really taken her to their hearts. Her artwork was displayed in the local gallery and selling well. She felt as if her heart would burst, she had so much to be thankful for.

She passed Jake, the postman, and pointed at the box in her basket. "You see... I got it!" she called. He grinned back at her and gave her a thumbs up.

Blake Simmons came out from his office, smiled and waved. "We must have that drink sometime," he said as she slowed up.

"You bet... I'll give you a call. I know work's got in the way. I haven't forgotten."

Caroline cycled on passing Ted Johnson the lighthouse keeper, now sporting a full thick black beard and glasses and gave him a friendly wave, which he returned.

On the corner where she turned off to cycle out of the small town, she passed another friend she'd made, a barman at the local pub, Steve, on his own this time. He stood there in his duffle coat and watched her go. He remained there for a while with a silly grin fixed on his face as if in a daze. Eventually, he shook himself in a bemused fashion and moved back towards the town square and the pub.

Caroline cycled on and burst into song. She felt alive and her heart was full. This small town had got under her skin, and she felt deliriously happy. For once in her life things were going really brilliantly. She couldn't quite believe how well her pictures were doing. They were selling. Tourists were buying them and so was Victor Channing. And, more importantly she was making her own friends not just taking on her sister's friends, which reminded her, she really should give her a call and catch up. She promised herself she'd do that and soon.

Even better she hadn't been plagued with calls from Philip Chapman although the last one had been very intimidating and now, he didn't know where she lived so she hoped his persistent pestering would cease. She was tempted to block his phone number but knew he could get to her through her sister so believed it would be futile. She just prayed that no one would tell him her new address, that's if he came looking for her. It was then her phone rang.

Caroline pulled over on the coast road and fished for her phone. The voice on the other end filled her with trepidation. It was menacing and threatening. She managed to gasp out, "Leave me alone. I've told you. I don't want to do anymore."

The cold tones returned, "Then I will have to speak to your sister. She may be able to persuade you, after all you don't want anything happening to her… or her cat."

Caroline bit her lip and submitted, "This will be the very last one. Do you understand?"

"Or what?"

"If you don't stop then I will be forced to go to the police and tell them everything."

"Really? Fancy a prison stretch, do you?"

"No… but I have had enough of threats. Leave my family alone and the cat."

"Then do the painting. Instructions will be sent on WhatsApp to you."

"And then that's it."

"If you say so." The receiver went down with a click.

Caroline cursed, mounted her bike, and pedalled away furiously, her good humour had vanished. She had one consoling thought that he didn't know where she lived but she realised that with the means he had at his disposal he would soon ferret out her sanctuary and that made her feel miserable.

The sun smiled down benignly bathing her upturned face with warmth and she made up her mind the brute was not going to destroy her happiness. There had to be something she could do and with that thought in mind she visibly calmed and cycled more genteelly back to the cottage. This would be the very last time and Caroline would put her own plans in place to thwart him. After all, she already had the evidence. But a voice in her head that was not her own seemed to murmur, 'Be careful…'

*

The night was black, and a terrible storm was raging. The 'Saucy Jane' was bobbing about in the treacherous swell. Forked lightning flashed down followed by an ear-splitting crack of thunder and the rain poured down in torrents swamping the deck as Adam and the rest of the crew tried to haul in the nets and lines. The boat was dipping and diving in the deep troughs of the brutal unforgiving ocean waves.

Adam had an image flash through his mind of a young man being tossed into the foaming sea from a towering, surging wave that just gathered him up and pulled him over the side into its clutches and of the boy sinking helplessly to the bottom.

Instantly alert, Adam glanced across at the newbie in the team.

He was a recent addition to the crew, a young eighteen-year-old lad, Billy Spencer. His face had turned a greenish white and he looked terrified. It was then the freak wave dashed over the bows and liberally flooded the deck. Billy screamed as he could no longer hold on, such was the force of the wave. He went sliding across the wooden deck, slippery with fish scales and water and aquaplaned towards the prow as it dropped down. Adam, risking his own life, waded towards him as the boat rocked and tipped. He grabbed the young man and hauled him to his side to prevent him from being swept over the edge. He dragged him to the rails and placed the boy's hands on the thick chandler's rope that ran along inside the rim where Billy held on tighter than he'd ever done. Adam stood next to him and holding on with one hand, with the other he helped to keep Billy upright and safe.

Billy shivered and nodded his thanks to Adam as any words would be lost in the wild cacophony of wind and swirling water. The violent storm continued to rage with streaks of white lightning sheeting down and thunder roaring as the storm was now directly above them and at its most dangerous.

Adam blinked his eyes against the stinging salt spray that seemed to penetrate his body when he received another flash of images like a film clip and his eyes moved rapidly back and forth unable to stop the vision that had started playing in his head. He could see his mother, Martha shuffling across the landing from her bedroom using a stick, and dragging her left leg. She was unsteady on her feet and moving awkwardly towards the stairs when there was a series of vicious lightning strikes and the deafening roar of thunder. The lights had begun to flicker as she reached the head of the stairs. She held on to the bannister and was about to step out when another fork of jagged lightning hit, and the house was plunged into darkness.

Martha's shriek was terrible to hear, all the more so, since she had made no sound since her stroke and she tumbled down the stairs, lit intermittently by the repeated streaks of lightning until she hit the hall floor.

Hot tears ran down Adam's face mingling with the salty spray and punishing raindrops. He knew his mother was dead. In his mind he could see her as she lay crookedly at the foot of the stairs. His father hurtled from the sitting room and rushed to her side and cradled her head that was now pooling with blood, and then held her tightly in his arms. A pitiful wail burst from his lips as he rocked backwards and forwards with her on the floor that was joined by Adam's own sobbing cry. Adam knew his father was now a broken man and his heart filled with sorrow for them both. The future didn't look so bright now. More importantly they had to get the 'Saucy Jane' safely back to the harbour. That would be a difficult enough task in itself.

*

Caroline's easel was set up. She was in the process of creating a picture in the style of Monet. Her look was harassed, almost tortured, as she tried to impersonate the same type of brush strokes as the original artist. She stood back, one paintbrush in her mouth whilst another was in her hand, and eyed it critically.

The phone rang and reluctantly she answered, "Hello?" As soon as she heard his voice she was irritated. "Philip, I've told you, no more. This is the last one. I do not want to get involved and I just want to focus on my own work... Okay, okay... But this is the last one... Yes, I'm almost done."

She muttered under her breath as she ended the call, "Why can't he just leave me alone? He's doing my bloody head in."

She stepped back towards the easel and continued to work until she was finally satisfied. Caroline set down her paintbrushes and paused to look at the completed picture. She gave a nod of satisfaction and flopped down onto her sofa.

The almost full moon's face shone brightly making a silver ribbon path across the gently rippling water. Occasional clouds scudded across the sky intermittently shrouding the light of the moon. Someone was moving stealthily across the cliff top. The barely discernible figure walked slowly towards the cottage and stood in the shrubbery and watched.

A song drifted on the breeze from an open window. Portishead's Glory Box, 'Give me a reason to love you', played. The poignant tones of the woman tired of playing with her bow and arrow lingered in the air and a long sigh was emitted from the watcher.

Caroline joined in the lines, "I've been a temptress too long." As she moved to the window and gazed at the magnificent vista a huge smile spread across her face. She picked up her art pad and flicked through her sketches and stopped, looking at another impressive portrait of Victor Channing, which reflected his charm and personality perfectly but set against the backdrop of the cliffs and sea. This made it even more dramatic. She took it out and placed it on the table, before taking one of her framed paintings and hanging it on the wall. Satisfied it looked just right she shimmied back to the table, when something caught her attention.

A Tiger moth danced against the window and a white feather floated down onto the portrait. Caroline exclaimed aloud, "Ghosts indeed!" As she spoke the framed picture she had just hung crashed to the floor. She gasped and spun around then laughed at herself. She ran to rescue it and examined it. The glass was intact and so she carefully rehung it. Content that it was safe she dreamily waltzed back to the table, picked up the feather and danced around the room.

Outside, hidden by bushes a figure stood watching her through the window, taking more photographs of Caroline. The person was hardly breathing and then the air escaped the watcher's lungs in a great whoosh.

Caroline was continuing her mesmerising dance still clutching the feather, when someone knocked at the door. She jumped and moved from the room towards the front door and opened it.

Jake stood there holding some letters and a small package. Caroline grinned as she received the post. "Why not leave them in the box?"

Jake grinned back. "Then I wouldn't get to see you and anyway, the package won't fit."

"Flatterer..." she said flirtatiously. "All flannel!"

"Perhaps you'd like to test me on that?" said Jake with a smile. He nodded at her and as the conversation didn't progress further he turned and walked back down the path. Caroline closed the door and wandered back to the sitting room turning over the letters in her hands. She sat and examined them more carefully before tearing open one of them. A cheque slipped out from between two sheets of notepaper. It was a four figure sum. She raised her eyebrows in delight just as there was another rap on the door. She tossed the letters, package and cheque onto the table and dashed back to the front door, opened it and looked outside. Nothing. She glanced around but could see no one. "Jake?" She stepped right outside and searched about her with her eyes. There was no one there. The gentle breeze ruffled her hair. Puzzled, she went back inside and closed the door firmly.

4

THE SUN SHONE ITS GOLDEN nuggets of light on the hot pavement, which sparkled as if impregnated with tiny crystals. Caroline walked up the High Street pushing her bike towards the main convenience store in the town. She leaned her cycle against the wall and picked up her folded shopping bags from the basket, together with her handbag, and shopping list.

The shop bell jangled as Caroline entered studying her list. She methodically walked up and down the aisles in order, selected some items and added a few more, not on the list, to her pull-along basket. She squeezed past two women deep in conversation, who didn't give her a second glance so involved were they in their gossip.

One of the women, with a plain and homely appearance, a Mrs Blewitt, drew the hushed conversation to a close and looked up catching sight of Caroline from the back.

She called out, "Well, there she is! Lisa! Lisa Devereaux!" but Caroline kept walking.

The other woman, thin, with sharp features, shouted out, "STOP!"

Caroline halted abruptly and turned to face the women who had pursued her up the aisle. They gasped and Mrs Blewitt murmured, "It's not her."

"I am so sorry," said Mrs Curtis. "We thought you were someone else."

"Yes," added Mrs Blewitt. "The resemblance is startling."

"I don't understand," faltered a confused Caroline.

"Oh… Young Lisa Devereaux has disappeared. Vanished into thin air. You look just like her from the back."

"We thought you were her… so alike. Please accept our apologies."

"No harm done," said Caroline with a smile and continued shopping. Then she stopped as she remembered the meeting on top of the cliff where Steve, the barman, had been walking with someone called Lisa. She was sure she had been introduced as Lisa Devereaux. Caroline shuddered and had to agree that there was a similarity between them. She hoped that wasn't a bad omen.

Mrs Blewitt and Mrs Curtis saw Caroline's hesitation as she stopped and exchanged a look before they fell back in to deep conversation once more.

Caroline chased her recollection from her mind and thought no more about it and carried on, adding groceries to her basket. Once she had everything and a bit more, she paid for her items and loaded them into her bicycle basket, which was fuller than she would have liked. It was then she noticed the board outside the newsagent, 'Local girl reported missing'. She made up her mind to buy a copy to discover what all the fuss was about.

Curious now, Caroline looked around and grabbed Steve who was walking past on his way to The Dog and Duck and she asked him to purchase a copy as she couldn't leave her bike. Happy to oblige, he did so and popped it in her basket, wedging it so it wouldn't fly out, when she started to cycle.

"How sad, about Lisa. What do you think happened?"

"I don't know. I've only just heard about it. It sounds really bizarre. I only worked with her yesterday and you met her, too, just the other day."

"Yes, I realised that. I didn't connect it before. Was she the sort of person who would just up and leave?"

Steve shook his head, "Nah, not Lisa. She had plans. It's weird. Nice girl. I reckon something's happened to her. It's not in her nature to just disappear."

"No, she seemed very pleasant. And you would know. You worked with her."

Steve sighed, "Yes, very sad. Just remember," he said, "come and visit the pub. There's a bit of a party here Friday night and you'd be welcome to come along. We all need cheering up after news like that."

"Thanks, I may just do that." Caroline grinned as she climbed on her bike and began to pedal calling out, "Bye, Steve. Catch you later."

Lisa Devereaux sat in terror. She was blindfolded, gagged, and tied to a chair, still dressed in her party clothes from the night before. She couldn't see anything, didn't know where she was and the person who held her sounded insane. He kept telling her that she would live forever, and her beauty would never fade. She would sit at his table for every celebration and party and be adored.

She flinched as he stroked her hair. "Blonde hair, so beautiful and not from a bottle. A rare English beauty." Lisa struggled to say something, she was desperate to go to the loo.

He loosened her gag, "Don't scream. No one will hear you anyway. We're miles from anywhere."

Lisa made some more small sounds, so he let the rag slip onto her chin, "I need to pee. I'm desperate. Unless you want me to wet myself."

"No, of course not. I'll help you." The nutcase, retied her gag, loosened her restraints to the chair but still kept her hands tied and the blindfold on. "I'll guide you. Don't do anything stupid, now," he warned. "I know what you young girls are like. Think you can kick me or bite me… Well, it's not going to happen. If you try, you'll regret it. Big time." He lifted Lisa from the chair and began to carry her. He was muscular and strong.

Lisa shuddered as she felt his arms around her. They seemed to move out of a room, at least, she heard a door open, then another and he stood her up. He lifted up her dress, pulled down her panties and sat her on a toilet. Lisa's expression was horror-stricken and full of humiliation. She began to cry, again.

"Don't cry. It makes you look ugly. Red eyes and cheeks are not attractive. Not attractive at all."

Lisa felt his arms around her again as he lifted her off and flushed the toilet. She knew she had to do something to buy her some time and work out how to get free. He pulled up her panties and smoothed down her dress before picking her up once more.

Whether it was a reflex action or not Lisa knew she had to get out of there and as he carried her she dropped the nut on him, hard. He staggered dazed and Lisa fell to the floor. She began to crawl, not knowing where she was going and tried to dislodge her blindfold. She heard him swear and felt a sharp blow to her head. Everything faded to black.

*

Lisa Devereaux sat looking dumbstruck. She was completely immobile. Her blonde hair tumbled over her shoulders, and someone had washed and dried her hair and was now brushing it. Her face was turned away from her captor and she had been forbidden to turn around. In fact, she was rigid with fear, more than that she couldn't turn around. Once her hair had been brushed a black hood was placed over her head. Her feet had been tied to the chair she was sitting on, and her jailer undid the bonds on her wrists. The urge to rub them was strong but she could do nothing about it and one arm was secured to the chair. The other hung limply, which the person behind her abduction, now placed on the arm of the chair and secured, leaving her hand free. This was taken and creamed and massaged lovingly, before her nails were painted and left to dry. The procedure was then repeated with the other hand and then her bonds retied. Lisa tried to speak, but she couldn't. The only part of her body she could move were her eyes. She was like a puppet in his hands. Whatever he had given her had made her completely immobile.

"I told you not to do anything stupid. But you didn't listen. That's why I have done what I have done. Even if I untie you, you won't be able to move. I have injected you with a brachial plexus nerve block rendering your arms immobile. The ketamine ingested will sedate you and you won't remember anything. You will learn to behave."

*

Caroline sat on the sofa, with her feet tucked up under her. She twiddled the telephone wire between her fingers as she talked to her sister. "It's a beautiful place, Sis. You'd love it."

"It sounds wonderful," said Vanda.

"You must come and visit."

"I will, I promise."

"Not only that the house on the other side of the cliff is for sale. You could move there, and we'd be neighbours. It is truly glorious. Look it up on line. Cliff Head House. You said you were looking for somewhere else to live."

"I did. Now the company is thriving I can work from anywhere. I might just take a peek."

"But you didn't call me to talk about the cottage or real estate, Vanda. What's up?"

"No... I'm concerned. Has Philip Chapman been in touch with you again?"

Caroline hesitated before answering reluctantly, "...Yes, but it's okay. I'm handling it."

"So you say, but the man's a snake. He's dangerous. He's mixed up with some very bad people."

"I'll be fine. You worry too much, Sis. I have one last item to complete and then I'll be free."

"I know him. You'll never be free... and if he knows where you live..." she left her words hanging in the air.

Caroline shivered. "Don't. You're scaring me."

"You should be scared. Don't say I didn't warn you."

"Sorry, Sis. Gotta run. Chat again later." Caroline put down the phone. Her hands were shaking. Her sister's call had really spooked her. "Deep breaths, Caroline. Deep breaths," she murmured, in an attempt to calm herself. She stood up and walked to her easel and surveyed the picture she had now completed. She nodded satisfyingly and sauntered to her CD player and pressed play, putting it on repeat. Portishead's Glory Box began to play as Caroline went upstairs to change.

A short time later, Caroline emerged wearing a white floaty dress with a blue ribbon sash at her waist. She danced down the stairs, swayed and twirled in the sitting room, lost in the music. She moved expressively as if no one was watching. Her blonde hair tumbled carelessly around her shoulders as she sang along with the music. With her eyes closed she spun towards the window and threw up her arms. She stretched them in ecstasy and opened her eyes. To her horror she saw a figure wearing a hoodie and face covering standing outside her window staring at her. Caroline stopped dancing and screamed. She ran out of the room into the hall and stopped. She was trembling and scared, unsure where to go or what to do. Her sister's words reverberated around her brain. 'You'll never be free... and if he knows where you live...'

There was a sharp rap at the door. She tiptoed towards it and quietly slipped on the chain. Trying to sound braver than she felt, she called out, "Who is it?"

"It's me, Blake."

Caroline opened the door with the chain still on and peered out to see, "Blake?"

"Have you forgotten?"

"What? ...Oh, sorry, our date... No, well, er ... yes... Was that you at the window? You frightened me half to death." She slipped the chain off the door and Blake came into the hall.

"I don't know. Was it?"

"Staring at me through the window." She eyed him up and down. "You're not wearing a hoodie."

"Should I be?" He lifted his arm holding a hooded jacket. "I'm carrying one." Caroline shuddered and Blake put his arm around her. "You really are scared."

"I am. Oh, I don't know... I just get the feeling I'm being watched. Maybe this isn't the place for me after all..."

"Come on. Let's go. I'll get rid of your fears. We've got a film to see."

Caroline nodded, then grabbed her coat, and bag. They went out and she locked the door. Her hands were still trembling, and she almost dropped her keys. Blake steered her to his car and opened the door. She got in and Blake looked around him. He saw no one. He finally shrugged, sat in his car and drove away.

A breeze caught the wind chimes at the door and a gloved hand batted them away with a hiss of anger.

*

The night promised to be wild. The inquisitive wind nosed its way into Adam's bedroom and whistled mournfully through the gap between window and sill, that Adam hadn't quite shut or secured the catch. He got up and closed the window firmly, stopping its whining complaint. He peered through the chink in the curtains. The sky threatened rain as dark storm clouds bruised the sky and the light of the moon was hidden by the billowing, increasingly black clouds burdened with its heavy load of rain. It seemed to Adam to be a portent of doom. He closed the drapes shutting out the growing storm and fell onto his bed. As the rain began to tumble from the sky, he slipped under the cover of his sheet and sighed.

Adam lay in his bed and stared up at the ceiling. He just couldn't fall asleep, no matter how hard he tried. He was worried. Worried about his father who had taken to wandering around the house calling his mother's name. At the moment, the boarding house was quiet with only the creaks and groans expected at night when the house settled down after the day. He thought about reading awhile to make himself drowsy, but was in no mood to read, he wouldn't be able to concentrate. Instead, he forced himself to turn over and closed his eyes tightly. He practised some deep breathing exercises to calm his rampaging thoughts and focused on centring himself. It seemed to work, and Adam eventually drifted off on a sea of dreams able to ignore the storm as it finally passed overhead.

Time ticked on.

The wind outside was still blowing although the rain had stopped, and the night sky was becoming clearer. The branches of the tree outside his bedroom window waved their scarecrow twig fingers against the glass and began to scrape and scratch stirring Adam. He lay there trying to get back to sleep, when there was a sound outside his door. The noise brought him back to wakefulness and he got out of bed in his boxer shorts. He tiptoed towards the door and could hear the sound of sobbing and a voice cried out in anguish, "Martha!"

Adam opened the door and stepped out onto the landing and watched his father, who moved as if sleepwalking, continually calling out Martha's name. Adam was filled with an overwhelming feeling of compassion. He ran to his father, and he tried to usher him back to his bedroom.

"It's okay, Dad. I'm here. I'll look after you. Come on, back to bed," and like a small child his father allowed himself to be led back to his room.

Adam took James back to his bed and helped him to get in. He straightened the bed clothes and tucked the sheets in resolutely, all the while making soothing sounds of encouragement. He stroked his father's head and dropped a kiss on his forehead, as a father would a child. Adam stepped back and watched as his father muttered his wife's name over and over again before he whispered, "As you looked after me I'll look after you, I promise."

For the next few months that was Adam's life, caring for his father as would a parent. He helped him dress and washed and changed him. He coaxed him to eat, but James was becoming frailer by the day. He had lost weight and it seemed as if he had lost his sensibilities since Martha had died. But Adam did everything possible to make him comfortable, then one morning he had a vision of his mother and father dancing together in a ballroom of light and somehow he knew what to expect. He went to his father's room and tried to wake him, but James Barrie had passed in his sleep and there seemed to be the semblance of a smile on his lips.

The next few weeks were a blur as Adam prepared for the funeral, and dealt with all the legal documentation and his father's financial affairs, which were relatively simple as everything was to come to Adam.

The day of the funeral dawned, and the weather was fitting for such a time as the sky was overcast and brooding. Grave diggers stood by when the coffin was carried from the church and gently lowered into the freshly dug grave placing his father's coffin with his mother's. The minister stood reading from a Bible. "Man that is born of a woman hath but a short time to live, and is full of misery. He cometh up, and is cut down, like a flower; he fleeth as it were a shadow and never continueth in one stay."

Friends and mourners stood around the graveside looking sombre. Adam waited with his head bowed clutching two roses. As the coffin came to rest Adam stepped forward and tossed his rose into the grave. "Goodbye, Dad. God bless. And this second rose is from Grandpa who was unable to make the journey to say goodbye himself." As he said these words the sun began to force its way through the heavy cloud and the true blue of the sky began to reveal itself. The grave diggers shovelled spades of soil into the pit and Adam walked away followed by the rest of the mourners.

*

Caroline and Blake sat in the reasonably busy Dog and Duck pub. She laughed at something Blake said and they put their heads together sharing a private joke before she picked up her glass and drained the last of her wine. Immediately, Blake picked up his beer and drank it down. He took the empty glasses to the bar to be replenished and Caroline gazed at the other customers in the bar.

Jake, the postman, was sitting alone at a table on the other side of the bar. He was watching Caroline, covertly, over his pint. He caught her eye, smiled and raised his glass to her as if toasting her. Caroline looked down shyly and looked up again. This time Jake's eyes were unashamedly locked on to her. He smiled engagingly and Caroline grinned back and acknowledged him with a friendly wave as Blake returned to the table with their drinks. He spotted Jake looking at them and gave him a hard stare. With a flash of annoyance he indicated the postman. "Is he bothering you?"

"No," said a surprised Caroline.

"Well, he's bothering me. His eyes roaming all over you. If he doesn't stop staring I'll say something."

Caroline looked horrified, "Please don't. He's my postman. It's embarrassing."

Blake immediately bristled. "Come on, drink up. I'll take you home."

"It's all right. You've been drinking. I'll get a cab. It's not a problem."

Blake insisted more forcefully, "I said, let's go."

Now it was Caroline's turn to look at Blake and she pursed her lips, "And I said, 'no'."

Blake was now seething. "Very well. You've made your position quite clear. Seems the rumours were right." He downed his drink and slammed his glass down petulantly.

"What rumours?"

"About you being something of a tease, a temptress."

"How dare you!"

"We've been going out a few months now and I don't enjoy you preening yourself in front of other men." He studied Caroline's shocked face. "I suppose I won't be seeing you again, then?"

"No. You most certainly will not! I am no one's property."

"Very well." Blake marched out of the door in anger without looking back.

Caroline heaved a huge sigh of relief and took a sip of her wine as Jake crossed to her and sat down.

"Are you all right?"

"As right as I'll ever be. Talk about a split personality. One minute all charm and pleasantries, the next a raging possessive jealous loon."

"A loon?" said Jake with a twinkle in his eye.

"Can you think of a better word?" said Caroline impishly. "I've had enough of controlling men, up to here," and she gestured with her hand raised horizontally to her nose.

Jake laughed and said, "Perhaps you've picked the wrong men."

"Perhaps I have," mused Caroline and raised her glass to Jake, who reciprocated, and they chinked drinks. "Now," said Caroline positively purring. "Tell me all about yourself," and she smiled mischievously.

At that moment, Philip Chapman entered the bar and spotted Caroline. He strode across to her and her face fell. "Philip, what are you doing here?"

"I came to talk business but couldn't find you at your flat. It seems you've moved." He stared at Jake. "Would you excuse us a moment please. I'd like a private word with Miss Mitchell."

Jake looked at Caroline, "Are you all right with that?"

Caroline nodded. "It's okay, Jake. I won't be long." Jake nodded and returned to his previous seat but continued to watch the exchange.

"So where have you moved to?"

"None of your business."

"That's not very nice. After all I have done for you."

"Done for me? Threatened me, more like."

"You've been paid well. You've always cashed the cheques."

Caroline flushed with colour. "Well not anymore. I have completed the last one. We had a deal, and this is over. Now, if you don't mind I'd like to continue my evening with a friend."

Philip ignored the last comment. "So, it's done?"

"It's done."

"When can I have it?"

"As soon as the canvas is dry. I will package it and send it to your business address. That suit you?"

Philip became aware that others were listening and so he nodded cursorily. "Very well. I will be in touch."

"No, you won't. Once this is over, I shall be changing my number. Goodbye, Philip. Haven't you got somewhere else to be?"

Philip Chapman rose. "Yes, I have. And a cab is waiting for me outside. Don't do anything silly, Caroline." He left quickly the veiled threat ringing in her ears.

5

DOWN THE COAST, VICTOR SAT at his desk in his office chair signing his last will and testament. His solicitor stood next to him, and Blake was present together with a nurse and his recently hired housekeeper. Victor looked ill and weak. He coughed occasionally and his eyes were sunken into his cheeks, he was clearly suffering from some respiratory complaint. His voice crackled like parchment and with a pen he tapped a letter in front of him. "My wishes are all in there. The house is to be redecorated and the wing that has a nautical theme be refreshed. My grandson loves the sea. See that the larder and bar are both well stocked."

Blake looked shocked and murmured, "You're speaking as if you are dead already."

"Just being prepared, Blake. I want to leave everything perfect. Leave nothing to chance."

"Come, sir," said his solicitor. "We need to get you back to bed and rest."

"Oh, tosh! Let me finish here, first. Bed can wait. I'll be in it long enough. In fact, I think I will enjoy a brandy with you all. Please humour me."

The nurse smiled and said, in her Irish tones, "Does that include me?"

"Of course. Didn't you tell me you had a penchant for a good brandy?"

"That I did. And being as you have been doing so well of late, I see no reason your request be denied. The antibiotics are starting to kick in. You are allowed a bevy or two with this variety. You'll soon be racing around again like a new man."

"Thank you, Nurse Rosalind. But, I doubt that. This has fair knocked the stuffing out of me."

"But you can't keep a good man down," she said with a twinkle in her eye.

"I don't think that's exactly the right saying. But, no matter. I'll take it," Victor responded with a smile. "In fact, I may even be up for a small dinner party tomorrow. How do you feel about that, Zoe?"

The housekeeper looking prim in her attire, grinned. "Sounds good to me. It will be lovely to have a few to cook for."

"Instead of this invalid garbage?"

"I didn't say that."

"No, but that's what you meant. We'll talk later about a menu and who to invite."

"It's very short notice, Victor," said Blake.

"Mmm, yes. I think you're right. We will give it a few more days. Something to look forward to. Now, how about that brandy? Let us adjourn to the drawing room." Blake rushed to help him. "Don't fuss, Blake. I'm perfectly capable of walking. I don't need a Zimmer frame yet."

A few hours later, Caroline returned to the cottage. She had refused a lift from Jake and had taken a cab home from The Dog and Duck. She had hurriedly unlocked the door as she heard the landline telephone ringing inside and was now in deep conversation with her sister, Vanda.

Caroline paced the room in an agitated fashion as they talked. The living room curtains were open, and the drapes lifted and fell in the night breeze.

"Just what has he told you?" exclaimed Caroline.

"Nothing concrete but I did get the feeling that he was being threatening about one of his artists."

"And he doesn't know we're related?"

"Not yet. I intend to keep it that way. If he is responsible for this major art fraud, and I believe he is, I need to catch him at it."

"As long as it doesn't involve me. I want no truck with the man. I've done enough already."

"You were foolish to do that. The man could ruin you. Wreck your career before you begin. I promise you, I'll do what I can to keep your name out of it. This is a huge scoop for me."

"I saw him tonight. I've finished the last piece for him. No more."

Vanda took a deep intake of breath. "He doesn't know where you live?"

"No. I don't think so."

"Think so? The man's a monster. Be careful. He could follow you and by the sounds of it he could easily get at you in your cliff side cottage."

Caroline didn't answer as she stopped pacing and peered through the window to the outside. A trickle of fear washed down her spine. She could feel the hairs on the back of her neck standing to attention. An uneasy feeling waved over her as she saw a shadow move outside. She snatched a breath and stifled a cry.

Her sister became alarmed by the silence and said more urgently, "Caroline? Caroline? Are you still there?"

Caroline lowered her voice. "There's someone moving around outside… again. I don't like this. Hold on."

Vanda insisted, concern flooding her voice, "No, Caroline. Hang up, lock the doors and call the police."

But Caroline had already set down the phone and she tiptoed to the door. She took out an umbrella from the stand, with a long spike-like ferrule and held it tightly. She slowly began to take the chain off the door and opened it, holding the brolly like a lance in front of her. She stepped outside.

"Hello? Anybody there?"

There was a sudden rush of wind that set the wind chimes tinkling. Caroline stilled them with her hands and looked around herself, but saw nothing. She turned to go back inside when someone moved rapidly and silently, almost in a blur, and attacked her from behind. Her brolly went flying and she struggled to breathe as an arm went around her throat in a stranglehold. Caroline scrabbled with her hands trying to free herself. She gasped for air and slid to the ground in a dead faint. A crack on the back of her head with a flashlight ensured she stayed down.

Arms tucked under her armpits and the unconscious form of Caroline Mitchell was dragged along the ground to the garden at the back. Caroline was placed in the potting shed and the door shut decisively and absolutely.

The wind chimes tinkled on the breeze.

The telephone connecting Caroline and Vanda lay on the coffee table and Vanda's voice could be heard calling her sister. "Caroline? ... Caroline?" A gloved hand belonging to a mysterious hooded figure, replaced the receiver disengaging the call.

The figure moved quickly and stealthily around the house and crept up the stairs to find Caroline's bedroom. A case was dragged from the top of the wardrobe and placed open on the bed. Clothing items were taken from the closet and tossed in the case along with underwear and tops from the tallboy.

From there the intruder hurriedly moved on to the bathroom and selected toothpaste and a toothbrush, toiletries, cosmetics, and a wash bag. These were removed and packed in the case, which was now closed and lifted off the bed. The attacker sneaked back downstairs and entered the kitchen, tore a sheet of paper off the memo pad and with the attached pencil scrawled, in capitals: 'SORRY, I HAD TO LEAVE'. The note was placed on the table and the figure left, took the case, and closed the door softly.

Night had fallen swiftly. The late evening sun had disappeared beneath the horizon, and marauding clouds had stolen the light of the moon. The shadowy figure carried the limp form of Caroline Mitchell along a rocky passageway, which opened out into a cave, where water dripped. Like a vampire from a horror movie the beast disturbed her clothing, covered her body with his own, and grunted like a bellowing elephant seal protecting his harem until he was satisfied. He rose up and sat back against the dripping rock wall and stared at her.

Caroline began to stir, her eyes fluttered open and she sat up. Her blouse was open, the skirt of her dress rucked up and her panties around her ankles. Blood encrusted her inner thighs. Her eyes widened in horror as she scrambled to her feet. A lonely cry of despair echoed through the cave as she tried to adjust her clothing. She hurriedly tried to pull up her knickers but stopped, feeling eyes upon her, watching her, observing her every move. She swung around and saw her assailant. "You! But why?" her shocked surprise was evident. She turned and began to run but he was soon upon her. She kicked and tried to scream but the sound was cut off as gloved hands caught her by the throat. Her face was a mask of terror as she struggled to breathe. Once more with her air supply cut off, her eyes flickered and shut, and as the hand was removed from her throat she tumbled once more onto the sandy floor.

An enraged voice rasped, "Why? Why did you have to do that? It could have been so perfect." He was prevented from saying anymore as police sirens could be heard outside. He hastily hauled Caroline up, slung her over his shoulder and retraced his steps to the back of the cave and passageway knowing he couldn't remove her safely until the police had gone and the tide was out. There was only one thing he could do, and he didn't want to do it, but he felt this time he had no choice. He rushed towards his hiding place, dragged Caroline who lost a shoe and lifted the lid of the chest, which fell back, and he roughly concealed her inside. His breathing was heavily laboured, and he mumbled wordlessly as he forced her form inside, secured the chest and locked it.

The assailant slipped away unnoticed, hiding from the police cars with their lights flashing outside the cottage. He left the cave and scrambled over the rocks and boulders to the clifftop path and melted into the darkness.

Outside the cottage, Victor in his night clothes and dressing gown was in conversation with two policemen. "Sorry, I can't help you. I expect she's in town. Quite a popular young lady. Her bike has gone; it's usually propped up against the wall by the front door."

"It must have been a crank call. It came from someone outside the town. She didn't give her name said she'd been talking to her when she heard some sort of ruckus and then the phone went dead. She tried calling back, but it just rang and rang. Sorry to have troubled you. If you hear anything please give us a call."

Victor watched as the police returned to their vehicles and drove away. A shiver ran down his spine and he turned to look at the cottage looking concerned. The wind chimes tinkled as he returned to his own house. He was filled with a feeling of dread and as if to confirm his suspicions he felt the whisper of a breeze on his face and the weight of a hand on his shoulder. He sighed, "Oh my dear, Elaine. Is that you?" The lights flickered and he continued, "I won't be long now, my darling and we will be together again, soon. Of that I feel sure." He imagined he heard a feminine sigh and words spoken inside his head, "Not immediately, but soon, my darling, soon."

Victor smiled and he murmured aloud, "Not soon enough for me."

As his door closed and the lights of the cop cars disappeared into the distance, Caroline's bike was wheeled from around the back garden and put into its usual place. The figure retreated once more into the ever increasing dark.

*

The next morning was crisp and fresh as Jake, the postman, came along the path whistling cheerfully. He smiled as he saw Caroline's bike propped against the wall and quickened his stride and rapped on the door. There was no answer, so he knocked again, this time a bit harder. He called out her name. Still nothing.

Jake moved towards the large bay window, where the curtains were open and peered inside, but he couldn't see anyone. The easel, now empty of the canvas was propped up against the sofa. The room appeared undisturbed apart from a few cushions scattered on the floor. He moved back to the door and hammered again, "Caroline!"

Puzzled, he shuffled through some letters in his bag and posted them in the relatively new box on the wall. He removed a package and shrugged before walking around the back to the garden and greenhouse, where he left the parcel. He moved to the small shed and tried the door. It was locked, padlocked securely. He called her name again, "Caroline!" He shook his head slowly as he returned to the front of the house. Her bicycle was there, she should be inside. Why hadn't she responded? This time he rattled the front door knob and set off the wind chimes as he knocked them. It was a strangely happy and spiritual sound in the middle of the day. Unexpectedly the door clicked open. Jake pushed the door with his finger and called again, "Caroline? Caroline are you in there?"

There was a sudden gust of wind that appeared from nowhere and the front door slammed shut in his face. He tried the door again, but it was locked. Jake was now feeling very unnerved. This was all too weird for him. He finally gave up and walked across to the big house next door. He took a bundle of letters and was just about to post them in the letter box when the door suddenly opened.

Victor looking somewhat frail appeared on the step.

"Mr Channing, you startled me…"

"Sorry. I heard you calling for Caroline."

"She doesn't appear to be here although her bike is in the usual place."

"That's strange. The police came last night, something to do with a crank call but her bike wasn't there then. I'm sure I heard her playing her music earlier." He caught Jake's concerned expression and added, "I'll get the key." Victor plucked a key from a hook on his hall wall and walked with Jake to the annexe.

Jake waited while Victor fiddled with the lock and opened the door tentatively.

"It's odd, the door clicked open when I was standing there and then slammed shut. I can't explain it."

"Must have been the wind," murmured Victor who peered inside hesitantly before calling out, "Caroline? It's Victor." He stepped inside the cottage followed by Jake. Victor stood in the hall listening and called again, "Caroline?"

Victor turned to Jake, "I'll check upstairs, something may have happened to her. You look around down here." Jake nodded and watched a moment as Victor began to climb the stairs very slowly and cautiously using the bannister to help steady him. As Victor reached the landing he saw the main bedroom door was ajar and he started to approach it when a cold gust of wind closed it suddenly. Victor shivered. The wind chimes outside began to play an abstract mournful melody. Victor opened the bedroom door.

He stepped inside to the feminine room with its bed neatly made and colourful patchwork cover. Victor opened the wardrobe door and saw the bare hangers. Her clothes had gone. The drawers of the tallboy were mainly empty, but cosmetics remained on the dressing table. Victor left the room, worry etched on his face and moved to the bathroom. Toothbrush, paste and soap had gone. Shampoo and conditioner still sat on the side of the bath. Victor was shaking his head in puzzlement when there was a shout from downstairs.

"Mr Channing! You need to see this."

Jake was in the kitchen reading a note. He looked up as the door opened wider and Victor walked in looking questioningly. Jake passed him the note, which Victor read. "Sorry I had to leave... It's not signed and doesn't say much. I don't understand..."

"I thought she was happy here."

"So did I... and written in capitals. I know her signature but it's not there. She's artistic... writing in capitals doesn't fit. Look at her shopping board." Victor pointed to a cork board on the kitchen wall with her notes for items needed. Jake went across to study it. "Her writing's very round and curly... she doesn't write in capitals. Do you see?"

Jake turned with a worried expression, "Do you think we should call the police?"

"Yes, I do. Come with me to my house. My housekeeper can make us a coffee and we'll decide what to do. Something is very wrong."

Rumours were flying around the small market town of Brinkworth. No one could understand why the popular young woman had absconded. Speculation was rife. Mrs Curtis and Mrs Blewitt were outside the supermarket gossiping about the incident.

"I heard she just upped and left. Didn't even take all her stuff," said Mrs Blewitt.

"Left owing bills, too."

"It doesn't make sense."

"Why would an artist leave all her paraphernalia behind: paints, canvases, brushes, pastels and so on?" said Mrs Curtis.

"And her easel. I heard she'd not even collected the money owed her in the gallery. It's all very odd."

"No one has heard from her..." Mrs Curtis stared as if a thought had just struck her, "Oh, you don't think...?"

"Another Lisa Devereaux?" said Mrs Blewitt.

Mrs Curtis nodded knowingly looking wide-eyed at her friend. "That's just what I was thinking... Coincidence, maybe?"

"I don't believe in coincidences." She paused and then added, "It's too odd for words. Makes me shiver thinking about it. Change of subject… I heard the big house has been sold."

"Cliff House?"

"That's the one. A young woman, divorcee or widow or something."

"Must have a pretty penny to buy that place."

"I heard she was wealthy and beautiful. The local men had better watch out."

"Watch out?"

"Well, if we have another temptress living here who knows what will happen?"

"Let's hope she's not blonde like the others."

"Why? Do you think there's a link?"

"Well, Lisa Devereaux is a blonde so is Caroline Mitchell."

The two women fell silent and eventually moved inside the supermarket together.

*

The cliffs were awash with warmth as the sun played hide and seek with the clouds, changing the colour of the cliff face at every small and subtle change through the day. A woman stood on the beach her blonde hair streaming in the gentle breeze as the incoming tide lapped gently at her feet. She threw up her arms and tried to let out a cry, but no sound would come. Tears rolled down her cheeks and she looked around her in utter despair. Eventually, she ran back to the cave and her footsteps vanished as she ran.

Detectives Vance and Jacobs sat in Victor Channing's kitchen at the table, with Victor who was looking very concerned. Worry was etched on his parchment wrinkled skin and he coughed intermittently, clearly suffering from some sort of chest infection, which was taking its toll.

Vance was a chunky well-built man, not fat but muscly. He had dark hair and piercing intelligent blue eyes, that searched Victor's face with every question.

"Why didn't you report her missing before?" Vance asked, studying the old man's expression and reaction.

"Because I wasn't sure. I thought she might have come back for the rest of her things and all her artist materials. Something is not right."

"It certainly looks like she just absconded. There's no sign of a struggle."

"But how did she leave? She rode her bike everywhere. Why did she leave it behind? I checked with the local cab company and no taxis came to collect her to take her to the station or anywhere. She's just vanished without a trace. And she would never leave behind her art equipment. It's her livelihood, for goodness sake."

"Someone must have picked her up. But, it is very puzzling. One of our officers went to the cab company. It seems she was quite well known down there."

"That's why it makes no sense," muttered Victor.

Jacobs who had been taking notes looked up and added, "It's all the more worrying with the disappearance of Lisa Devereaux," at which Vance shot Jacobs a warning look.

Victor asked, "Do you think they're linked?"

Vance frowned. "It's hard to say. There are similarities, hair colour, height, age, and so on."

Jacobs continued, ignoring Vance's glare, "But, it's a totally different M.O. Lisa was snatched but it seems Miss Mitchell just left."

Vance interrupted before Jacobs could say anymore, "We'll file a report. But, I'm afraid there's nothing more we can do."

"Can't you put out an amber alert or CRA or something?"

"Amber alerts are only used in the States and Child Rescue Alerts are for children only. Miss Mitchell is an adult. If she chooses to disappear and it looks like that's what she's done, then she can. And there's nothing anyone can do about it."

"And if she hasn't and it's something more sinister?" said Victor.

"Then we will have to deal with that when it's confirmed but for now we cannot do anything," asserted Vance.

6

VANDA SULLIVAN, STOOD OUTSIDE BLACK Head Ridge House and stared curiously. She was tall and leggy with rich auburn hair, and startling aqua-green eyes. She had an aura of composure and poise. She looked like she knew what she wanted and how she would get it. She moved towards the annexed cottage and smiled when she saw the wind chimes and murmured to herself, "You always loved those...They always reminded me of your laugh."

A sudden breath of wind blew and ruffled through her hair. The chimes tinkled. Vanda sighed and turned back towards the big Black Head Ridge House. She reached for the door knocker and rapped loudly. A shuffling gait was heard and the door slowly creaked open. Victor stood there a shadow of his former self. He seemed shrunken and tired. His silver white hair graced his shoulders, and his eyes were now rheumy with cataracts. It was clear he couldn't see too well. He peered out at her, and a hopeful flicker of recognition crept into his expression. His face broke into a smile, and he exclaimed delightedly, "Caroline?"

"No, I'm sorry. It's Vanda. Vanda Sullivan." Unnerved, Vanda was taken aback at the mention of Caroline's name. "I'm the new owner of Cliff House. As we're neighbours I thought I'd introduce myself."

He opened the door wider. "Please, come in. Sorry for the confusion. I had hoped it was... but never mind..."

Vanda followed Victor inside and she gazed around at the decor as Victor closed the door. "Why. It's lovely. Like being on a boat."

"That's the intention." Victor walked slowly to the sitting room and politely ushered Vanda inside.

She looked around the room in its nautical colours as he gestured her to sit. "Were you in the navy?"

Victor laughed, it was a warm rich sound. "No, nothing like that. It's for my grandson, Adam. He worked on the boats along the coast after his parents closed their boarding house. He loved this place and the sea. It's my little gift to him. I transferred the property to him over seven years ago but he's not aware of it, yet."

"Lucky man. I'm sure he'll love it."

"How can I help you, Miss Sullivan?"

"I'm just trying to get a feel for the area and the people. I thought you, as my closest neighbour might be able to help me."

"What do you want to know?" Victor picked up his spectacles and put them on. "That's better, now I can see you. You know, you bear a startling resemblance to Caroline. Oh, the hair is different but…"

"Who's Caroline?"

"She used to rent the cottage next to me. An artist of much talent. I have a number of her paintings; that's one of her pictures there." Victor gestured to a seascape in oils gracing his wall.

"It's lovely. What happened to her?"

Victor shook his head sadly. "It's a mystery. Still upsets me to think about it."

He began to tell her all about Caroline and Vanda listened carefully. She asked an occasional question without revealing her relationship to Caroline but agreed that it was all extremely odd.

"But who would have wanted to harm her?"

"I have no idea. She seemed well settled and liked in the town. Maybe she did just up and go. Maybe there was something else going on, which forced her to leave."

*

Months had now passed since Caroline's departure and Victor was now restricted in his mobility and forced to use a wheelchair. He looked even more delicate and more than that, he looked desperately ill. The doctor had confirmed that his heart was weak, and he was experiencing regular breathing difficulties. In fact, Dr Webb was astonished at the rapid decline in the old man's health. Blake silently cursed as he felt Caroline's departure had contributed to Victor Channing's ill health. But Victor knew he was fading and for that reason he summoned his solicitor, Brian Dakin, his estate agent and friend, Blake Simmons, as well as his doctor. His personal carer and nurse was also at his side. He knew that he was coming to the end of his life and wanted all his affairs, everything, to be put in order.

Brian Dakin passed a number of legal papers to Victor to sign, including his last will and testament. It was as if the effort of holding a pen was almost too much and he coughed occasionally as he spoke. "My final wishes are all there. There are some small bequests to each of you who have given me friendship and care." He turned to the nurse, "Rosalind, my dear, you have been a stalwart companion and I know you always put others before yourself. For that reason, you must promise me that the money I leave you must be spent on you, for living and life. Champagne and diamonds, dear Rosalind. Do something frivolous, diamonds are not only beautiful but a good investment and champagne, ah – enjoy the bubbles. Blake, I know I can rely on you, please ensure the house is well stocked for my grandson's needs as he is to inherit this house and the bulk of my estate. I have left enough for you to buy the property you now lease as your agency. I have already spoken to the leaseholders, and they are agreeable to the purchase price so that your future will be secured. You have been a good friend to me and for that I thank you." He coughed again before proceeding around the rest of the assembled company.

The room fell quiet, and Blake interrupted, "Oh, Victor… I hate it when you talk like that."

"Maybe so. I just want things to be right."

Dr Webb added, "I think that's enough for now. You need to rest."

"Not yet! Give me a little longer."

Blake ignored the doctor and continued, "What about the cottage? It's been over a year…"

Victor sighed heavily, "I'm sorry Caroline has gone. She was a delight; a good neighbour and her pictures were sublime."

"So what do you want to do?"

"Leave it empty. I don't want to rent it again... besides, I'm still hoping she might come back. If she doesn't then it will be my grandson's decision."

*

Adam Barrie, Victor's grandson sat in his kitchen on the phone. He had matured and there was an energy exuding from him that was hard to describe. He seemed to be charged with ambition and had an aura of strength and resilience surrounding him.

"Well, Brent, you always said you wanted first refusal..."

"We most certainly do. And please accept our condolences. We were so sad to hear of your parents' passing. We have missed coming down the last few years."

"Thank you. It's much appreciated. My solicitor will be in touch. Bye."

Adam curtailed the call and set down the phone. He picked up a letter sitting next to him on the table and read it again. His grandfather's voice echoed in his head.

"If you are reading this then you will know that I am no longer in this world. Don't be sorry. I have had a good life and reached a great age. For you, Adam, my dear grandson this is your time. You will now have the opportunity to do whatever you wish. You will have the means to follow whatever dream is uppermost in your mind and closest to your heart. I hope you will choose to live in my house that I know you have always loved. It and its contents are now yours. The annexed cottage will provide you with a good income should you decide to rent it out."

Stifling a sob, Adam dropped the letter letting it fall to the table and he gulped hard to prevent himself from crying. He rose quickly and hurriedly wiped his eyes stopping the tears from spilling out down his cheeks. He was now well and truly alone. He looked around the kitchen and the waiting empty boxes and murmured to himself, "I better crack on."

It was at this point that he became filled with an otherworldly energy and began to move with purpose. He quickly selected items from the house that he wanted to keep in the kitchen and packed them away before going to the sitting room and staring at the family photographs of his mother and father and wrapped them carefully in bubble wrap and placed them in yet another box. He paused in his endeavours and moved to gaze out of the window across the garden and was aware of a shimmering of light. The more he tried to grasp the image in his mind, the more elusive it became until he heard his mother's voice. "You won't remain alone. Your destiny awaits." It was an odd choice of words but as the sun peeped out from a weeping sky the speckles of light that had danced before him in the rain ceased and Adam could just make out the willowy form of a woman with luxuriant hair. The features, however, were indistinct. Adam just had a feeling that someone important was to enter his life. As he grappled with that thought, the mirage dissolved and he felt an uncanny fluttering in his stomach, of excitement mingled with trepidation.

*

The low skies with their leaden loads had finally blown away and the day was looking bright and full of hope especially for Adam as he carried the final few boxes to his car and packed them in safely. A number of neighbours had come out to watch his departure. It was the end of an era and people were clearly sorry to see him go.

There was an air of finality as he firmly closed the hatchback's door. The clunking sound seemed to punctuate the ending of a lifetime in service. Adam turned and leaned against the door and appraised the folks who had come out to say goodbye. He walked towards the neighbours and friends in the street and shook their hands.

Old Mr Pettigrew from next door put out his hand, "Sorry to see you go, Adam." There were murmurings of agreement amongst the others watching, who in turn said their goodbyes.

Brent and his wife, Rhonda stood by the 'For Sale' board now crossed with a bold banner reading 'sold' in scarlet writing. Adam went to them last flourishing a large bunch of keys, which he passed to Brent. "The time has come for new blood to take over. I wish you all the very best. I know you'll do us proud." He turned to the assembled company, "This is Brent and Rhonda Underwood. They have been visiting us for many years. I would just like to ask that you embrace them and help them to settle in by extending the hand of friendship to them as you have always done with my family." The folks nodded and smiled at the couple in welcome.

Brent shook Adam's hand and smiled. "You're welcome to visit and see how we're getting on at any time."

Rhonda continued, "That goes without saying. If you ever want to come back and work..."

Adam smiled trying to contain his emotions. The departure was bittersweet, he didn't trust himself to speak and anyway, he had no words. He looked at the people gathered there and took a last look at the house before forcing a smile and getting into his car and driving away. He stuck his hand out of the window and waved, without a second look, giving them all a thumbs up.

The car purred away and out of sight. Adam had a very physical lump in his throat that made him swallow hard as he tried desperately not to cry. The people standing in the street watched him go until the car could no longer be seen and they flocked around the new owners, introducing themselves and offering to help them whenever it was needed. The boarding house was, it seemed, in good hands.

The sun slipped towards the horizon turning the sky a vivid red as if it was ablaze. Adam had left the madness of the motorway and had liked driving on the open road. He was somewhat off the beaten track now, and enjoyed crossing the moors. As the road became narrower he met very few vehicles, a feeling of exuberance and freedom encompassed him and he began to sing, Nina Simone's, 'Feeling Good'. His voice was melodic and full of tone colour. He had obviously inherited his mother's musical talent. He could almost feel her approval as he sang.

Adam had reached the halfway mark on his journey as it was now dusk. He still had some way to go and so stopped in the fading light to refuel and grab a bite to eat as the petrol station had a small shop and café attached. He also needed to get a few essentials. He understood that provisions had been bought for him on his grandfather's instructions but was uncertain whether any fresh produce like milk and bread would be available as he hadn't told the agent when he would be arriving, and he didn't want to search out a supermarket after the long drive.

Adam filled up his car and moved off the forecourt to the shop and café, where he ordered a burger and fries together with a coffee. Feeling somewhat fortified he did a small shop in the adjacent store and whistled as he went back to his car. He stopped as he put his hand on his car door handle. 'What am I whistling?' It was nothing he recognised. He tried to recall the tune. Was it something he had invented? Adam shrugged off the feeling and the word temptress entered his mind. He decided he'd Google the word once he had settled in. He didn't know what to expect and a fluttering of trepidation made him wonder what he was going to experience at Black Head Ridge House.

Twilight succumbed to the darkness of late evening. His lights were the only ones on the road. His headlights picked up road signs to the small market town of Brinkworth and Black Head Ridge. The silver moon was now out and almost full. He turned off to the left and began to follow the coast road to the secluded Black Head Ridge.

He passed a few isolated cottages en route where lights burned brightly and one primitive shepherd's cottage that sat in darkness on the headland in the distance. Its white walls were picked up by the headlights as Adam drove on. He opened his driver's window a little and could smell the fresh sea air. He smiled in pleasure and anticipation that some of his dreams were coming true. He was going to live right by the sea in a house with its own private beach. Thanks to his grandfather he was now a man of means and he felt the urge to sing again.

He stepped on the accelerator as he turned into the approach to Black Head Ridge House. His expression was one of wonder as the lights turned onto the magnificent property, which had been silhouetted in the moonlight and he caught his breath. It truly was a glorious building. He slowed down on the gravel outside, parked and switched off the engine. He paused for a moment looking out across the silver moonlit ribbon striped sea, which shimmered in the calm belying the treacherous rocks that surrounded the headland with its cross currents and rip tides that looked calm and serene in the benevolent starlit night and gazed out at the lighthouse on top of the cliff its friendly beam shining bravely out to sea.

Adam stepped out of the car and breathed in deeply and smiled. He had a good feeling about this place and his move. He was keen to get inside. The lamps on either side of the porch were lit. He walked towards the front door and stooped down beside a colourful flower tub and foraged amongst the foliage where he knew the key was kept.

Wind chimes tinkled in the gentle breeze and startled him. He laughed at his foolishness and inserted the key in the lock and gently opened the door, which creaked in complaint on its hinges. It was an eerie sound in the night. There were strains of a tune on the whispering breeze that sounded remarkably like the tune he had heard in his head and had whistled. He shivered yet the night was mild. He propped open the door with a lump of hardwood that looked as if it was used as a door stop.

Adam returned to his car and fetched his things. He left them in the hall and returned for his laptop bag and locked his car. He stepped into the hallway, closed the door, leaned against it and sighed with relief. He was finally here. It had been a long drive. He glanced to the side of him in the gloom and spotted the light switch. The hallway flooded with light, and he gasped at the changes that had been made since his last fleeting visit with his parents. A smile tugged at his lips, 'How like Granddad,' he thought as he put his car keys on the board of hooks for keys. The wall by the stairs displayed family photographs and there was an excellent portrait of his grandfather. On the other wall were nautical pictures of seascapes with different fishing vessels, and in a recess next to the stairs was a grand piano.

Adam crossed to the portrait of Victor Channing and traced his fingers around the artist's initials and breathed them out, "C.M." As he said this he felt suddenly alert. A tingling ran down his spine and he shivered. The wind chimes tinkled again. Adam moved around to the Steinway piano and lifted the lid. He tapped his fingers on the keys. It was in tune and had a fine tone. Adam sat and began to play. He was a little rusty. He hummed the tune of 'Empty Chairs'.

"That will give me something to do. I'll relearn the piano."

Almost as if someone had taken him over he tapped out with one finger the song he'd heard fleetingly in his head, and he hummed along. He stopped and closed the lid, picked up his bag and walked up the stairs. He stopped as a phrase of Portishead's Glory Box could be heard very faintly and melted away as if it had never played. Adam wondered if he had imagined it and shook his head as if to clear it. He moved purposefully to what he had chosen as his bedroom and opened the door.

As he opened the door, the room was flooded with moonlight. He placed his bag on the bed and strolled to the window and looked out. He sighed as he saw the ocean stretching into the distance. The lighthouse on the promontory shone out brightly and the silvered glow of earth's satellite bathed the rocky steps down to the beach. Adam sighed contentedly, he had a strong feeling that his life was to change dramatically but now he was dead on his feet. The long drive had tired him out. He'd leave the unpacking until tomorrow. Now, he needed to sleep.

Fingers of platinum moonshine managed to prise their way through a chink in the curtains as Adam slumbered. A haunting voice and melody penetrated his subconscious. Strains of Portishead's Glory Box teased him to wakefulness and as he stirred he heard the words, 'I've been a temptress too long, just… Give me a reason to love you. Give me a reason to be a woman…' He was suddenly awake, no longer in that half asleep world where dreams and reality met. He had shaken off the last remnants of sleep and his ears were now alert for every sound. It was that same song, he was sure, the one he had whistled unconsciously, although he didn't know it. Did he dream it? He wasn't sure as the music had now faded away. Adam glanced at the bedside clock and sat up. It was 4:05 a.m.

He rose and walked to the window, pulled back the drapes and opened the window. The sound of the sea as it crashed against the rocks assailed his ears and he smiled in satisfaction when a movement caught his eye.

A woman with long fair hair was walking along the cliff top. She ran down the rocky steps to the beach and as if she felt eyes on her she stopped and turned and stared at the house with a look of abject sorrow on her face.

Adam shook his head in disbelief and the wind chimes tinkled again. He peered closer into the night as a dark cloud began to creep across the face of the moon, but the woman had vanished. The cliff top was empty as was the beach where the sea continued to roll in. The cloud moved further out to sea and the moon shone brightly again, as did the lighthouse, whose welcoming beam warned sailors at sea of the treacherous rocks. Adam stood there reflectively at the window, waiting for the woman to reappear. Was she real? Was she part of a dream? With questions raging in his head he returned to his bed, and tried to empty his mind so he could fall asleep once more.

It was ten o'clock before he awoke. He came to gently, yawned and stretched before getting out and disappearing into the en suite and setting the shower full on. He divested himself of his boxer shorts and didn't have long to wait before the shower came up to the right temperature. He stepped in and luxuriated in the steaming hot water as he soaped his body. He began to sing 'Fire and Rain' when another tune could be heard in the background mingling with the splashing water and his voice.

Adam stopped, shook his head like a wet shaggy dog and the soap suds flew. He stopped singing and could still hear the music filtering faintly into the bathroom. The words, 'Give me a reason to love you', reverberated around his head. He switched off the shower to listen more closely, but the music had died away. He murmured to himself, "I must have imagined it."

A short while later, Adam trotted down the stairs, freshly showered and in clean clothes, his travelling gear was now tossed into the washing basket. He looked smart but casual and decided it was time to explore the house before his brunch. He certainly couldn't call it breakfast, it was far too late for that.

He opened the doors from off the hall and peered inside each room. One was a dining room all laid out as if expecting guests, another was a library with an amazing array of books that he vowed he would check out another time and next was the study, with its desk and filing cabinets. Adam disappeared inside.

Adam sat down in front of the mahogany leather topped desk with its ornately carved legs and leaned back as he stroked the tactile leather surface and sighed contentedly. On the desk was a photograph of his grandfather and grandmother with his own mother as a little girl. Adam picked it up and gazed at it wistfully. Another framed picture showed Adam as a little boy with his mother and father and another of them all sitting on the beach below the house. They were happy times. He had no one left in the world now and his grandfather had ensured he would never want for anything, but he still had a gaping void in his heart. With no family who was there to care? As he sat in the black leather office chair, a small white feather floated down and landed in front of him on the desk. He picked it up and twirled it in his fingers and he felt a warmth and calm spread through his body. His melancholic demeanour vanished, and he felt somehow renewed and rose to study a wall of mounted seascapes and landscapes from the area. They all bore the artist's initials of C.M.

Adam returned to the desk and opened the desk drawers and examined the contents. Lying on the top of the first drawer was a white lace handkerchief. He picked it up and smelled it. It was fragrant with an unusual perfume, and he wondered if it was his grandmother's. He replaced it in the drawer and closed it, before opening the drawer to check the handkerchief again only to see it had vanished. "What?" he exclaimed. He opened the other drawers, but the hankie was not there either. "Adam, you're going mad. You need to talk to someone, living in your head like this will send you nuts. You're on your own."

He would have to get used to it. He had no cousins, in truth no friends. The few friends he did have were all at Smugglers' Cove and that was a long way away now. He would need to make new friends and start a new life. He resolved he would make a start on that as soon as he could, otherwise he would end up as a lonely recluse. But, enough of those thoughts. It was time for brunch. He had worked up quite an appetite, he thought he may even get himself a dog or cat. Dogs were good in helping people to meet others and make friends especially when out walking and it would give him a chance to explore the area. He would think carefully about it. But now... his tummy rumbled reminding him it was time for food!

The kitchen was well equipped and the larder and freezers well stocked. Adam enjoyed selecting the produce to cook and getting to learn how everything worked. His grandfather had quite a few gadgets that he hadn't used before. Adam thought how some of them would have been useful at the guesthouse, certainly with the preparation. He whistled happily as he cooked on the smart burgundy red, Rangemaster. He could get used to this, he thought.

He stopped as he realised he was whistling the same tune he had running in his head from the night before. He turned down the power and left the bacon sizzling, he liked it crispy anyway and left the mushrooms sautéing lightly in butter whilst he opened his laptop on the kitchen table and fired it up. It connected with the internet. 'Good. At least the password hasn't changed since my last visit.' In the search bar he typed in the words, 'song temptress, and give me a reason to love you'. Immediately the words Glory Box and Portishead came up in the search. Adam hit play and the plaintive melody filled the kitchen. Adam returned to the stove while listening to the music, which he found poignant and haunting. He knew he had never heard the song before and hadn't heard of Portishead. Why was this tune invading his mind? He dished up his brunch and closed his laptop once the tune had finished. He ate with great relish not realising how hungry he had been. His plate emptied and his tummy satisfied, he set to clearing away. His years in service at the family boarding house had served him well. The kitchen was soon as clean and sparkling as when he had sat down to eat.

Adam sighed, time to make a move. He stared out of the window at the clear blue sky and the glittering sunshine bathing everything on the ground in a golden glow. He decided there and then that it was the perfect time for him to take a stroll along the cliff path. He picked up his binoculars and slung them around his neck. He donned a lightweight linen jacket, grabbed his keys and locked up as he left the house and headed towards the cliff path. He breathed the sea air in deeply with a look of extreme satisfaction on his face and watched the mewling gulls in the sky with their familiar chuckles and calls. There were a couple of small fishing boats out in the bay and Adam smiled wistfully. He had enjoyed his time at sea especially on the 'Saucy Jane'. He thought back to the time of the storm and the young man he'd prevented from being washed overboard. His sixth sense had certainly come in handy then.

Adam reached a point on the cliffs where the road came down to join the path and he stopped to look at the panoramic view. He lifted up his binoculars and swept them across the vista and paused at the red and white striped lighthouse. From the base of the lighthouse was a twenty foot, small metal ladder that led to a door, partway up, for entry into the lighthouse. Above that, surrounding the huge light, was a catwalk allowing the keeper to walk all the way around the top of the structure.

The lighthouse keeper was busy vigorously cleaning the reflective and rotating lens assembly. He stopped to wipe his brow as the sun came out and smiled down on him; it was hard work. Once he had finished that he picked up another dry cloth to polish the glass until it was gleaming. The sun caught the sparkling glass and almost blinded Adam as he watched through his binoculars.

The keeper completed his task and gathered together his cleaning stuffs ready to take inside. He twisted from side to side to ease his back pain from the stooping, bending and stretching and paused. He sighed deeply and bent down to pick up his threadbare duffle coat that lay on the ground beside him and put it on. Adam felt a rush of sympathy as he felt the man had little in his life and not much money. He could almost feel his loneliness and wondered would he end up being as alone as the man in the lighthouse?

The keeper disappeared from the catwalk taking his cleaning items with him and minutes later came out of the small door twenty foot from the base and began to descend the ladder. Adam continued to watch the keeper who had now reached the ground. He observed him as he got into an old van that had seen better days and drove away.

Adam removed the binoculars from his eyes and watched the waves, no longer crashing on the rocks but gently caressing the seashore. It was a beautifully calm day. Adam studied the panoramic view and turned to walk back. He glanced across at the other very grand house majestically overlooking the sea on the other side of the bay and put the binoculars to his eyes again and in curiosity began to study that house.

The front door opened and a striking looking young woman with glossy chestnut hair with fiery lights stepped outside and stood gazing at the ocean. She walked towards the edge of the cliff where sea thrift grew, a purple wild flower that was in abundance there. It was interspersed with evening primroses. The woman stopped to pick a small posy of them and other flowers and took them inside. Adam lowered his binoculars. Moments later they were up to his eyes again as she emerged and shook a small pot of something that rattled as the contents hit the side of the pot. She called out, "Elsa! Elsa!" and her voice echoed across the cliff to him. It was a resonant voice full of colour.

A fluffy tabby cat came running to her with her tail puffed out straight up in the air and dived through her legs, and into the house. The woman turned and followed the cat inside. Adam removed his binoculars and strolled back to the house at Black Head Ridge with a smile playing on his lips and went into his house. The wind chimes on the door of the annexe tinkled daintily.

7

BLAKE SIMMONS GLANCED AT HIS watch. It was time to leave, if he was to keep his promise to Victor. He looked out of the window. At least it wasn't raining. He locked up the agency, hopped in his car, travelled the coast road, and turned off at the lane that led to Black Head Ridge House.

He slowed outside spewing gravel as he braked. He cast a reflective look at the annexed cottage with its wind chimes and sighed regretfully before alighting from his car. Blake walked up to the impressive door and rang the bell. Adam soon opened the door and looked out curiously, "Yes?"

Blake extended his hand and fixed a big smile on his face, "Blake Simmons… Estate agent."

"Adam Barrie," replied Adam taking his hand and shaking it.

"Yes, I know. Your grandfather asked me to prepare the house for you and get everything ready. This is just a courtesy call… to see if everything is okay?"

"It's all fine. Well, more than fine. Thank you. Would you like to come in?"

"Ah… no thank you. Another time, maybe. I have a viewing in Brinkworth and the chap's a bit brusque. I daren't be late."

"Okay, well thanks for taking the trouble to come out."

"No trouble. It was what your grandfather wished. We were good friends. I may see you again sometime." Blake gave a cheery wave and started back towards his car.

"Wait! Can you tell me who it is that lives in the big house over there?"

"Cliff House? That'll be Vanda Sullivan."

"Miss or Mrs?"

"Miss. If you listen to gossip, she's a bit of a mystery woman. Well, if that's it, I'll be off?"

"Of course and thank you."

Adam watched as the estate agent drove away. He murmured to himself, "*Miss* Sullivan… Things are looking up."

A short while later, Adam was busy unpacking his last few boxes. He had moved on to a box of trinkets and family memorabilia. He took out a photo of his mother and father and set it on a shelf above the fireplace. Next to it he placed his father's seaman's whistle. He took out a folio of sheet music and laid it on the coffee table. This gave him a feeling of sadness as he remembered his mother and father. He sighed, "Oh, Mum… I wish you were here as you always were before your fall. I miss you and your angelic voice. There's a piano here… We could have had some great musical evenings." At that moment, the wind chimes tinkled, and Adam snapped out of his wistfulness. He rose as the chimes tinkled again and yet there didn't seem to be a breath of wind. He followed the sound to the front door and opened it. The chimes came again. He searched with his eyes for the sound but saw nothing. The air outside was still, not a leaf in the shrubbery moved and the tinkling faded away.

Adam stepped forward towards the beach when a movement caught his eye. He stared down at the sandy cove and shaded his eyes trying to see who was there and breathed out the name Vanda Sullivan. This was his opportunity. He gulped and tried to steady himself. Looking more confident than he felt he made his way to the steps that led to the beach.

Adam tried not to look too eager and stepped out onto the rocky hewn steps and set foot on the sand. He approached the woman who was absorbed in doing something on her iPad. As soon as she became aware of him she closed her iPad and put her sunglasses on the end of her nose and peered at him.

"Sorry to intrude. I've just moved into Black Head Ridge House and spotted you here. Thought I'd introduce myself as I believe we are neighbours. I'm Adam Barrie."

The woman placed her iPad in her beach bag and scrambled up. "I know who you are. News travels fast down here. Bush Telegraph I call it. Pleased to meet you." She extended her hand, "Vanda Sullivan." They shook hands.

"Have you lived here long?"

"Not long. Twelve months or so. I find it peaceful here and perfect for my work." She resumed her seat on the blanket covering the sand, and was almost dismissive without being rude.

Adam persisted, "What is it you do?"

She clearly didn't want to talk about it and rebuffed the question by asking, "I'd rather hear about you. There are so many rumours flying around."

"Oh? Do tell me."

Vanda became playfully coy, "Oh, I couldn't possibly repeat them. Some may be true. I'd rather form my own opinion."

Adam grinned, "Not much to tell, really. What you see is what you get."

Vanda chuckled, "How disappointing, then you are not some millionaire recluse?"

"Hardly. I inherited the place from my grandfather with a little bit of money and with the sale of my family home I have enough to live on until I find a renter for the cottage and then I can decide what to do. Whether I'll go back to sea... or..."

"Or?"

"I'm not sure. I've not made up my mind yet, but I'll have to do something. Everyone needs a focus in life. I can't just do nothing."

"No, that's not a good idea. Everyone needs a reason to get up in the morning."

"So, what gets you up in the morning?"

"Ah, now that would be telling."

"Then perhaps I'll become a detective..."

Vanda laughed. "I am really not inclined to say anymore. I'm sure you can invent something far more exciting and glamorous than the reality. Besides, I like to keep people guessing."

"Fair enough. Then shall we talk about the weather, the small town of Brinkworth and Black Head Ridge?"

"Then you'd better join me and sit down."

Time passed and late morning stretched into afternoon. Vanda and Adam chatted like old friends. Vanda looked out across the water and saw that the tide had turned, and the waves were galloping in towards the shore. She sighed dreamily and murmured, "Isn't it beautiful?"

Adam agreed nodding, "We're so lucky to live here."

Vanda glanced at her watch and scrambled up gathering her things, "Oh my goodness. Look at the time! I must go."

She dashed to the foot of the rocky steps and Adam watched her wistfully as strains of Portishead's music Glory Box with the words 'Give me a reason to love you' were heard on the breeze. Vanda stopped suddenly and turned.

Adam asked, "You heard it, too?"

"Strange, I've heard it before…" The music faded. "No matter. I have to go."

Adam nodded and followed her with his eyes as she ran up the rocky steps. A fluffy tabby cat, Elsa, appeared from behind a rock and ran alongside her mistress.

Adam shrugged as he watched her go and made his way back to the house. In truth, he was feeling a bit hungry. He decided to make himself a snack to stave off the rumbling in his stomach and then he would explore the house again and see if it held any more secrets for him.

Time marched on and Adam returned to the kitchen and began to prepare his evening meal as he thought about his earlier meeting with Vanda. She was an enigma, and he knew very little about her, yet she seemed to draw from him his life's story. He worried, perhaps he had talked too much? She did dash off in a hurry and yet in his heart he felt that they had made a connection and that she had enjoyed his company as he had hers, but then again, he could be wrong. The angel and devil sitting on his shoulders continued to argue with each other and carried on into the night, long after he had eaten his solitary meal, and long after he had cleared away. They interrupted his thoughts as he tried to play his music and relax with a drink. It was no good, he must drive those thoughts away and get upstairs and hopefully find some solace in sleep and he plodded up the stairs to his room.

He gazed out of his window at the night sky and his eyes flicked across to Cliff House. The property was shrouded in darkness with no visible sign of any lights burning. Adam sighed, removed his jacket, and began to unbutton his shirt, which he untucked.

The grandfather clock downstairs began to strike its melodic notes. Adam glanced at his bedside clock and saw that it was now midnight. He turned to his window again and it had begun to rain. The drops hit the glass and ran in rivulets like tears down a child's face. As he stared through the droplets of unhappiness, that mirrored his mood, a cloud crossed over the night sky and partially obscured the face of the leprous moon.

He turned his gaze towards the beach when a movement caught his attention. Adam gasped. On Black Head Ridge beach, the figure of a woman dashed madly down the rocky steps to the sand. Her long blonde hair tangled in the breeze and streamed behind her blowing wildly in the wind. She sprinted across the golden sand now pitted with raindrops and turned to look back at the house. Her face was a picture of melancholy and as she ran she dropped a white lace handkerchief.

Adam raced down the stairs and dashed out of the house jacketless with his shirt open and the tails flapping in the gathering wind. He spun around and stared frantically around him and rushed towards the beach. He hurried across the sand in the direction he had seen the woman run. Whispering cries filled his head and he scanned the beach, caves and cliffs looking for a movement or sign of the fleeing woman, before he called out, "Hey! Please… I'm not going to hurt you. Where are you?"

Adam spotted the white lace hankie on the wet sand, rushed towards it and picked it up. He studied it curiously before stashing it in his pocket and looking out at the water. The waves appeared to crash against the rocks more violently. The sound of the surf seemed to increase in volume and Adam's head began to spin. Strains of Portishead's Glory Box, 'Give me a reason to love you' reverberated around his mind. Was it real or was it his imagination?

Adam's heart rate increased, and the sound of its metronome beat seemed to thump in his head. Adam examined the sand around him where he picked up the handkerchief. There was only one set of footprints … his; and it was way above the line of the retreating tide. 'How can that be?' He raised his hands to his head that was pounding unbearably and collapsed on the sand as he tried to make sense of things.

A voice came out from the dark, "Are you all right?" It was Vanda. She knelt down beside him. "I heard you shouting."

Adam, looked up. "I saw a woman on the beach. You *must* have seen her."

Vanda shook her head in puzzlement. "No, nothing. But I heard that music again… If there was someone else here, there would have been footprints. The tide is just on the turn. It can't have washed them away. The only ones here are yours and now mine."

"Sorry, this is so bizarre, but I know what I saw. Or… have I imagined it?"

"Come to the house. I'll get you a drink."

Adam sighed and rose unsteadily. They walked up the rocky steps to Cliff House. Still shaken up Adam allowed himself to be helped along by Vanda who led him in through the door to the sitting room. She helped him to a seat and walked to a drinks' cabinet and poured him a glass of brandy, which she passed to him. "Here, you look as if you could do with this."

Adam sipped it thoughtfully. "Good brandy," he said appreciatively.

"I like to think so."

"And what else do you like?" asked Adam.

Vanda continued, "I like to watch the ocean at night, even on a dull night like tonight. I was sitting in the dark when I saw you rush down to the beach. When I heard you calling out I knew something was wrong."

Vanda poured herself a glass and sat next to him on the sofa. Elsa jumped up beside her and settled herself. Vanda sniffed the air and then his clothes. "You smell of patchouli oil. That brings back memories. I used to wear it in my Bohemian days. Haven't smelt it in a while."

"I don't even know what patchouli oil smells like," said Adam feeling somewhat better.

"Like you, now," said Vanda laughing.

"Maybe it's this." Adam reached in his pocket for the handkerchief he'd picked up, but he couldn't find it. "That's funny. It's not there."

"What?"

"She dropped a hankie, the woman I saw, I picked it up and put it in my pocket."

"Maybe you imagined it. You could have been dreaming. Tell me exactly what happened." So Adam started to launch into the events as he saw them, and Vanda listened. He was halfway through when she interjected, "Curiouser and curiouser as Alice said."

"Alice?" questioned Adam his train of thought broken.

"Alice in Wonderland, although if Lewis Carroll wanted to be grammatically correct he should have said 'more curious.' You must have some kind of sixth sense or something, if you're seeing ghosts."

"I don't know what I'm seeing. I just know there is some kind of mystery here and I will do my best to discover what it is and try and solve it."

"Bit of a detective are you?"

"I wouldn't say that."

"Well, what would you say?" said Vanda cheekily.

"Let's just say, I try to understand the unexplained."

"That's very cryptic."

"It will have to do, for now," said Adam with a grin. "Do you want to hear the rest?"

"Please continue," said Vanda with a wry smile as Adam carried on relating his experiences.

On the outskirts of Brinkworth twenty-four-year-old Luke Armitage had his arm around his girlfriend, Angie Hartman as he walked her home. They were a picture of a couple very much in love as Angie nestled into Luke's shoulder while they strolled along the deserted road.

The night air was still with hardly a breath of wind. They paused under a street light and kissed tenderly. Luke ran his hands through Angie's long blonde hair that tumbled freely over her shoulders, and he drew her into him again. He gently released her, and they continued walking, passing a property towards the end of the road that had extraordinarily high hedges and tall trees, which obscured the house. Standing in the shadows was a man wearing a balaclava who was watching the couple. He sighed in longing as his eyes ranged over Angie's body.

Oblivious to this Luke kissed Angie again. Angie heard the town clock's chimes, which told her it was midnight, "Gosh is that the time? You have to be up at five."

"It doesn't matter."

"But I can walk home from here. You don't have to come all the way. I'll be fine," she reassured him.

"But I don't like leaving you all alone."

"You worry too much. You've got to be up really early…"

"Well, yes. But it's no problem, honestly."

"Go on with you. Get yourself back home. I'm a big girl now I can walk the rest of the way myself. Go on… go."

"But…"

"No buts… go!"

Luke ginned bashfully, "Only if you're sure?"

"How many times do I have to say it? Go on, go."

"See you tomorrow?"

"You can count on it."

Luke kissed her again before leaving her side and stepping away to retrace his steps. He whistled as he walked and looked back at Angie at the split second she too, turned to gaze at her boyfriend. She blew him a kiss before walking on.

He popped his headphone buds in his ears turned the corner and disappeared from view. Angie strolled down the leaf strewn lane with a dreamy expression on her face as the man moved out from the shadows and crept behind her furtively. He held a thick piece of cord in his hands tied with a square knot. He tested its strength.

Angie heard a twig snap behind her. She didn't look back but laughed. "Changed your mind? I said I'd be fine." She turned smiling broadly but the man was upon her. The cord slipped around her neck, which he pulled tight.

Her face suffused with colour as her feet scrabbled on the ground and she struggled to release herself from his vice-like grip. It was no good. He was too strong, and Angie blacked out.

He dragged her still form to a vehicle and bundled her in the back, where he climbed in beside her and taped up her mouth and bound her hands and feet. He clambered out and pulled off his face covering and got into the driver's seat and started his motor. He drove back along the empty road passing Luke on the way, who was happily whistling along to a tune on his headphones. The man grinned to himself as he turned off and headed out of Brinkworth.

At Cliff House Adam was feeling marginally better. He drained his brandy glass, which Vanda whisked away and poured him another. She sat next to him and stared at him intently, "That's some story."

"I know. Makes me sound deluded or high on something."

"And are you?"

"No. Of course not." He sighed heavily, "I know what I saw."

"In that case... I think you *have* seen a ghost. What did she look like?"

Adam screwed up his face as he thought. "She had long blonde hair and was wearing a white floaty dress, with a ribbon sash tied at the waist... Vanda I don't understand it. I saw her. She was beautiful but so sad. I felt she was crying out to me for help."

"But there was no one there when you searched?"

"No."

"And no footprints?"

"No. I know I sound crazy." He turned his face quickly to Vanda's and their heads were disconcertingly close. Vanda hesitated as there was a moment between them, which she broke by rising and walking away to the window.

Vanda gazed out at the now peacefully benign beach with the waves gently kissing the sand and the stars shining brightly in the night sky where the moonlight travelled across the water in a pearlized silver path. "You've had quite a shock... You need to go home and rest."

Adam felt suitably chastened. "Of course. I've already taken up too much of your time." He gulped down his second brandy and rose a little unsteadily.

Vanda caught his arm and helped him to the door. As she opened it there was a rush of wind and wind chimes could be heard on the breeze.

Adam bade her goodnight, swallowed hard, and made his way back along the cliff to Black Head Ridge House. He could smell that strange aromatic scent again on the salty air. "Get a grip, Adam," he murmured as he approached his front door.

He tumbled inside, confused. What was happening to him? Premonitions he had dealt with all his life but this… this was different.

8

THE FOLLOWING DAY, THE SUN slunk up over the horizon bathing the sky in its crimson hues. Adam had finally slept, and he was late getting up. He grabbed a shower turning the dial to cold to wake him up. Thirty seconds of blasting cold water was enough to make him fully alert. He quickly dried himself and dressed, before walking downstairs to the kitchen. He could see he was nearly out of his favourite breakfast cereal and so after he had finished off the remainder in the packet he began to make a list of everyday items that he needed.

Partway through writing, the pen he was using stopped working. He scribbled with it on the desk blotter but there was nothing. He rubbed and rolled the implement hard between his fingers and blew on the end of the pen, yet it still didn't work.

Frustrated, he tossed it down and opened the desk drawer to look for another pen. There inside, on top of other stationery items was the white lace handkerchief. He picked it up. It was still damp from the wet sand. A few grains dropped from it onto the desk. He put it to his nose to smell and murmured as the distinct aroma of patchouli oil pervaded his nostrils. "Patchouli oil... what the hell is going on?"

Adam shivered in spite of himself. He placed the hankie back inside the drawer and stared thoughtfully ahead. Something or someone was calling to him. Something otherworldly. It was as if he was a receiver for spirit messages from the other side and Adam knew that he was being tormented to solve some kind of mystery. How did he know that? As he gazed at the study window, shooting ice of frond like ferns, travelled across the window pane and an unseen hand wrote in the frost, 'Find me. Help her.' Adam felt the chill of the air that travelled through his bones, and he stood up abruptly. "I am not going mad." He shouted out, "I will discover the truth of this, wait and see." The papers on his desk were ruffled by an unseen hand and a white feather floated down onto the desk. Adam rose in an agitated fashion. He grabbed his list, marched outside and took a deep intake of breath to calm his thumping heart. He was feeling incredibly unnerved. In all his life, with all of his premonitions and sensitivities he had never experienced anything as intense as this and whoever it was, that was speaking to him from the grave, would not leave him alone.

The wind chimes outside the annexed cottage played although there was no wind and Adam asserted, "I will help you. I will find you. I promise."

There was a whispering reply that Adam couldn't quite make out. He went to the hall cupboard to get his coat and saw hidden at the back an artist's easel. Adam frowned as a whispered voice stretched out the word, "M-i-i-i-n-e." He locked up and went to his car where on the misted windshield words formed, before his eyes, 'Thank you'. He dived into his car and took off driving faster than was safe.

An hour later, Adam was walking down the High Street with his shopping bag picking up non-food items from his list. He paused outside a convenience store and entered the mini market and walked up and down the aisles gathering bread, milk, eggs, bacon and his favourite cereal, Weetabix, before joining the line of customers waiting at the till. As he waited to be served he listened to the conversations around him.

The shopkeeper, fiftyish Bernard Norton was particularly excited about something. His eyes gleamed with a fevered light as he replied to something Mrs Curtis had asked. "Gone missing. That's what they said. Really strange. Not like her at all."

Mrs Curtis put her basket on the counter for Bernard to ring the items up on the till. "Well," she said, looking around to garner the attention of those around her. "She told me that she was saving for her wedding to young Luke.

The poor lad's totally distraught. She's just vanished. It's really bizarre."

"It's the third girl in three years. If you ask me, there's something more going on here."

"All pretty lasses, too. It's a real travesty."

Another lady, Mrs Blewitt decided to chip in, "If you ask me, something's happened to them. The cops are doing nothing about it. Reckons they've run away and don't want to be found. It's something more sinister than that."

Adam interrupted, "Excuse me, I couldn't help overhearing. Did you say a girl has gone missing?"

"Yes, young Angie Hartman," said Mrs Blewitt. "Her mother's beside herself. Vanished two nights ago."

"What does she look like?" asked Adam.

"Petite girl. Pretty. Long blonde hair. Worked for Mr Norton, here. Always wore jeans and oversized shirts. Why? Have you seen her?"

"No, no. Nothing like that. I was just curious. I'll keep an eye out for her."

"Do," said Bernard Norton. "It's so out of character. You mark my words… Something has happened to her."

Adam gathered his purchases and left the shop. He packed them into his car and set off down the street looking for the estate agents' office. He stopped outside the shop front of 'Morrison and Simmons' and entered.

The office bell clanged in his wake, and he walked towards the receptionist Becky Sharpe, her name plate told him, who was working at the computer. "Yes?" said Becky with a smile. "Can I help you?"

"Is it possible to speak to Blake Simmons?"

"I'll just see if he's free. She picked up an internal phone and punched in an extension number. "Someone here to see you, Mr Simmons." She put her hand over the mouthpiece, "Who shall I say it is?"

"Adam Barrie."

"Adam Barrie, Mr Simmons… Yes, sir." She replaced the phone. "You can go through. His office is right at the back."

Adam followed where Becky gestured, walked to the rear and knocked politely on the door and opened it.

Blake was standing ready to greet him and shook his hand warmly. "Mr Barrie. How can I help?"

"Adam, please."

"Adam."

"I was wondering, who was the last person to lease the cottage annexed to the house?"

"That would be Caroline Mitchell."

"What was she like?"

"Lovely girl, we went out a few times, but she did a bunk and left owing utility bills and so on."

"Oh?"

"Your grandfather decided not to lease the place again. He was quite fond of her."

"I don't suppose she left a forwarding address?"

"Sadly, no. It was all very sudden and strange. Most unlike her. Although, she was a free spirit... She seemed to love it here. Bit of a puzzle really," said Blake with a frown. "Why?"

"No reason. I believe she left some things behind, that's all."

"Yes, so I understand. Her pastels, brushes and paints."

"Um, yes and I found an easel in one of the cupboards."

"Yes, as I said. It was all very odd."

Adam stared hard at Blake. He felt something didn't sit right with him but brushed his feelings aside, thanked him and left the office.

He continued down the High Street and stopped outside The Dog and Duck. He gazed up at the sign swinging in the breeze and decided to check it out. He walked up the steps and entered to be met by a happy buzz of chatter amongst locals at the bar. Adam smiled in greeting to them as he moved through them to the counter. Steve was behind the bar and grinned broadly. "What can I get you?"

"I'm driving. Got any non-alcoholic beer that tastes reasonable?"

Steve laughed and passed him a drinks' menu. "There's a list there. See if there's something you recognise."

"Can you recommend anything?"

Steve shook his head, "Sorry, mate, I'm not one for those beers, I'm a Doombar man myself. Not seen you in here before. You on holiday?"

"No, I live around here now."

"Oh?"

"Yes. Just outside Brinkworth."

"Right. Anyway, I'll give you a minute and you can tell me what you fancy. Run a tab?"

Adam scrutinised the list and decided, "Beavertown Lazer Crush Alcohol Free IPA. Sounds good to me."

"Coming right up."

Adam took his beer and sat at a table close to the bar and tried to listen to the chatter that filled the bar. The inconsequential snippets of conversation rose around him when he heard the name Angie Hartman, and he focused on the person talking and listened with interest.

A big bluff man with a wobbly chin, supped his pint and said, "Just don't understand it. Nice girl, too. Why disappear?"

A scrawny twenty something workman in blue overalls replied, "If you ask me, I think there's more to it."

"What do you mean?"

"Three unexplained disappearances."

"Yes, but that first girl ran off, didn't she? Owed money, I heard."

"Maybe. But what about Lisa Devereaux?"

"That was odd…"

"Wasn't she seen hitching a lift up the coast?"

"So, someone said."

Adam continued to listen. He drained his glass. The beer was actually quite good. He signalled to Steve for another, which Steve placed on the counter.

He got up to retrieve his pint and stood next to the jovial man and said, "Excuse me for interrupting but I couldn't help overhearing. What can you tell me about Caroline Mitchell?"

The bluff man, who he learned was called Geoff, responded, "That was the second girl, wasn't it? Ask Steve here. He took her out." Adam looked with renewed interest at the barman.

Steve sighed as he remembered her. "Caroline was a beauty all right. Something of a temptress. Oh, not knowingly but she set lots of the local lads' hearts a flutter. I used to tease her about it."

"Really?"

"Yes, a real beauty and she didn't even seem aware of it. Went out with me twice but nothing came of it. She was too wrapped up in her art. We were just too different."

"What about Blake Simmons?"

"Yes she saw him, too. He was really taken with her. He didn't like it when she broke it off. Too possessive, she said."

"I see."

"Don't forget Jake," said Geoff.

"The postman?"

"Yeah. He broke his heart after her. Couldn't understand it. They were getting along really well. Used to walk the cliff tops together."

"I don't believe she just left," added Steve. "There was something wrong somewhere. Too sudden and after all the speculation the explanations seemed just too pat."

The conversation went on and Adam continued to listen with interest. He learned more about each girl that had vanished and the men she had been friendly with. Adam decided that Caroline Mitchell was something of an enigma. The picture that had been painted of her certainly intrigued him. She sounded fascinating, talented and someone he would have loved to have met.

*

The sun was slipping towards the horizon and bleeding out across the sky. It was a perfect evening. The developing night sky was a proliferation of stars, and the moon shone brightly. Adam had returned home and was doing what he loved best, standing at the window and looking out across the water and the vista with his binoculars.

He swung his eyeglasses across to the red and white lighthouse standing proudly on the headland where the lighthouse keeper's old, battered van had just pulled up. Adam murmured aloud, "He's late today."

Adam continued to watch. He was fascinated by the man's movements and the extreme care he took over keeping the light shining brightly, always cleaning and polishing the lenses and reflector glass. He was clearly a man proud of his work and the important job he held. Adam made up his mind that at some point he would make himself known to him. He had always seemed friendly enough with a kind wave when he spotted him. He knew he would have to pluck up the courage to ask if he could look around the lighthouse. He would love to see inside the building and have all the workings explained to him. The man cut a solitary figure against the tall structure.

There was a small wrought iron ladder that led about twenty feet up to a small access door. This was clearly designed to guard against inclement weather, so that the stormy sea couldn't crash over the base of the building and flood it. Adam continued to watch the man. He could clearly see the worry lines etched on his face. It was a kind face and one that seemed to have seen much sorrow in his life. He had heard in the town that the man had no family to speak of and was pretty much a loner who had only a few friends. But those he did have were full of praise for the man who had devoted his life to saving others by his work, as his father had before him.

The keeper, Ted would always play Father Christmas at the local primary school and children's ward at the local hospital. He had many a good yarn to tell and Adam thought one of these days he would persuade him to tell him some seafaring tales of vessels and the lives the lighthouse's friendly beam had saved. But, he thought, it was a lonely occupation and Adam made up his mind that he would try and make friends with him.

Adam panned the binoculars across to Cliff House but could see no activity there. There were no lights burning, but Adam knew that Vanda used to enjoy watching the sea when night had begun to fall, so she may be at home after all. He sighed wistfully and pulled the binoculars back to watch the lighthouse keeper who had now alighted from his battered van. He was standing as if mesmerised by the rolling waves, rushing in to strike the rocks and the sea spray flew up.

He moved abruptly towards the small external ladder that led to the little door that would allow him to enter the building. He began to climb it. He struggled to place his hands on the rungs and slipped a little but managed to regain his hold.

He started to climb again but began to lose his hold on the rungs that seemed slippery with sea spray. He was almost at the top when he lost his grip completely and plummeted to the ground. He didn't appear to be moving.

Adam gasped as he watched through the binoculars. He set them down quickly and ran out from the house and along the ridge and cliff top down the grassy path to where the grass met the rocks where the man had fallen. As he approached the lighthouse he heard the keeper groan as he started to come to.

Adam called out, "Wait! Don't move." He reached the man's side as he attempted to sit up.

"Whaaa? Who are you?"

"Adam Barrie. Black Head Ridge House. I saw you fall. You shouldn't move in case you have broken something."

Ted, the keeper waved away Adam's concern, "I'm all right. Thank you. Nothing's broken. See." As if to prove his words he rose and brushed himself down.

"Just thought I could help. It looked like a nasty tumble."

"Nah. I'm fine, really. But thank you. These eyes of mine are not so good these days. I have trouble seeing with these new-fangled spectacles. Everything seems too close makes me feel giddy. It's no wonder I fell. My old ones are much better, were much better."

"Then why not wear them?"

"Oh, I lost them a while back... never found them. Damned nuisance, really. These are so strong, everything's blurred."

"You should get your old prescription and have them made up with new frames," suggested Adam.

"That's a good idea. Thank you." He thrust his hand out, "Name's Ted Johnson."

Adam took it and shook it, "Adam Barrie."

"Why yes, from the big house. I've seen you walking the cliffs."

"That'll be me," said Adam with a grin.

Ted nodded amiably. "Well, now... sorry, I must get on."

"No problem. I'll see you safely up. Don't want you taking any more tumbles."

"Thanks."

Adam watched as Ted climbed the ladder again and this time he disappeared through the small door. He popped his head back out and gave Adam a small wave before closing the door. Adam remained until he saw the lighthouse beam shining out brightly into the ever growing dark and smiled to himself before retracing his steps to Black Head Ridge House.

As he opened the door he heard the wind chimes tinkle. He was getting used to the sound now and smiled. He stepped into the hallway and the portrait of his grandfather, Victor, created by Caroline Mitchell tumbled to the floor with a clatter. Adam hurried across to it and was relieved to see the glass wasn't broken. He lifted it up and inspected it before he rehung it carefully. The picture cord was intact, and the hook on the wall was safely in place. Adam was puzzled. "Why did it fall?" he murmured aloud. Adam shook his head. 'Did it mean anything? If so, what?' Adam walked to the sitting room. "Time for a nightcap, methinks."

Adam strode to the big bay window to draw the curtains and hesitated as he saw the moonlight pick out someone walking towards Cliff House. He strained to see who it was but couldn't quite make the figure out. He moved away to collect his binoculars and strode back to the window. He scanned the cliff top and steps to Cliff House but could see no one. Whoever it was had vanished, and it wasn't his mysterious woman, at least, he didn't think so. But, he needed to be sure. He dashed from the room and went back outside.

Adam hurried along the cliff path towards the imposing house belonging to Vanda Sullivan. He hesitated as he saw lights on in a number of rooms. There were several cars parked outside. He peered through a chink in the curtains and saw Vanda entertaining a group of people. One man, had his arm around her shoulders. He was acting as if he knew her very well. She laughed at something he said and appeared to be enjoying his attention. It was clearly some sort of party and feeling foolish, Adam walked away and returned along the path to Black Head Ridge House. He halted at the steps to the beach and gazed down, the moonlight silvering the golden sand shimmered.

He sighed, he had no reason to be upset. He hardly knew Vanda Sullivan. He wasn't going to be offended that she hadn't invited him to her party and anyway, she seemed to be involved with someone. Best put her out of his mind, he thought. Pity, he really liked her.

He continued looking at the gentle waves, which were lovingly lapping the shoreline. He seemed mesmerised at the sight, and the sound of the soft seawater was soothing, especially now. He instantly felt better.

~ 9 ~

ADAM HAD HAD HIS NIGHTCAP and gone to bed where he was in a fitful sleep, tossing and turning. He was close to becoming awake when the sound of wind chimes woke him, and he sat up in bed yawning loudly. Although bleary-eyed, Adam felt drawn to his window; he stretched and swung his limbs out of bed and padded towards the window and pulled back the drapes with a flourish allowing the moonlight to spill onto the floor.

He gazed out across the water to Cliff House where only one light was burning now. To his horror a scream reverberated in the night air sending the gulls up from their roosts to call in alarm in the night sky. Adam wasn't certain but he felt the cry had come from Cliff House. He hurriedly tugged on his jeans and grabbed his shirt and shoes. He dressed quickly. Had something happened to Vanda? He fled his room, raced down the stairs, and dashed along the coast path to Cliff House. As soon as he reached the door he hammered on it. He could hear someone inside undoing the bolts. It was Vanda, she opened the door, her face was ashen as if she'd suffered a terrible shock. Elsa, her cat, ran to her as soon as the door opened and rubbed herself around her legs.

"Adam?" she said questioningly.

"I heard a scream," said Adam wondering if he'd done the right thing by coming there.

"There was someone here, looking in on me."

"Who was it?"

"I couldn't see. He ran off when he heard me scream."

"I'll take a look around. Go back inside and lock all the doors and windows. I'll knock when I've searched around."

Vanda nodded and picked up Elsa and closed the door. Adam waited until he heard the bolts being drawn across. He darted off, moving stealthily around the house.

As he entered the gardens at Cliff House the moon was eclipsed by clouds that stole away the light. Adam cursed for not bringing a flashlight or torch. He squinted in the dark and could see a shed in the gloom and wondered if, whoever it was, that had scared Vanda, was hiding in there. He stepped forward carefully and stopped, sure that he had heard someone behind him. He turned, but there was no one; he thought it was just his imagination playing tricks with him again. He had set off once more, when he heard a twig crack. This time he had definitely heard something, he started to turn but was hit from behind with something heavy. Adam fell forward and collapsed onto the gravel path that edged the grass, grazing his hands, and his knees where the denim had torn.

Moments later Adam came to, rubbed his head and staggered up. His hand was covered with blood. He swayed unsteadily on his feet and almost fell again but managed to stumble back to the front of the house and hammered on the door. Vanda's voice called out, "Who is it?"

"Me, Adam."

The bolts slid across, and Vanda opened the door, keeping it on its chain. As soon as she saw him she released the chain and fell into his arms. Although taken by surprise, he instinctively held her close before they stepped back into the hall and she secured the door with bolts and the chain, once more.

Once in the light of the hall, Vanda saw Adam's head was bleeding profusely. His hair was congealed with drying blood. The shock on Vanda's face was apparent and a note of fear entered her voice, "What happened?"

"Someone jumped me."

"So, it wasn't my imagination?"

"No, you were right. Someone was watching you."

"I was so frightened. Especially after all that has been happening in the town." She studied Adam's head. "Here, let me see to that. You're bleeding."

Vanda helped Adam into her kitchen and sat him down. She rushed around, fetched a bowl of warm water, cotton wool and antiseptic, and bathed his wound, cleaned his hands, and mopped up the congealing blood. Once the dirt had been cleared from the injury she liberally applied an antiseptic spray and covered the gash up with gauze and sticking plaster. Then she turned her attention to his knees, removing the bits of gravel from the graze, before washing that, as well.

Elsa mewed and Vanda settled her cat by giving her a saucer of milk, which she lapped comfortingly. It was a reassuring sound in the light of what had just happened, a sign of normality.

Vanda finally asked, "You're going to have a banger of a headache."

"I've already got one," said Adam and winced as she applied some TCP to his knees.

"Sorry."

"You never did tell me, what do you do?"

"Oh, this and that," she said evasively.

"That's not a proper answer. You know all about me... Is there anyone special in your life?"

"There was, not anymore."

"Oh?"

"Be patient. I'll tell you sometime."

Adam looked stung by Vanda's comment and rose. He was feeling somewhat frustrated.

"Thanks for your help. I'd best be getting back now." He started for the door.

Vanda stepped in front of him and stopped him. She exclaimed, "You can't."

"Why?" said Adam puzzled.

"He may still be out there. He could attack you again." She hesitated and then continued, "And I wouldn't feel safe." Adam stared at her questioningly. She finally blurted out, "I don't want you to go."

Adam sighed and returned to his seat, "Then I won't leave."

"Thank you." Vanda stared around. "I can't expect you to sleep on the sofa. Take the spare bedroom. I think we both need a good night's sleep after tonight. Things will definitely look better in the morning. You should report the attack to the police."

"I can't think straight at the moment," Adam said abruptly. "Better show me your spare room."

Vanda nodded and led the way upstairs. She showed him the bathroom and then the spare room. It was tastefully furnished, and it had a wash basin in it. "Old fashioned, I know," she said; "but I quite like there being a sink in the bedroom, especially for guests and you'll find a new toothbrush and paste in the cabinet underneath. I collect all the freebies from hotels where I stay so there's soap, shampoo and everything a guest could need if they have come to visit unprepared..."

"Like tonight," Adam said ruefully. "Thanks, that makes it easier. At least I won't have morning breath," he said with a laugh.

"There's a bathrobe on the door and fresh towels. Like a boy scout, I am always prepared." She stopped and added, "And thank you."

"What for?"

"For staying. It really does make me feel better." She studied his face, "You look bushed. Sleep well. I'll see you in the morning."

Vanda bid him goodnight and closed the door after her. Adam moved to the window and looked out. The sky was inky black but filled with a myriad of stars and the moon was being chased by a clump of prowling clouds that played with its silver face letting it shine one minute and then obliterating it the next as if in some kind of game. He opened the window slightly to hear the soothing sound of the surf. He watched a while longer, his eyes searching the desolate beach as the tiny waves innocently rippled along the shoreline, before closing the drapes and shutting out the night. It was hard to believe there was someone out there, on a night such as this, someone ready to cause trouble. He touched his head where he had been struck and winced as he felt a lump.

Finally, Adam yawned and began to undress down to his boxers. He pulled back the bed covers and slipped between the cool sheets and lay there quietly, not moving, in an attempt to fall asleep, but sleep eluded him. He would doze for about ten minutes and then awake with a jolt. He tossed and turned but just couldn't seem to settle. He assumed it was because he was in a different bed and yet, he had had no trouble settling into the new bed at Black Head Ridge House when he had arrived.

Adam sighed heavily, again. He just could not sleep. He propped himself up on his elbow and looked at the bedside clock, which read 3:40 a.m. The ends of the curtains were gently blowing in the breeze from the half open window. The air had become distinctly chilly, so he slipped out of bed and crossed to the window. He tugged open the drapes and just as he was about to close the window he heard the same strains of the Portishead song on the night air. He opened the window further to listen as the line, 'Give me a reason to love you', burst out. Adam strained to listen to detect where the sound was coming from. It appeared to be coming from the direction of Black Head Ridge House. But that was impossible. There was nothing there.

There was a knock on his door. Adam turned and Vanda entered in her dressing gown. "Do you hear it?"

Adam nodded. "I couldn't sleep. But where is it coming from?"

"Across the cliffs from your annexe. I've heard it before."

"But why? And why that song?" Vanda shivered. "You're cold. Why don't you go back to bed?"

"Put your arm around me, please."

Adam put his arm around her. "You're freezing."

"The temperature has dropped in here, too."

Adam hugged her close in an attempt to warm her up. She tilted her face up to his and unable to resist, they kissed; tenderly at first but then the caresses became more urgent and the kisses more passionate. They stepped back and fell onto the bed. Entwined together they began to make love. Adam explored her neck and face with his lips, and they shyly consummated their relationship before Vanda fell into a contented sleep.

Sometime later, Adam still held Vanda close. She lay sleeping in his arms, her head on his shoulder and he eventually closed his eyes. As they slumbered together, the tick of the bedside clock increased in volume as if warning of some impending doom. It grew louder and the temperature dropped considerably so that their breath could be seen clearly, as if on a cold and frosty night. Fern fronds of ice shot across the window pane, and slowly, at the side of the bed, the apparition of Caroline Mitchell began to manifest and stood at Adam's side of the bed. She appeared to glow with an inner light, still wearing the white floaty dress with a blue sash. The scent of patchouli was in the air.

She whispered, sighing through her words in ethereal tones, "Find me... Save her."

Adam stirred and began to shiver. He opened his eyes and saw the spirit of Caroline Mitchell. As he opened his eyes wider the apparition dissolved from view but her words lingered in the air, "Find me... Save her."

Adam sat up abruptly disturbing Vanda who groaned as she looked at the clock, which read 6:30 a.m. Adam sniffed the air and muttered, "Patchouli oil, again."

"Six-thirty," complained Vanda. "Oh, what? Wake me up when it's proper morning..."

"She was here," said Adam. "In this room."

"Who?"

"Whoever it was that needs our help. Look!" He pointed to the floor where a few pools of water led in a trail from the bed to the door. "Tell me that's my imagination."

Vanda stepped out of bed and followed the water trail, which ended on the landing. "It stops here. Why is there nothing on the stairs? I don't understand it."

"Because she's not from our world. She wants us to search for her. If only we knew who she was..."

"None of it makes any sense to me." Vanda came back and grabbed her wrap. "I'll get dressed and start breakfast. I'll give you a shout when it's ready."

Adam nodded in resolution. Who was this ghost and why was she haunting him? It was no one he knew or recognised. He desperately needed more sleep, but that was impossible now. He was fully alert and arose. He padded into the shower and quickly bathed himself.

He dressed quickly and glanced at the frosted window pane in the bedroom, which now had something traced on it. He could clearly see the finger marks and the word, 'help', in block capitals. The frozen crystals were rapidly melting, and it looked as if someone had shed tears over the word, which left the window sill pooling with drips from the weeping rivulets of melted ice.

There was a shout from downstairs where Vanda was cooking breakfast. Aromas of bacon wafted up the stairs. Adam yelled back that he was coming and trotted downstairs to the kitchen where the table was laid, and coffee percolated.

Vanda had laid out sausages, bacon, hash browns and eggs. "Fancy some breakfast?"

"I'd rather have you!" he said with a laugh.

"Behave yourself," she reprimanded, waving a spatula at him. "Tuck in."

Adam sat and helped himself to coffee and poured a mug for Vanda and pushed it across the table to her. He raised the mug to his lips and took a sip before cradling the mug in his hands. "We need to get to the bottom of this business, or I'll go mad."

"You're not going mad. I've heard the music and smelled the perfume, too. Tell me, what have you discovered? What do we know?"

As they ate, they went through their various encounters with the troubled spirit recalling the music, the perfume, and visitations, to see if there was any pattern. There wasn't. At least, nothing that they could think of, except that the otherworldly contact seemed to have accelerated since the disappearance of young women from Brinkworth.

"I think these vanishings are all linked and linked to our mystery apparition," said Adam.

"What? … Do you think we have a serial killer in Brinkworth?"

"It's possible. It can't be a coincidence that three young women have disappeared, two in quick succession, can it?"

Vanda screwed up her face looking concerned, "And maybe whoever it is, is now after me."

~ 1 0 ~

THE DAY WAS CRISP AND fresh after an unexpected cold snap had set in. Adam had scraped the frost off his windscreen and determined to venture into Brinkworth to the local garage and buy a car cover for his vehicle as well as going into town for some groceries. He planned to have Vanda across for dinner sometime this week.

He heard his mother's voice in his head telling him to wrap up warm, so he set the car running with the heater blowing full blast and went inside to grab his coat and find his gloves. He enjoyed the drive into town seeing the frost covered meadows that glistened in the early morning sunshine. The road sparkled with its icy frosting as if crushed diamonds had been sprinkled on the black tarmac. Everything looked so different and clean. He arrived at the local garage with its accessory shop and was able to purchase a waterproof all weather car cover that had come recommended. He paid for it and travelled on into Brinkworth.

Luckily, he managed to park in the town square and proceeded to walk down the High Street with his shopping bag, his head down studying his shopping list. Ted Johnson emerged from the chemist, fairly loaded and Adam crashed into him. There was a clank of glass bottles as Ted pulled up short trying to protect his purchases.

Adam coloured with embarrassment and apologised, "I am so sorry…"

Ted looked at him and touched his hat respectfully, "Oh, it's you."

"Hello, Mr Johnson. My fault, I wasn't looking where I was going. I hope I haven't damaged anything?"

Ted beamed at him. "I haven't thanked you properly for the other day. You were very kind… it's nice to know that if it had been more serious then someone would have been on hand to help. Thank you."

"No need. Anyone would have done the same."

"Maybe. But it's pretty isolated over there with only two houses in the vicinity. It's reassuring to know you're there." Ted sighed heavily and placed his bags gently on the ground. "They're a bit heavy," he murmured.

"Let me give you a hand with them. Where's your van?"

"That's very kind of you. I'm parked by the clock tower on the square."

Adam picked up one of the bags, "Goodness, they are heavy. That's some load you have here."

Ted picked up the other bag and they began to walk back to the square.

"Sounds like you're going to have a party, or planning on building a distillery," said Adam with a laugh.

"Nah! Nothing like that. Just a few items for my hobby. I have lots of time on my hands when I'm not on duty. I learnt from my father. He's dead now."

"Oh, I'm sorry."

"No, it's all right. He passed a long time ago, but he taught me to do a bit of taxidermy. It sort of keeps me close to him."

"Wow!"

"I keep the practice well away from my house. Don't want to upset the neighbours. A lot of people think it's odd."

"Taxidermy, eh? Gosh."

"Sounds creepy, I know. I often pick up dead seabirds. It means they live again, albeit in another form. They are beautiful creatures. The art is trying to capture them as they were in life as if in flight or so on. Ah, here's my van. Thank you for your help."

Ted opened up the back door of his van and packed his shopping inside, cushioning it all with a soft rug. "Just in case…" he said with a smile. "Don't want anything to break."

"No, I should imagine it's quite an expensive pastime."

"It's not cheap, that's for sure." He extended his hand in thanks to Adam, who shook it and as he did so, he had images of wild seabirds suspended on wires and cords from a ceiling looking as if they were circling the sea ready to descend and ride on the waves.

Adam watched the lighthouse keeper drive off and gave him a friendly wave before he returned to complete his shopping trip.

Later that night at home in Black Head Ridge House after he had cooked himself a good meal, he poured himself a brandy and settled back in his chair and sipped it thoughtfully. Images tumbled through his mind that he was struggling to make sense of when there was a thunderous knocking at his door.

Adam put down his brandy and rose. He glanced at his watch. It was 9:00 p.m. Who would come calling at this time of night? Adam entered the hallway as the bell rang this time, quite insistently. He opened the door and was surprised to see Vanda standing there. He opened the door wider to admit her and asked, "Whatever's the matter?"

"I don't know. It's just this feeling of unease. Stupid, I know."

"Not stupid at all. Come on through. My turn to get you a brandy."

Vanda padded after Adam in to the lounge and sat on the settee while he poured her a brandy, which she took gratefully. "Remy Martin, my favourite."

"Mine, too."

"Something else we have in common," she said taking a sip.

"So, what's wrong?"

"I've a lot to tell you. You'll have to forgive me…"

"Why?"

"I had some people over the other night, and I didn't ask you."

"So?"

"There was a reason. I couldn't."

"Why?"

"There is so much you don't know."

"Then tell me what you can."

Vanda sighed, "Where to start, that's the problem."

Adam smiled gently and coaxed her. "Try the beginning…"

Vanda took a gulp of her brandy and looked at him. "I keep myself to myself and try not to arouse any suspicion."

"Rumours abound. In Brinkworth you are a woman of mystery."

"With good reason." Vanda took a moment and paused. Adam didn't press her just looked questioningly. She then announced, "I'm an investigative journalist."

Adam's tone was measured, "Okay... An investigative journalist?"

"Yes."

"Then who were those people and what are you investigating?"

"Hmm... Philip Chapman. He runs a major gallery up the coast and likes to think he has a chance with me. He doesn't. But he tries to intimate that we are close. The others are all hangers on and old acquaintances of my sister..." she took a deep breath, "Caroline Mitchell."

"Caroline Mitchell? What? How?... But you are Vanda Sullivan?"

"Yes, I kept my married name after my divorce. I didn't want anyone to connect me with Caroline."

"So, you're investigating her disappearance?"

"Yes. And what was happening to her morally. Philip was trying to involve her in a fraud."

"What sort of fraud?"

"It's complicated. But very lucrative in the world of art."

"Try me."

Vanda went on to explain how Philip Chapman inveigled an innocent Caroline to produce replicas and copies of an artist's style in the guise of improving her reputation as an artist and then, how once she discovered the truth, he started to blackmail her to force her to continue. It was a sordid story.

Adam whistled between his teeth, "That's some tale. Why didn't she just go to the police?"

"She was afraid and after I had tried to convince her, she just disappeared."

"So, you don't know whether she took herself off to escape his clutches or whether this Philip Chapman has done something to her?"

"Exactly. But then these women began vanishing. I didn't know what to think. I already have quite a file on this man, Philip Chapman. I just needed some more information to complete my exposé on him. Caroline was going to help me, but by then she had gone. However, now I am thinking it could be something far worse."

"You don't know that for certain. You have to have hope. And now, you have me to help you."

They continued talking. The lights burned late into the night. Adam yawned, noisily, "Oh, excuse me. Sorry."

Vanda heard the grandfather clock begin to strike and stood up. "Damn and blast! It's really late. I must get back. Elsa will be starving. I have to feed her. See you tomorrow?"

"You bet. Look, I'll walk you back."

"You don't have to."

"I do. And anyway, I want to."

"I know you're tired."

"Not a problem."

Adam helped her on with her coat and he accompanied her to the door, grabbing his keys as they left.

The moon was shining brightly and the smell of salt on the air was strong as they strolled along the path to Cliff House. They walked silently, without a word. There was no need, they were in tune with each other. They stopped outside Vanda's front door and Vanda tilted her head and as Adam bent to kiss her their faces were bathed in an ethereal silver glow.

Elsa came running up from the steps leading to the beach and wrapped herself around their legs, purring loudly. Vanda smiled up at him and whispered, "You didn't have to do this."

"What? Kiss you?"

She batted him playfully as Elsa mewed. "No, silly. Walk me back."

"What? After your scare the other night? No way I'd let you walk back alone. Especially after what you've just told me. Besides, Elsa would never forgive me."

They kissed again and Vanda opened the door. Elsa shot inside mewing in delight running straight towards the kitchen and her dish.

Adam laughed. "Best, go and feed her. I'll get back."

Vanda nodded and mouthed, 'thank you' and closed the door. Adam began the walk back to his house. He had an odd feeling. Something told him he was being watched. He quickened his step and hurried back, glad that he hadn't left the door on the latch.

Once inside he poured himself another drink. The walk back had woken him up and he no longer felt sleepy. He opened his window a fraction so that he could still hear the lulling sound of the ocean as the waves washed in and out from the shore, but closed the curtains, and sat on the settee to mull over all Vanda had told him and about this art expert chap, Chapman. So many thoughts rambled through his mind he felt he needed a distraction.

He sat back on the sofa and switched on the television and flicked through the channels, but there was nothing he wanted to watch. He pulled up a recording of an old film, something his grandfather must have liked and recorded. He thought he'd check it out. He quite liked old black and white movies and he settled down to watch Casablanca. He curled up on the couch and partway through he became drowsy. Sleep overcame him and he drifted off on the sound of the water and the smell of sea air.

Hours later the wind had begun to get up outside. Leaves on the outside shrubs brushed against the window. The television was now reduced to white light as the film had since ended. Wind chimes tinkled outside, and the cold fresh air rushed into the room blowing the drapes by the window. Combined together they were a powerful rousing force and Adam began to stir.

He sat up and rubbed his eyes and using the remote he switched off the TV. Adam shivered. He stood intending to close the window. He strolled across still feeling sleepy. He needed to get to bed. He yawned as he moved the drapes but was startled by a woman's face at the glass window pane; pale and twisted in torment.

Her anguish moved him as she mouthed, 'Help me'.

Adam stood there in numb astonishment, rooted to the spot as the woman's face faded into the darkness. Final strains of Portishead's vocals, *'Give me a reason to love you'* mingled with a tortured scream. Adam was uncertain whether it was the brandy or remnants from a dream or that he had just imagined it. He shut the window firmly, pulled the curtains closed and supressed the urge to wander outside. He made his way to the foot of the stairs and went up to bed and attempted to sleep, which thankfully he did, as soon as he settled under the covers.

Next morning, Adam was up and about earlier than he expected after the events of the previous evening. He stood at his window cradling a cup of coffee and surveyed the scene outside. He never seemed to tire of it. He was alerted by the sound of an engine and watched the lighthouse keeper's old van drive along to the lighthouse and stop. Adam put down his half-finished coffee grabbed his jacket and keys, slipped out and strolled towards Ted who was alighting from his vehicle.

Ted shaded his eyes suspiciously as he saw a figure approach him and muttered, "Can I help you?"

"Morning, Ted. Beautiful day."

"Oh, it's you," he murmured as he recognised Adam.

"I was wondering…"

"Yes?"

"I hope you don't mind but I'd be fascinated to see some of your work."

Ted immediately lightened up and grinned broadly with pleasure. "Really? Most people wouldn't want to know." He closed his van door. "Come on up."

Ted started to climb the ladder leading to the small door of the lighthouse. Adam followed eagerly and waited while Ted unlocked the door and entered, closely followed by Adam.

Inside, there was a spiral staircase that led up to a couple of rooms before the catwalk. Ted stepped out into one. He invited Adam inside. "The room on the other side is where I can sleep if I need to. This one is where I have some of my exhibits."

Ted opened the door, "Voila! My exhibit room." He entered and Adam followed.

There was a mixture of stuffed birds, some in flight, suspended on cords attached by square knots. Others stood on the wooden bench. There was a variety of seabirds from black headed gulls, to kittiwakes, cormorants and even a puffin. A cat with glassy eyes stared at him, its paw raised as if batting at a gull.

Adam stared around him in amazement. "This is incredible. It's like a museum. What a great job you do. Fascinating."

Ted flushed with pleasure, "Thank you. I do odd jobs for some in the village who want to preserve their pet cat or dog. I find it a bit strange, but they pay me, and it helps to supplement my income."

"You're very talented. These are amazing. I expect it's a lonely occupation here and this hobby must be very satisfying and helps to occupy you."

"It does. Thank you. Are you interested in the sea?"

"Interested? I should say so. The sea has been my life."

"Then come on up. Have you been in a lighthouse before?"

"No, never."

"Follow me."

Ted stepped out of the room and began to mount the spiral staircase. He stepped up towards the catwalk followed by Adam who was more than intrigued. Ted set foot onto the catwalk and Adam followed, now puffing a bit at the ascent. He emerged a little behind Ted. "Phew! That's quite a climb. You must be fit."

"You get used to it."

Adam gazed out at the vista and the sea, totally immersed in his surroundings. "This is stunning." The wind ruffled his hair as he drank in the magnificent view. He walked around the catwalk and marvelled at what he saw. "Tell me, have you ever noticed anything odd around here?"

"Odd?"

"Yes, people you didn't recognise, strangers or visitors?"

"No." Ted looked puzzled.

"What about a young woman who frequents the beach?"

Ted shook his head, "No. Seen no one at all except for the lass over yonder. I sometimes see her, reading on the beach. Used to see another who would sit and sketch. Not seen her for a long time."

"No. I believe she used to rent my grandfather's cottage, but she upped and left suddenly."

"Yes, strange that. I'd sometimes see her on the cliff top sketching or painting. Why?"

"No matter. Just curious. Wondered if you'd seen anything suspicious that could shed light on her disappearance."

"Sorry, no. What are you? Some kind of cop or private detective?"

Adam laughed, "Goodness, no. Just interested in the local mystery."

"Ah… the vanishing women."

"Yes. What's your take on it?"

Ted thought a moment. "Don't really know. Reckon young lasses like that just probably upped and left."

"Mm. Possibly."

"Do you want a coffee or something?"

"Er, no thanks. I'd best be off. I know you have work to do, polishing and cleaning the reflective glass and such. Thank you for showing me around."

"No problem. Thank you for showing an interest. Not many do."

Adam beamed and shook Ted's hand. "I'll get out of your hair, now." As he did so he had a flash of an image of Ted falling. He shivered and added, "Just take care out there. We don't want you falling, again."

"Thank you. I'm sure I'll be fine, but thanks for your concern."

Adam nodded and smiled and made his way back to the spiral staircase, through the door, down the ladder, and back onto Terra Firma. He had an urge to speak to Vanda, something was bugging him. He strode purposefully to the house and picked up his phone and called her.

She answered sleepily, "My, you're early."

"Sorry. Didn't mean to disturb you…"

"No, go on," said Vanda sounding more alert.

"I've been thinking about what you told me… about your sister." As he said those words, a shiver ran down his spine and he heard the wind chimes tinkle.

"Yes?"

"Can you come across for coffee and …."

"Yes?"

"Do you have any photographs of Caroline?"

"I do."

"Can you bring one?"

"Sure. But why?"

"It's just a feeling… and anyway, I would love to see the face of the artist that painted these glorious seascapes and my grandfather's portrait."

"Okay. Give me a chance to shower and dress and I'll be across."

~ 11 ~

ADAM GLANCED UP AT THE kitchen clock, she would be here in a minute. The coffee was brewing and he had set out a plate of biscuits. He was eagerly looking forward to seeing Vanda and more importantly seeing what her sister, Caroline Mitchell looked like.

The doorbell rang and Adam hurried to admit her. She followed him into the kitchen where he poured her a mug of coffee to her taste, and they sat together at the kitchen table.

"Well? Did you bring it?" asked Adam anxiously.

"I brought what I thought was the best." Vanda opened her bag and took out a number of snapshots of her sister and passed one to Adam who pounced on it to study.

"This is her," he said excitedly. "This is the woman I've seen. Her hair is a little longer but it's her, I swear."

"Are you sure?"

He gazed at it again, "Positive. There is no mistaking her."

Vanda's eyes filled with tears, "In that case…" she hesitated, "I had hoped … then, she must be dead."

Adam fell silent realising that his recognition and confirmation of the woman he had seen, had cruelly taken away Vanda's last vestige of hope of ever seeing her sister alive again.

In some ways he wished he could unsay it, but he knew that was impossible. "I'm sorry, Vanda. This is definitely who I have been seeing. Did she wear patchouli oil?"

"She did, but I haven't seen her for so long. I was stupid not to connect that."

"No, not stupid. No one would want to imagine their missing sibling was not alive. I'm so sorry."

Vanda drained what was left of her coffee and gathered up the remaining photographs sitting on the table. "These are even more precious now," and she replaced them into her bag.

"So what now? What do you think it all means?"

Adam considered for a moment. "There has to be a reason that her spirit is still here. I believe the key to the mystery is here, this house."

"Or more likely, the annexed cottage, where she lived. Have you ever been in there?"

"No. I keep meaning to, but something seems to get in the way. No excuse I know."

"Life's like that."

"I will have to inspect it if I've any chance of renting it out for some extra income. That was my grandfather's plan for me. I've got the experience in that field. It would be easy."

"Come on, get the keys. Let's check it out."

Adam left the dregs of his coffee and went to the hallway where all the keys hung and picked up the ones labelled for the cottage.

They left the house and stood outside looking at the front of the place. Adam rattled the key in the lock. "It's a bit stiff... no cracks, please," he said with a laugh.

"It needs some oil. Try again."

Adam jiggled the key in the lock, and it finally clicked open. He turned the knob and pushed open the door and they stepped inside. The air was still, and cobwebs hung from the lights. They heard the sound of wind chimes tinkling, and a gust of wind blew the front door shut with a bang making them both jump.

They went further inside to the door of the sitting room. "Voila! It's still furnished. Could do with a good clean but it would make a great holiday let. It would be different from your boarding house, you wouldn't have to cook any meals, just keep it clean and change the linen. Much easier."

"Yep, you're right. But, that aside, let's have a good look around and see what we can find," said Adam.

They gazed around at the furnishings. There was a pack of pastels on the coffee table and some sketches. "The smell of patchouli is everywhere. She must have always worn it." Vanda touched an Indian designed throw that was over the settee. "I recognise this. We bought it at a local craft market when we went to India many moons ago."

"If it meant something to her, why would she leave it? And why leave her pastels and artwork behind? It doesn't make sense. Let's find the kitchen."

They crossed from the living room, across the hallway to the kitchen. On the kitchen table was a sunshine yellow mug with a smiley face. It seemed grotesque within the stillness of the house and situation.

Adam pointed to the countertop where there was a spoon and an open tea caddy and a teapot. "It's as if she was waiting to make herself a hot drink. Look."

"Mm, that's bizarre. What about upstairs?"

Adam and Vanda approached the stairs and climbed up them to the main bedroom and stepped inside. A variety of rough cut crystals sat on the dressing table and at the window was a dreamcatcher.

"Wow!" exclaimed Vanda.

"What?"

"This is so her. The dreamcatcher and crystals. She was a true free spirit."

"Until someone cut her life short." As Adam said those words strains of Portishead's Glory Box drifted up the stairs. They stopped and stared at each other before rushing from the room and racing back down the stairs.

They entered the living room where the CD player was playing, 'Give me a reason to love you....' Vanda crossed to the machine and switched it off.

"It's giving me chills," murmured Vanda wrapping her arms around herself.

"But there's nothing here. How could..." A flurry of wind blew through the room and the sketches on the coffee table shifted, lifted and fluttered to the floor. Vanda gathered them up and sifted through them.

Adam peered over her shoulder as she looked through them. There was a picture of Adam's grandfather, Victor, looking happy and smiling, one of the cottage, another of the lighthouse, and one of sea thrift and primroses. Vanda placed them back on the table.

"She really was very talented. Do you mind if I take the one of my grandfather?"

"They're not mine to give. They're in your property."

"But she's your sister."

"I'm sure Caroline would have wanted you to have them. I'll take the wild flowers on the cliff. They look like the ones around my house." Vanda sighed and smiled. "Right. What's next?" She picked up a torch on the table and tested it. "This still works."

"So?" said Adam puzzled.

Vanda rolled her eyes. "We have to get to the bottom of this. The police obviously went over the cottage. There's not a lot to see here. It doesn't make sense she would leave the tools of her trade. What's outside?"

Adam was slightly confused at the change of subject and hesitated. "Er... A greenhouse and an old tool shed... I think."

"Then this torch may be useful. Let's go and have a look."

"No time like the present. I warn you, I don't know what's out there. I haven't set foot outside."

"Come on." Vanda was eager to get going. They went out through the kitchen to the back door and drew back the internal bolts and stepped out into an overgrown and neglected garden.

Avoiding the nettles that were encroaching on the garden path, they picked their way through to the greenhouse and peered inside. Vanda shook her head sadly as she saw the rows of dead plants that mouldered on the shelves. "Caroline would never have left her plants to die. She loved flowers. Used to help Dad with all the gardening at home." Vanda switched on the torch and played the light on the inside. "No one has been in here in months. The dust is thick and undisturbed. Don't think we'll find anything here."

"Nevertheless, best to be thorough," said Adam stepping inside and looking around the decaying plants. There were bags of compost and a tomato grow bag. But even though Adam scanned the area with his eyes, nothing appeared to be out of the ordinary. "Okay," he murmured. "Next stop the shed."

Vanda followed Adam to the bottom of the garden, through the brambles and long grass to a gap in the hedge at the very end where the shed was housed. Vanda groaned, "Oh no! Now what?" The door of the hut was bearing a stout padlock, and it was securely locked.

"I'll soon fix that," said Adam, refusing to be beaten. He moved off to the rockery and picked up a large quartz rock and returned to the shed. "Stand back." Adam began hammering the padlock. The rock finally did its job, the padlock smashed, and the wood splintered. He threw down the rock and pulled at the door, which reluctantly creaked open and he stepped inside followed by Vanda. She switched on the torch, and they examined the interior.

Dust motes floated in the air like tiny alien parasites. This shed, like the greenhouse, looked forgotten. Old tools lay on a workbench. Vanda shone the torch around the space. The one window with an opaque pane was covered in grime and refused to let in any light.

Adam refrained from swearing and muttered, "There must be something, surely?"

"I would have thought the house and cottage would have had a cellar, a basement or something…"

"Me, too. But, we didn't see anything."

"Wait a minute. Why would a shed's dirt floor have a carpet? It's not like a cement floor that would be cold underfoot. It doesn't make sense."

Vanda stooped down and pulled up the old rug. Something flipped up with a ping and landed under the bench. Disturbing the motheaten rug sent clouds of dust flying up into the air making her cough. She scraped at the layer of dirt that was under the mat and gasped in astonishment. "Look!"

Adam stared in amazement at a trapdoor that had been hidden by the earth and carpet. He bent down on one knee and tugged at the round handle. It was refusing to budge. He heaved again and it became a little looser. A further tug and it finally gave. He pulled it open, and it revealed steps going down into the dark.

Vanda shone the torch down the uneven steps. "They disappear into the earth. It looks inky black down there."

Adam giggled, "I feel like a kid about to embark on an adventure."

"Me, too," Vanda agreed. "Let's see where they lead."

Cautiously they started down the stone steps with Vanda lighting the way with the torch. Their footsteps echoed hollowly as they walked down them. At the bottom, was a rocky tunnel. "I bet this was used by smugglers years ago," she whispered.

"I don't think my grandfather knew about this. He would have told me."

They continued through the passageway. The walls were wet with dripping water, and roots of plants trailed down. The secret route opened out into a cavern and the sound of the sea could be heard clearly. There was a well camouflaged door in the rocks, which Adam spotted. He hurried to it, and it opened easily. "Must be in regular use," he murmured.

Behind the door was a small room. As they set foot in the little chamber, the aroma of patchouli oil grew stronger and Adam swore he could hear wind chimes. In the corner was a huge chest. It had a large, insulated cable leading from it and going upwards.

Vanda shivered, "I don't like this. It feels bad."

Adam grasped the handle on the heavy chest and lifted the lid. Once opened he stepped back in horror. Inside the refrigerated chest, wrapped in polythene and covered in frost was the twisted body of a woman.

"Oh my God!" exclaimed Vanda. "Caroline."

"Don't touch anything. Call the police."

"That's if I can get a signal."

Vanda took her phone from her pocket and walked towards the cave entrance until she finally managed to get through, by which time, tears of despair streamed down her face. She rushed into Adam's arms and sobbed, "I always knew it was a possibility but even after the photographs, somehow a corner of me hoped I was wrong."

"What did they say?"

"They'll be here as soon as possible. We are to wait outside the house. We'd better move."

Adam nodded. "I know it's a tragedy but at least, you know now for sure. And now, we need to find the bastard who did this."

Further down the coast, on a cliff in a remote shepherd's cottage a light was burning. Inside, a pretty young woman, Angie Hartman, bound and gagged was sitting on the floor looking terrified. Her oversized shirt was ripped, and her appearance dishevelled. Sitting at the table, but not moving, was Lisa Devereaux. She stared ahead, glassy eyed, holding a knife and fork, but ignoring the meal in front of her. It was as if she was paralysed with some sort of drug, that had made her mute and immobile.

Footsteps could be heard approaching the door and Angie tried to make herself as small as possible, cringing away from the person who opened the door. She whimpered and screamed in terror as the man came into the room. He knelt down beside her and said softly, "No need to be afraid. You're part of my family now," and he gently stroked her cheek. She flinched as if burnt and twisted her head away as tears filled her eyes.

She whispered, "Please, don't hurt me."

"Hurt you? Why, that's the last thing I'll do. I am going to make you more beautiful than you could possibly imagine. I will love and honour you forever." The way he said those words made her shiver. "Oh dear, you're cold. Don't worry, I'll fetch you a nice warm rug. Wait there." He laughed and added, "Of course, you won't move. You can't." With that he stood up and laughed some more as he walked out of the room.

Outside Black Head Ridge House was a hive of activity. Two police cars with lights flashing were outside along with an ambulance and another large white van belonging to a team of scene of crime officers or SOCOs as they were known. A white marquee type tent had been erected as police and Forensics moved in and out of the annexed cottage, garden and house. Paramedics emerged with a gurney and figure in a body bag, which was wheeled to the ambulance and whisked away. Officials talked in hushed tones with each other.

Inside Black Head Ridge House, Vanda had set mugs out on the counter top and coffee was brewing. Here, too, a constant stream of people moved in and out, bringing with them blasts of cold air as the doors were all wide open. The crisp morning sunshine probed its way into the kitchen and washed the tiled floor a linseed yellow but there was no warmth in it.

Adam was being interviewed by Detective Andrew Harding. Vanda thought the questioning seemed quite intense as she poured coffee for another policeman, Paul Jacobs, who had just entered. He grinned at her, as she passed him the coffee, "Just what I could do with. It's cold out there." He cradled the mug in his hands in an effort to warm up.

Vanda crossed to Adam and the detective, giving them each a coffee. "Sugar's on the counter top if you need it."

She heard the detective say, "Good job you're a newcomer to the area and this house. It crosses you off the list of suspects."

"Suspects?" exclaimed Adam. "Do you have any?"

"Not yet. But we will."

The Medical Examiner, fifty-six-year-old , Jon Culshaw crossed the kitchen to the lead detective, Ricky Vance, a man in his forties who was studying his notes. He looked up, "Well?"

"After a cursory examination, it looks as though the girl was raped and strangled. Of course, I'll know more when I get her back to the lab. But the bruising on her neck suggests some kind of knotted ligature. Trauma to her thighs shows a violent assault."

Vanda overheard and bit back her tears, which threatened to run down her cheeks. She stifled a choking sob and turned it into a cough.

"Don't suppose we can get a time of death?"

Culshaw shook his head, "No, sorry. I'll get an approximation to you when I've finished my tests."

"Understood. As soon as you're done, let me have the report." Culshaw nodded, turned and left the kitchen. Vanda watched him go, apologised and fled from the kitchen.

Adam's face furrowed in a frown, and he turned to the detective, "Are we done here?"

Vance rose and approached Adam and Andrew Harding. He nodded at the detective, effectively dismissing him and spoke to Adam. "Mr Barrie, we'll be out of your hair soon. Please leave the place locked up. It's a scene of crime. My officers may still have to access the building and grounds. You understand?"

Adam affirmed and followed the detective to the door. Vanda was already there, and her shoulders were heaving as she tried to suppress her emotions. Adam put his arm around her, and she nestled into him. No words passed between them. Vanda didn't trust herself to speak and Adam didn't know quite what to say. They watched the police leave and the Forensic team as they dismantled the tent and packed it away in the white van. Elsa appeared and wrapped herself around Vanda's legs with a small mew. The SOCOs boarded the van and they, too, left the premises. Vanda was a little calmer now. They returned inside to the living room, followed by Elsa. Adam sank into an armchair in relief as Elsa jumped up onto Adam's lap and began purring and kneading his thighs making herself comfortable. Vanda observed from the doorway.

"She likes you. Can't think why…"

"Get on with you," said Adam good naturedly.

Vanda swallowed hard, she sat opposite him on the settee. "It's so hard. Not just that she's dead but to die in such a horrible way. I mean, raped and strangled and then frozen… why? Why her? What did she do to hurt anyone?"

"I don't know. Do you think this Philip Chapman had anything to do with it?"

"I'm not sure. He's not a pleasant man. He's done some terrible things but rape … I don't know. I just don't know."

Vanda stood up and moved to the door. "I have to get out of these clothes and shower. The smell of death is all over me. It's stuck in my throat. You know, my mother always used to say she could smell a coffin when someone died. I never understood what she meant, but I do now. It's disgusting. I can even taste it. I don't want to throw up in here."

"Don't worry, I've got a mop," he replied trying to lighten things. "But, I know what you mean. You get yourself back, do what you need to. It's been a shock for both of us. I'll catch up with you later. It's a lot to get your head around." Adam yawned, "I'm bushed. It's going to be an early night for me."

"Well, at least it's over. No more visions or music in the night. I'll see you very soon." Vanda walked across to Adam and kissed him tenderly before picking up Elsa who mewed in complaint.

"Thanks for everything, Vanda. You've been a tower of strength today. I don't know what I would have done without you."

"Nor I, you … Just think, if we hadn't decided to have a good look around, she might never have been found…"

"Doesn't bear thinking about."

"At least I can give her a proper burial."

"Yes, I'll help you with all that. I've been through all the form filling etc. Not an easy experience."

"Well, at least we found her. Her soul can rest now. And now, I must go." Vanda blew him a kiss and left with Elsa. Adam sat back in his chair and thought, 'Yes, at least it's all over.'

~ 12 ~

ADAM LAID IN BED WITH Vanda who was breathing steadily at his side. He was on the cusp of sleep and wakefulness. His eyelids were heavy and closed and he willed himself to slip away into a dream filled sleep that bore no terrors or imaginings. As he dozed, the bedside clock began to tick ominously, growing in volume becoming louder and louder with each passing second.

Adam stirred. Wind chimes tinkled in the air. Adam's eyelids fluttered open bringing him to full consciousness and he groaned, "What now?" He laid there a moment longer, but his eyes were drawn to the window. Unable to help himself, he slipped out of bed, careful not to disturb Vanda, and pulled back the curtain. He gazed out at the lighthouse standing proudly on the cliff its strong beam shining out across the water.

As he stood there a terrible cry carried across the water on the wind to where he stood. A cry so full of melancholy that it made the hairs on the back of his neck stand to attention. He glanced back at Vanda sleeping peacefully. Had she heard anything? It didn't seem so. Was it all in his head?

He turned back to the window again and focused on the beach and was shocked to see the figure of a woman on the beach running across the sand. She was wearing the same white floaty dress with a blue ribbon sash at her waist. Her long blonde hair streamed behind her as she ran. He shook his head and gasped, "It can't be."

It was almost as if she heard him. She stopped and turned, and stared straight at Adam with a pained expression on her face, which appeared closer and closer as if viewed through a magnifying glass. The closer she came, the more he could see her face and the sadness reflected in her eyes. There was no doubt the ghostly apparition was Caroline Mitchell. But why? Wasn't her body now found and she would soon be laid to rest? Adam tried to reason with himself but then she shot him a pleading desperate look of agony. She mouthed the word, 'Help'. As she said this, the wind chimes tinkled and Portishead's poignant notes echoed around him so much so, that Vanda woke from her sleep and sat up in bed. She saw Adam standing by the window and was filled with alarm. She called out huskily, "What is it?"

"It's not over. Not yet."

"What do you mean?"

"There's something else. Something far more sinister behind this and we have to find it. She wants something more from us. She's asking for our help."

Vanda shivered as she responded, "But not tonight. Please. Come back to bed."

Reluctantly, Adam turned away from the window and gazed at Vanda's beseeching eyes. He looked back at the beach, but Caroline was gone. There was no sign that she had ever been there. Adam sighed and returned to the bed and allowed himself to be embraced by Vanda who wanted to know exactly what he had seen. He tried to explain, and she listened carefully, nodding and murmuring encouragement after each of his sentences. When he finished there was a silence between them, a silence filled with apprehension.

Vanda finally spoke, her voice was soft and gentle, "She's gone now. There's nothing we can do. It will have to wait until morning."

Adam sighed and nodded his agreement. He tried to sleep but he was feeling unnerved. Vanda stroked his skin gently until her tender, soothing touch ceased, and she had fallen back to sleep. Adam remained awake for some time, felt her heart beating against his chest and he listened to her breathing that was deep and even, until suddenly the smell of patchouli oil filtered into the room. Adam knew, Caroline Mitchell would not let him rest until he had fulfilled her wishes. But what was it she wanted? Adam puzzled over this for over an hour until the need for sleep overcame him and he finally drifted away in a dreamless sleep.

The next morning, Adam rose quietly. Something had woken him from his deep sleep and although he was tired he simply couldn't settle. He didn't want his restlessness to disturb Vanda, so he crept from the room, grabbing his clothes and showered in the family bathroom rather than the en suite so as not to wake her. Turning the shower onto cold for the last minute had done the trick. He was invigorated and alert. He tiptoed down the stairs and set to making breakfast in the kitchen. A cup of coffee was what he needed first and after yesterday's activities he realised he was quite hungry. So, Adam began to prepare a full English with bacon crisping in the pan, golden hash browns, button mushrooms, fried tomatoes and he would put the eggs on last.

He set the table and made a fresh pot of coffee. The aroma of fried bacon and fresh coffee must have wafted up the stairs as Vanda appeared in the doorway dressed in one of Adam's shirts and his bathrobe, which she was in the process of tying. She yawned noisily and immediately apologised, "Oh, excuse me! Sorry."

She glanced at the table laid with napkins and even a small posy of wild flowers and smiled. She moved to the table and sat. "Something smells good."

Adam finished cooking the eggs, took the plates from the warming oven and dished up two mouth-watering breakfasts and joined her. No one spoke for a moment as they both tucked into the food. Adam raised his eyes and watched Vanda enjoying her meal, which pleased him, and he carried on eating.

It was clear something was bothering him, and he stopped mid forkful. "I have heard that souls won't rest until justice is done... I think this might be it. She's asking us to find her killer."

"How on earth do we do that? Surely, that's a job for the police?"

"Maybe, but she trusts us. That's why these strange happenings keep occurring. She wants *our* help. So, there has to be a way."

"That's going to be tough. We don't have any clues. Nothing. The Forensic team will have taken prints off that chest, the polythene and the wire. I doubt if they'll share that information with us."

"Probably not. They won't want anyone interfering in their investigation. But, she trusts us. I feel she will help lead us to her killer. And what else was it she said?"

"I don't know. You're the one who has picked up on her, not me. I've never seen her."

"She said, 'Find me. Save her.' So there's someone out there being held prisoner or something…"

"Well, other girls have gone missing and perhaps they are still alive?"

"Then, why say 'Save *her*'? Seems to me only one is possibly still around."

Adam took another bite of his bacon and shrugged, "Whatever she meant we have to do something."

"Shame we can't just conjure her up and ask her."

"It doesn't work like that."

"No, more's the pity. So, what do we do?"

"Finish our breakfast," said Adam, mopping up the rest of his egg with a slice of bread.

Outside the convenience store in Brinkworth stood a board advertising the local newspaper. There was a glaring headline, 'Body found underground at Black Head Ridge'. A group of people were together outside discussing the story.

Blake Simmons was reading the article with a hint of sadness. "It says here, she was found in a refrigerated container in some sort of underground room." He looked up, "Black Head Ridge; must be the cottage, it has to be Caroline Mitchell." He shook his head, "I can't believe it."

The postman, Jake chipped in, "Poor kid. She didn't deserve that."

"No. She was beautiful, a real temptress," said Blake.

"How do you mean? Why use those words?" interjected Steve, the barman at The Dog and Duck.

"Well, you have to admit, she was something of a flirt," said Blake defensively and then added, "… but gorgeous with it."

"I suppose, I just saw her as a fun loving woman, with great charm. Talented, too," said Steve.

"You know what this means?" said Jake looking around.

"What?" chorused the others.

"Well, to me… it looks like we have a murderer on the loose."

Blake surmised, "A serial killer, more like. Look at all the other disappearances and the resemblance between the women."

Steve looked uncomfortable as he posed the next question, "Do you think that's what happened to Angie?"

Blake shrugged and pursed his lips, "Who knows? But someone's responsible and it seems it's someone from around here."

The group looked suspiciously from one to another and fell silent. They were each weighing up the possibility of it being someone they might know.

Steve broke the silence. "We've not had anything like this happen before. What about that new bloke who's arrived at Black Head Ridge House?"

"No," said Blake. "He came here a long time after Caroline's disappearance."

"Maybe it runs in the family and his grandfather did away with Caroline. If her art was that good it would be worth twice as much now she's dead," said Steve.

"Definitely not," said Blake. "Victor Channing adored Caroline. He was championing her artwork and commissioning more pieces."

"Maybe the grandson did it on one of his visits," argued Steve.

"I don't believe that," interjected Jake. "Mr Channing was a lovely old boy. Always a delight to talk to, as is his grandson. No, it's someone else. Someone hiding in plain sight. Could even be someone here in this group." The men fell silent once more.

Further along the coast, in a shepherd's cottage along the cliff, Angie Hartman, sat at a table next to Lisa who remained silent. There was a plate of food in front of both of them. Angie picked at the food miserably and turned to her captor pleading with her eyes and voice, "Please, let me go. I won't say anything I promise." Angie looked around the room and implored, "I don't even know who you are or where I am. You could blindfold me and drop me in the town or where you found me. No one need ever know what you've done. Please."

Her masked captor remained silent, whilst his hands played with two thick pieces of cord. One piece in each hand. The right end passed over and under the cord in the left hand; then the cord in the left hand passed over and under the one in the right hand. The knot was menacingly tightened as both running ends were pulled tightly together to form a distinctive square knot.

Angie asked again, this time tears ran down her face. "Please." He said nothing. "You can't be all bad, you're feeding us and giving us something to drink. You must have family somewhere, too. I am supposed to get married this year, start my own family. Please." But her words fell on deaf ears that refused to listen and didn't want to listen.

Angie fell silent as the daylight hours dwindled into twilight and the inevitable darkness that followed. Her captor rose suddenly, and she flinched. He left the room and Angie looked about her for anything she could use to help her escape. She couldn't take the cutlery that would be noticed. There were two other places set. Who would be joining them? Her legs were bound tightly to the chair but her hands for the moment were free. She thought about not eating, but that would be stupid. The girl next to her wasn't eating. She was still in some sort of drug induced stupor and Angie could elicit nothing from her.

Angie grabbed a pickle fork in the centre of the table hidden by the condiments. Would he notice? It was worth a try. She needed somehow to be free of her bonds, but how? And how long would her kidnapper be away? Angie decided to eat her meal to keep her strength up and tried to formulate some sort of plan to escape. She had no idea how long she had been missing or if anyone had missed her yet. These and other thoughts spiralled around her mind, and she stifled a sob in her utter and abject despair.

Angie stuffed the pickle fork down her trousers at the front. It just poked out of her waistband. She pulled her oversized shirt down to cover it and tried to formulate some kind of plan. She knew he'd carry her to the loo and pull her trousers and pants down. Maybe that wasn't such a good idea. Where else could she hide it? She removed it from her trousers and contemplated trying to secrete it in her bra, when he returned. He saw the fork in her hands and said quietly, "Let me help you with that. You want some pickle?" Angie nodded, she could hardly say she didn't when she was holding it, and she wasn't very keen on pickle.

Her captor opened the jar and forked out a large, pickled onion. "How many?"

"Just one, please. Thank you." She didn't want to antagonise him and felt politeness was best. She didn't want to be drugged like Lisa. He duly deposited one onto her plate, which she attempted to cut and eat trying to disguise her dislike as the malt vinegar spices hit the back of her throat and she coughed.

"Here, have some water," he filled a glass from the jug and passed it to her, which she gulped from gratefully.

In Angie's mind the best way to stay alive was to humour him and be pleasant and that's what she endeavoured to do.

"I have to go," he said abruptly.

"Do you have to?" she asked sweetly. "It's lonely here and she won't talk."

"No. She can't," he said. Angie went to speak but he raised his hands. "No more questions now. I'll be back soon enough. We'll talk then." He said it almost genially and rose up tossing the pickle fork into the centre of the table, tantalisingly close but just out of reach of Angie's fingers. Inside she was praying he would leave her there, but it was not to be. Angie slumped back in despair and her captor grunted as he dragged her, in her chair, away from the table and put her next to the wall. Once there, he tied her hands behind her back again. Angie tensed her wrists and hands hard, in the hope that her bonds would be looser once he'd gone, and she relaxed. At least that is what she'd seen in films and read in books. She was unprepared for what he did next. He loosened her bonds to the chair and pulled her off it, moving the chair out of the way, returning it to the table. Then, he bound her legs with another piece of rope. He connected her hands behind her back, and threaded it up and around her neck. She had no chance of stepping through her bonds and untying her feet. She was well and truly stuck.

Vanda was entertaining Adam at Cliff House. They were just finishing a meal Vanda had prepared. The aroma of spices and herbs wafted in the air from the curry she had cooked. Adam took another gulp of his red wine and sat back, patting his stomach. "That was great. Thank you."

Vanda shook her head, "It was nothing special."

"It was special to me, because you cooked it."

"Flatterer."

"Well, I want to be invited again," he said with a laugh. He rose from his seat and wandered towards a coffee table where Vanda had laid out a number of paintings. He picked them up and started to go through them. "Wow! She did all these?"

"Yes, she was very talented."

"I've seen a lot of her work in the house, my grandfather really valued her as an artist. Beautiful seascapes and landscapes and some impressive portraits. She painted in so many different styles."

"Yes, that's what set her apart from other artists. She painted and sketched what she was passionate about and wanted to see. She wouldn't be forced into a box like many other artists who were only known for one thing, but she could create anything."

"Which is why she's so valuable to Philip Chapman?"

"Yes, she could mimic the old masters… anything. But, she didn't want to do it. She was duped into producing some pieces and then coerced into doing more by being blackmailed. It seems originally Caroline was being pressured to produce copies of famous paintings and then forced to create new artwork in the style of the artist which was then being promoted as original."

"Surely, they couldn't get away with that?"

"Oh, Philip was resourceful. He had precious crystals ground down to make the paint used, just as the grand masters did years ago, and then she painted over old canvases."

"Ingenious. So, do you think Philip Chapman or one of his hangers on could be responsible?"

Vanda screwed up her face as she thought. "I don't know. I don't think so. It would be like killing the goose that laid the golden egg. But, I'm not discounting it. Also, her own work is attracting a lot of attention. Philip could make a mint out of her now she's dead."

"Maybe he felt she knew too much and couldn't be trusted to keep quiet."

"Yes, it's a possibility. But he did seem genuinely upset when I talked to him the other day to let him know her body had been found. He then started pressuring me to let him have all her other work to sell."

"What did you say?"

"That I wasn't ready to do that yet."

"Hmm. If I were you, I would put all her work somewhere safe. We don't want to invite a burglary of some sort... you never know."

"No. You're right. Philip can be ruthless and unscrupulous, as I have seen many times. I know he's mixed up with some very bad people."

"Then you'd better be careful. And remember, some nut out there, is watching you. You just never know. So we both have to be careful, you especially."

"Thanks, for that!" she replied tartly. "I don't need reminding."

"Sorry, I'm just saying that's all," said Adam apologetically.

"No, I'm sorry. I shouldn't have snapped. I must admit the thought frightens me."

"No problem. You've just lost your sister in a most horrible way. You're bound to be spooked. The attack on me and you being watched was not imagined," said Adam ruefully.

"So, what do we do?"

"I don't know. But we have to do something. Come on, let's brainstorm and talk about everything we know. Got any paper?"

Vanda nodded and walked to the bureau. She took out a pen and some notepaper. "Right, let's get started."

Night fell.

A hooded figure wearing a duffle coat plodded along the cliff path. The sky was shrouded in fog and drizzling rain fell from the sky covering the grass and land in misty drops that bedecked spiders' webs and blades of grass with nature's jewels. The figure tripped on the uneven ground and regained his balance striding on with determination. The mysterious person continued on, and disappeared into the ever increasing mist. It appeared to be headed for Cliff House.

The walker approached the grand house and Elsa rushed out from the rocks and hissed at the stranger before hastening back down the steps to the beach. The stalker moved stealthily towards the big bay windows. Good, the curtains were not drawn. The miscreant could see inside the house to the living room quite clearly. Vanda was pacing around gesticulating with her hands as she spoke on the phone. A sigh escaped the watcher's lips. She was so much like her sister, Caroline, except for the hair. That woman had been denied him, he'd been forced to kill her and put her on ice until he could safely move her and now that would never be. The police had seen to that. A snarl of anger rose on his lips. The figure moved in closer to watch some more.

Vanda put down her phone and appeared to be crying. The door opened, and Adam walked in and comforted her. The figure hissed in anger as soon as Adam came into view and the watcher disappeared back into the dark.

"Are you okay?"

"It's that awful Philip Chapman with his veiled threats."

"What do you mean?"

"Oh, nothing concrete just the hint of menace. He said things like, 'It would be a pity if people found out about your sister that she was not all she seemed to be.'

"I told him if they did, it would ruin him, too, and he twisted things to make it seem like I was threatening him… Oh, I don't know."

"What does he want?"

"The remainder of Caroline's paintings and sketches. Well, he's not going to have them. He put the phone down in anger and said, I would be very silly indeed, to refuse."

"Sounds like he's got over his initial grief, then?"

"Huh! Crocodile tears just for my benefit. I don't know what to think."

Adam embraced her and cradled her in his arms. He didn't like what he was hearing. This Chapman character seemed dangerous. "I don't think you should stay here at the moment. We know someone is watching you. You will be safer with me."

"What about Elsa?"

"She can come too. Get a bag with some things and stay awhile. If you need anything from the house, I will come with you to collect them."

"Oh, I don't know…"

"Come on, Vanda. You know it makes sense." Vanda nodded her agreement. "No time like the present. Come on, get your things. We'll walk back to mine. I'll help with Elsa's bits and bobs. Just leave a light burning in your room, people will believe you're home." As he said those words, wind chimes could be heard tinkling and a white feather floated down and landed on Vanda's shoulder. "There you are!" exclaimed Adam. "It has your sister's and my grandmother's seal of approval."

Later that night, the stalker returned to Cliff House. He could see just one light on upstairs, but the rest of the house was in darkness. 'She must be in bed. That would be perfect.' He grinned to himself. He peered in through the ground floor windows but could see nothing. So he switched on his flashlight and shone it into the rooms. There was no one sitting in the darkness, so he moved on. He tried the front door, it didn't open. He moved to the back of the house and tested all of the windows and the back and side doors to the property, but they were all securely locked, all except for one little window that Vanda had always left open for Elsa. He clambered onto the window sill and put his hand through the small open window and stretched down to the big window. He fiddled with its catch and jiggled it. He sighed gratifyingly as he managed to release it. He pulled back his arm and slid the sash window up. It creaked a bit as it shifted, obviously it had not been used for some time and he paused not wanting to alert anyone inside. No one came. All was still and quiet. Good. He put one leg over the sill, bent double and crept inside. He shone his torch around the area and looked about him. So far so good.

The intruder slipped into the hallway and looked up the stairs to where he could see a narrow beam of light beneath one door. He mounted the stairs carefully, slowly edging his way up, keeping his tread close to the bannisters believing they would be more likely to groan nearer the centre of the step. Beads of sweat were now forming on his forehead as he reached the landing. He inched along it and stopped outside the door.

Was she awake or asleep? If the light was on, it was likely she was reading. Was she alone? The thought of her being with someone began to excite him but also filled him with trepidation. He put his ear to the door and listened. There was nothing. Slowly, he began to turn the door knob until it clicked. The sound it made almost made him jump but he managed to control his fear. He gingerly opened the door until it was just ajar and listened. Nothing… maybe she had fallen asleep? But, he could hear nothing. He pushed the door with his fingertip, and it swung open. Holding his breath, he ventured into the room.

It was empty.

The intruder searched through the rest of the house, but it was clear no one was home. He smiled wryly. He could afford to take his time. He returned to the main bedroom and rummaged through Vanda's wardrobe and chest of drawers. He selected a few pieces; she could wear these, when he finally captured her, and a couple of clothing items that might suit his other girls, he had no change of clothes for them so these would do very well.

The stalker picked up a lipstick from Vanda's cosmetics. This would also do very nicely. He went back down the stairs with his prizes and left through the front door, leaving it unlocked and was soon gone having disappeared into the night.

AT BLACK HEAD RIDGE HOUSE Vanda was sitting at the kitchen table watching Adam prepare a couple of sandwiches. She seemed lost in a world of her own. His voice interrupted her thoughts, startling her as a thought occurred to him. "Vanda?"

"Yes?" she cast her eyes back at him. "What is it?"

"Remember when we were in the shed and pulled up the carpet?"

"What about it?"

"There was a ping as if we'd disturbed a stone or something?"

"No, not really," said Vanda with a puzzled frown as she thought back to their time in the shed.

"Well, perhaps ping is the wrong word. Something got flicked up. I'm now thinking it might be important."

"Surely if there was anything the police would have found it? They were pretty thorough and hardly likely to tell us, if they had found anything."

"Maybe."

"But we can't go back in there. It's a crime scene. Everything's taped off."

"Possibly, but..."

"Why do I feel I'm not going to like what you say?"

Adam shrugged, "Perhaps if we do what they do and cover our feet and clothes etc we could go in without contaminating anything."

"And what if we get caught?"

"We won't. Come on, it's worth a shot." He looked pleadingly at her as he carried the sandwiches across, sat and joined her.

"Okay… so if I agree and I'm not saying I do, mind. Just how do we cover ourselves? We don't have forensic suits."

"We have all we need, plastic bags, hats, surgical gloves… we can improvise."

Vanda laughed, "Okay, as soon as we have finished our sandwiches we'll see what we can do."

Adam grinned; "Looking forward to it!"

They munched on their tuna and cucumber sandwiches, drank their tea and then Adam rummaged in a drawer in the kitchen and produced a number of items. They put freezer bags on their feet over their shoes secured with elastic bands, plastic bags encased their hair and were knotted at the front to keep them fixed. Elastic bands covered their surgically gloved wrists holding their shirt and blouse sleeves in place. They were already giggling at their ridiculous appearances, looking like refugees from a plastic factory. Vanda used a lint roller to remove any stray hairs on Adam's coat and he did likewise to Vanda. After giving each other the once over, and with Elsa streaking off, with a yowl, as soon as she saw them, they gave each other a nod and disappeared out of the door.

They moved around the back to the cottage garden and made their way to the old tool shed. They ducked under the yellow crime scene tape, opened the door and stepped inside. Vanda held a larger flashlight and shone it around the shed. It looked the same. Adam knelt down on the earth floor and patted the carpet under the bench. Vanda stopped and shone the light in that area.

Right at the back, Adam spotted something. He stretched out his arm towards the object, grabbed it and pulled it out. He stared at it and showed it to Vanda; it was a wooden toggle. He examined it and popped it in a plastic bag.

"Do you think that's it?" asked Vanda.

"Has to be. There's nothing else is there?"

"Best be certain," said Vanda. They spent another fifteen minutes, scouring the shed floor and the bench and flower pots. They discovered, nothing more, apart from some small pieces of pea gravel used for drainage for potted plants, which belonged there.

Adam sighed as he stood up. "A gardener I would never make. My knees are killing me. Come on, let's get back to the house and have another look at this beauty."

They trekked back to Black Head Ridge House and returned to the kitchen. He held the object up to the light. "It's a toggle." Still looking ridiculous in their homemade forensic plastic outfits, they scrutinised it in the bag.

"Looks like someone's lost it from a waterproof coat or bag."

"Or a duffle coat," said Adam.

"Caroline used to wear a duffle coat, sometimes," said Vanda.

"That doesn't help."

"No, there wasn't any sign of a coat with the body."

"Was there one with her clothes that were left?" asked Adam.

"I don't think so."

"Damn! Then we're no nearer." Adam ripped off his plastic knotted head covering and threw it in the kitchen bin in frustration.

"Well, let's think… who do we know or who have we seen wearing a duffle coat in Brinkworth?" suggested Vanda.

Adam thought for a moment, "Crikey, I've seen a few."

"Who? And which ones knew Caroline?"

"Um… Jake. He wears one sometimes."

"Jake?" asked Vanda looking puzzled.

"You must have met him… Our postman. He would have known Caroline. I hear they used to walk the cliffs together. I can't believe he'd have anything to do with it."

"Never say never. It's often someone you'd never suspect."

"Only in story books," said Adam dismissing the thought. "Also, the barman, Steve at The Dog and Duck. He went out with her."

"Hmm. I've seen your friend Blake Simmons, the estate agent, wearing one of those Parka style coats with a hood. They often have toggles, and he knew Caroline. He went out with her, too."

"Um… And our friendly lighthouse keeper."

"He went out with Caroline?"

"No," laughed Adam. "But, he wears a tatty duffle coat. I'm not sure he would have even met Caroline."

"We can't discount anyone. Let's get out of this ridiculous garb and make a list." They divested themselves of the plastic bag paraphernalia. "Oh, no!" exclaimed Vanda.

"What?"

"I meant to take a picture of you for posterity."

"Then it's a good job I've binned mine."

"Spoilsport. Gosh, is that the time? I must feed Elsa."

"Where is Elsa?"

"She's been going between here and Cliff House. I think she's a bit confused as to where her home is. I had better get back."

"Wait. I will come with you. You never know. It's not safe."

"I'll be fine. I'll come straight back, I promise. I just need to check on Elsa."

"No," he was adamant. "I'm coming. The list can wait. You never know we might think of some more people as we walk."

Vanda smiled, "Come on then."

They left the house and walked the cliff path to the house. "Look," said Vanda. "You can see the sun and moon in the sky at the same time. I wonder what that means?"

Adam looked up, "It's quite a rare phenomenon, I think. But the moon can be illuminated by the sun when it's really bright."

"Oh? I bet it has a special name. Does it?"

"I expect so, but I don't know it. We can Google it when we get back."

Vanda frowned. "Adam? Look."

Adam followed the direction of her finger and saw the open window. He put a restraining arm out to Vanda. "We have to be very careful. Open the door and let me go in first."

"Do you think whoever it is, is inside?"

"I don't know, but best to be prepared."

Vanda opened the door and they stepped into the hall. They looked about them warily. They moved into the sitting room and Vanda crossed to the window to close it, but Adam stopped her. "No. Don't touch it!"

"But, I can't leave it open," she protested.

"No. But put gloves on. You never know. Whoever opened it may have left prints."

"I never thought of that. Wait. I've got some surgical gloves in the kitchen for when I'm chopping chillies. I'll get them."

"We'll go together," asserted Adam. They moved back to the hall and into the kitchen. "Nothing seems to have been disturbed here," said Adam. "Tell me, why do you wear gloves chopping chillies?"

"Oh, on one occasion I rubbed my eye after doing that and I paid for it. Chilli burns the eye and any other sensitive area. It was horrible. My eye closed up with the swelling and irritation so now, I use gloves."

Adam nodded. "I see. Well, put them on and then you can close the window. I suggest you shut the top one as well. That's obviously how he managed to open it."

"Agreed." Vanda put on her gloves and returned to the sitting room where she ensured both windows were firmly closed and locked.

"Look, there's some sand here," said Adam.

"That could be nothing. Elsa often traipses sand into the house when she's been on the beach."

"Or it could have come from the intruder," said Adam. "Best keep an open mind."

They inspected the other reception rooms but found nothing untoward. "I suspect, our burglar has gone now but we had better check upstairs," said Vanda sounding more confident than she felt. She started for the foot of the stairs and crept up them slowly to the landing. They checked the spare bedrooms and family bathroom before entering the master bedroom. Vanda gulped. Someone had clearly been in here. Two of the drawers in the chest of drawers were open and her underwear had been rifled through. The wardrobe door was open, and Vanda looked inside. "Some of my clothes are missing," she exclaimed.

"Are you sure?"

"Most definitely. Some of my underwear, too. Damn, he's taken my favourite dress," she muttered.

"What is this guy? A transvestite? A drag queen?"

"Maybe. Or maybe, he's taking clothes for his other victims. Oh, I don't know. All I know is that someone is taking an unhealthy interest in me, and I don't like it."

"Do you still think it could be Philip Chapman?"

"Philip doesn't wear a duffle coat."

"No. But you said that Caroline wore one sometimes."

"Yes. She did. What are you thinking?"

"Maybe it was Caroline's toggle and so it doesn't mean a thing."

"Perhaps you should give it to the cops? Let them check it out."

"Then they'd know we entered their crime scene."

"Does that matter?"

"Possibly. Can you make a list of what's missing? Then we can decide what we need to do."

Vanda went to her dresser and opened a drawer and removed a small notepad. She sat on her vanity stool and started to make a note of missing clothes. She glanced at her cosmetics and frowned. She searched through her lipsticks. "Oh bum!"

"What?"

"My new lipstick. That's gone, too…"

"That settles it. Get what else you need and lock the house up. No toing and froing. You stay with me until this fiend is caught."

"I'm not arguing," said Vanda. "Let's get back. I feel defiled, somehow."

Once back at Black Head Ridge House, Adam called DCI Vance. He began to explain about the break-in at Cliff House. Vance listened attentively.

"I was going to call you," said the sharp tones of the detective.

"Oh?"

"It doesn't matter for now. But, this interests me. I'll get a man on watch just to be safe and send a team to check the point of entry. Someone will be along shortly. They will collect the evidence you have found. Who knows, it could well be a lead. But, I need to remind you, no more encroaching on the crime scene. Stay away."

"Yes, sorry. But we did take precautions. We can't have contaminated it."

"For your sake, I hope not. However, if all you say is true then Miss Sullivan may well need protection. I'll see to it."

Adam thanked the detective and returned to Vanda. "All in hand, Vance is sending someone out. I told him everything."

"Everything?"

"Everything," Adam affirmed. "Someone will be along shortly to pick up our find from the shed. And go through your house where you were broken into."

"I hope they find something that will get the creep responsible for all this." "Me, too, Vanda. Me, too."

Blake Simmons was at the police station undergoing what he would describe as an interrogation. All that was missing was a spotlight on his face and a foreign accent in his ear. He was becoming extremely uncomfortable under the scrutiny and his anger was building.

"I don't understand why I am here," he said brusquely.

"Tell me, Mr Simmons, where were you on these dates?" and Vance reeled off three dates.

"I don't know. I'd have to check my calendar. I can't remember off the top of my head. I doubt whether you could either," he said tartly.

"I don't need to remember. You will have to check your calendar and get that information. We will of course follow up on this."

Blake bristled at the question. "I don't like what you're implying."

"And what exactly is that?"

"You're treating me like a suspect."

"Everyone is a suspect until proved otherwise." Vance leaned forward in his seat, "You went out with Caroline Mitchell, yes?"

"Yes, I did. But not for very long."

"And why was that?"

"We weren't compatible."

"Yes, I heard."

"I don't know what you've heard…"

"Quite a bit, Mr Simmons. I know you were very possessive with her and tried to control her. In fact, you caused quite a scene in The Dog and Duck on one occasion." Blake Simmons fell silent. "Tell me, Mr Simmons, do you own a duffle coat? Or a waterproof coat with wooden toggles?"

Blake looked surprised at the question. "Why do you ask?"

"Answer the question."

"Er… yes I have a rainproof hooded jacket with toggles. Caroline wore one sometimes, too, a duffle coat, that is."

"I see. Can you bring your jacket into the station for us to see?"

"I can but I'd still like to know why."

"Not your concern." Vance terminated the interview. "You're free to go."

Blake rose and looked at Vance. "Look, I had nothing to do with Caroline's disappearance or any of the others. You are welcome to search my house and business premises."

"Oh, don't worry, Mr Simmons. If we need to, we will."

Vance watched Simmons leave and rubbed his chin thoughtfully. He called to his sergeant, "Jacobs?"

"Sir?"

"Who else is on the list of duffle coat, waterproof jacket wearers?"

Jacobs consulted his notebook. "Um, quite a few, Jake … Macready. Postman on the Channing's and Mitchell's round...Steve Barker barman at The Dog and Duck. Geoff Merryweather, Ted Johnson and John Grey."

"Remind me again, who are they?"

"Geoff Merryweather runs the hardware store, Ted Johnson is the lighthouse keeper and John Grey runs the gallery where she sold her artwork. Those are the ones who she either knew or men that lived and worked within a reasonable distance of her home. But if you want to include everyone that has waterproof coats with wooden toggles you'd be looking at more than half of Brinkworth."

"Hmm. Let's start with those listed and get them in for questioning."

VANCE LOOKED AT THE MOTLEY collection of men waiting to be interviewed. John Grey shuffled his feet nervously. Rick Vance pointed at him. "Mr... Grey? Come this way."

John Grey rose. He was dressed casually in an open necked striped shirt with a cravat and chinos. He carried a waterproof jacket. He rose hesitantly and felt the eyes of the other waiting men watching him. He followed Vance into the interview room and sat where indicated.

Vance launched into a list of questions, while Jacobs scribbled down his responses. "You knew Caroline Mitchell?"

"Why, yes. She was one of my artists. I sold a lot of her work at the gallery."

"Where were you on..." he consulted his notes, "the thirteenth of April."

John Grey thought for a moment, "In Nice. I was at an exhibition of artwork to buy for my gallery. I was there for the week, meeting other art dealers and returned home on the 22nd."

"You can prove that?"

"Certainly. I have my airline ticket and hotel bookings plus plenty of people in the art world who saw me. Oh, and my wife accompanied me, too. They can all vouch for me."

"Thank you, Mr Grey. If you can give my sergeant here a list of the people who saw you and the name of the exhibition centre in Nice. I don't expect we will have to bother you again."

John Grey rattled off a number of names including his contact details for his wife and the name of the hotel where he stayed in Nice. This appeared to satisfy Vance.

"Thank you, Mr Grey. We will check out all this information and probably not have to see you again. Thank you for your time."

John Grey immediately looked relieved. He rose and shook hands with Vance and then added, "You might want to check out Philip Chapman."

"And he is?"

"He's a dealer, and from what Caroline said to me, she was afraid of him. He doesn't live in Brinkworth, but he would turn up at odd times to see her."

"Thank you, Mr Grey. Do you have his details?"

"I can give you his number." John Grey, took out his mobile phone and ran through his contacts and passed on the dealer's number.

"Thank you. You have been most helpful." John Grey nodded and left the room. Vance turned to Jacobs. "I think we'll be able to cross him off the list. Has Blake Simmons returned with his coat?"

"He did, earlier this morning."

"And?"

"The jacket had different colour wooden toggles from the one found in the potting shed. I would say he's not our man."

"Did he reveal his whereabouts on the dates in question?"

"Yes, but no one could corroborate his alibi as he was home alone."

"Hmm. Then we can't dismiss him completely. Let's get the next one in." Jacobs nodded and went to the door and waved in Jake Macready.

Jake shuffled in looking uncomfortable and sat down awkwardly, gazing around the sparsely furnished interview room and the two detectives facing him.

"Mr Macready? Jake Macready?" Jake nodded. "Can you please vocalise your answers."

"Sorry, yes."

"Mr Macready can you tell me where you were on the thirteenth of April?"

Jake looked confused, "Sorry… no, I don't know…"

"Have you any way of finding out?" questioned Vance.

"Maybe. Can I ask… What's this in connection with?"

"The disappearance of Caroline Mitchell."

Jake coloured up. "Oh, of course... that's when she left, wasn't it?"

"It was. What can you tell me about her?"

"Caroline was..." his expression turned dreamy. "She was special. A real darling. I liked her, a lot."

"Did you ever take her out?"

"No. We were friends and often walked together. Things were going well."

"But you'd have liked to? Take her out?"

"Who wouldn't? She was lovely."

"I understand that you and Mr. Channing discovered her missing, is that correct?" Jake launched into retelling the events as they had happened that day while Vance listened, and Jacobs made notes. "Tell me, do you own a duffle coat?"

"Why yes, a comfortable hangover from my student days. A bit tatty now but still warm especially on the coast here with the winds that come off the sea."

"We'd like to see that coat, if we may? Can you bring it in?"

"I suppose so, yes. Why do you want it?"

"We'd just like to see it. It will eliminate you from our enquiries."

"What? You think I would have hurt Caroline?"

"I didn't say that."

"But, it's implied," said Jake crossly.

"It's nothing personal. Please understand, we have to check out everyone who knew her."

Jake appeared to calm down, "Yes, of course. Anything to help." The interview continued and Jake rose and shook hands with the detectives. "Get the bastard who did this, won't you?"

"We will certainly do our best." Jake nodded and left.

Jacobs went to call the next person in when Ted Johnson stood up and apologised. "Sorry, but can I come back later? I have to go on duty at the lighthouse and I have a lot to do. I'll happily come in when my shift is over."

Jacobs looked at Vance who hesitated then nodded. "Yes, understood. We will reschedule at a time to suit. Speak to Jacobs here and book a suitable time." Vance dismissed him and called in Steve, the barman from The Dog and Duck.

Vance had begun his questioning when his phone rang. He left Jacobs to continue and went outside the interview room to respond. "Vance…"

"Tom Bailey, Path Lab."

"Tom. What have you got for me?"

"Well, we have to wait until the body becomes unfrozen before I can perform the autopsy."

"Yes. Could take a week you said?"

"Yes. In a refrigeration unit at thirty-eight degrees to prevent decomposition of the outer body and extremities but we have found something, or it could be nothing…"

"Yes?" Vance perked up. This sounded interesting. "What?"

"In the folds of her frozen dress, we pulled out a pair of glasses, wire framed. Did our vic wear glasses?"

"No idea. I'll find out. Thanks, Tom."

Vance went through the men he'd already interviewed. None of them wore glasses. Did Adam Barrie or Vanda Sullivan wear them? Or maybe Victor Channing? That may be more likely. He was an old man. Vance retreated back into the interview room and continued questioning the barman from The Dog and Duck.

Steve was both evasive and defensive on all the questions to do with Caroline. He snapped sharply, "You'd be better off questioning Philip Chapman rather than me. He had some sort of hold on Caroline, she said as much."

Vance kept his face impassive as if he had never heard Philip Chapman's name before, "What did she say?"

"That she didn't like the man, but had no choice but to work for him and she wished she didn't."

"Why did she say that?" Vance was trying to elicit as much information as possible.

"I asked her that same question. She told me, she owed him and couldn't get out of a contract. Go pester him. I would never hurt Caroline. I am not so sure about him. You know he broke into her apartment when she lived in Brinkworth. He was intimidating and she was in trouble."

"I see. Where can I contact this Chapman?"

"Try John Grey at the gallery that sold her work. He'll know. He's well up in the art world. I'm surprised he didn't mention him. He's quite an unsavoury character masquerading as someone a cut above, if you get my drift?"

"Thank you." Vance appeared dismissive but his eyes gleamed. "Now, back to my first question... where were you on the night Caroline disappeared?"

"Home," he answered with a hint of belligerence.

"Can anyone corroborate that?"

"No. I was home alone all night after I finished work."

"You didn't talk to anyone, phone anyone?"

"No," he said glumly. His face was grim.

"You'll have no objection to me taking a swab?"

"A swab?"

"Yes, for your DNA."

"I don't expect I have a choice?"

"You can refuse. But it wouldn't look good."

"Very well."

Steve allowed Jacobs to scrape the inside of his mouth with a cotton bud, which was sealed in a tube.

"Thank you. You're free to go, Mr Barker."

Steve couldn't get out of the room quickly enough.

"That's it for the moment." Vance turned to Jacobs. "When is Ted Johnson coming in?"

"He said he'd return in two hours once he'd checked everything over at the lighthouse, but he wouldn't have long with us, he would need to return again after the interview."

"Find me when he gets here. I have some calls to make."

Vance immediately rang the number he'd been given by John Grey. The metallic clipped tones of Philip Chapman answered, "Yes?"

"Mr Chapman, Philip Chapman?"

"Who wants to know?"

"Detective Chief Inspector Vance, Brinkworth Police."

His voice immediately lost its brusqueness and became more oily and subservient. "Inspector…"

"Chief Inspector," Vance corrected.

"Sorry, Chief Inspector. What can I do for you?"

"Caroline Mitchell."

"What about her?"

"We are investigating her disappearance and murder, and your name has cropped up in our enquiries. Can you come into the station for an interview?"

"Depends when. I am a busy man."

"As are we all. You will have to make time for this. It is most important."

"Very well." Chapman's tone became more clipped. He was clearly irritated. "When?"

"Shall we say tomorrow at 11:00?"

"Let me see…" Vance could hear the man shuffling some papers. "I can alter a couple of appointments." He paused. "Very well. 11:00 tomorrow. I hope this won't take long."

"It will take as long as it takes," said Vance cryptically. "I'll see you tomorrow," and he replaced the receiver thoughtfully. He didn't like the sound of this man and he wondered if he wore a duffle coat.

Two hours later Ted Johnson appeared back at the station and looked nervous. He shook hands with Vance and sat opposite looking awkward and he kept studying his watch.

"Do you have to be somewhere, Mr Johnson? You keep looking at your watch."

"The lighthouse, I don't want to be late for my shift. I have a lot to do."

"I appreciate that as I know you came in earlier. This won't take long." Ted nodded. "How did you know Miss Mitchell?"

"I didn't. Oh, I knew who she was, of course. I often saw her sketching on the cliffs. If I was on the catwalk polishing the reflector lens she always gave me a friendly wave. Looked a really nice lady."

"You never came across her in town?"

"Well yes, but just to nod at, like. Not to talk to."

The questioning continued. "Do you own a duffle coat or waterproof jacket?"

"I do."

"Could you bring it or them in please, to be examined?"

Ted shrugged, "Of course. Will there be anything else?"

"Just a question of where you were on these dates."

Vance reeled off a list and Ted Johnson shook his head. "I haven't a clue. I expect I would be on duty at some time during the day, otherwise I'm pretty much on my own apart from my trips to town for shopping and so on. I often get a take-away to take home. Not much of a cook, see. They'd remember me. Sorry, I can't think at the moment or be of more help."

"Do you have anyone that could verify where you were on any of the dates?"

"I'd have to check back on my old duty rosters. Sorry. Except…"

"Except?"

"The day Miss Mitchell vanished."

"What about it?"

"I went to the chippy after my shift, they might remember me."

"Thank you, Mr Johnson, we will check."

"Lucy or Brett would remember me… yes, definitely."

"Thank you, we will pay them a visit. In the meantime if you could bring in your duty list when you bring your coats."

"Of course. I can do that."

"Thank you. Here's my card, if you think of anything else."

Ted nodded and left.

Vance returned to his office and studied the messages on his desk. He stared out of the window as his mind ticked over with what he'd learnt and considered the men he'd interviewed. He reached across and picked up the phone, checked a number on his list and dialled.

Vanda, still in her nightgown and dressing gown, sat with a fully dressed Adam, in the kitchen enjoying a cup of coffee when the phone rang. Adam went to answer it. "Yes?"

"Mr Barrie?"

"Speaking."

"DCI Vance here. I was just wondering... have you lost a pair of spectacles?"

"No, why?"

"What about Miss Sullivan?"

"No. Neither of us wear glasses." He glanced across at Vanda and she shook her head. "No, definitely not."

"It could mean nothing, but it might just mean a break in the case."

"The wooden toggle wasn't any help then?"

"Not yet. But it could be. I have a list of people who wear jackets and coats with toggles that Miss Mitchell knew. They will be bringing them in for us to examine."

"I see. So, why do you need to know if we wear glasses?"

Vance hesitated uncertain how much to say and divulge to him, "Did Miss Mitchell wear glasses?"

Adam referred to Vanda again. "Did Caroline wear glasses?"

"Not that I'm aware of; mind you, I hadn't seen her in a while."

"Miss Sullivan doesn't think she wore glasses."

"Thank you for confirming that. I'll be in touch."

"Wait! Why do you want to know?"

"I'm afraid I can't say anymore in case I compromise the investigation." Vance ended the call.

Adam replaced the receiver and sat back at the table. "Well, that was weird. Vance wouldn't say why he wanted to know if any of us wore glasses."

"What do you think it means?"

"I'm not sure, but it must be important."

"So, the toggle wasn't any use?"

"Doesn't look like it, at least not yet."

Adam sighed heavily, his brow creased up in a frown as something was eluding him. Something he couldn't quite remember. "What if a pair of glasses were found with the body or in their first search of the shed. They wouldn't tell us."

"Maybe that's why they thought they could have belonged to us or Caroline?"

"Yes, it's very puzzling."

"They could have belonged to Caroline… I'm not sure if she wore them or not. Maybe she did for close work but I'm sure I would have known… or…"

"Or…?"

"Maybe the police think they could belong to her killer," mused Vanda.

"You could be right," said Adam, when suddenly, he remembered the elusive fact he was struggling to recall and exclaimed, "I've got it… I wonder…"

Vanda looked at him curiously. "What?... What aren't you telling me?"

"If the glasses belonged to the killer then I think I know who killed Caroline." Adam rose and walked to the kitchen door.

"Who?" Adam shook his head and said nothing. "Then phone Vance and tell him your suspicions." Adam didn't respond. "Adam! Tell the police," she said insistently.

"I need to be sure. I don't want to accuse an innocent man."

"Can you at least tell me…?" Vanda called out as Adam went into the hall.

Adam opened the front door and shouted back, "If I'm not back in fifteen minutes, call the cops."

He opened the front door as Vanda shouted, "No, wait!" She ran to the hall, but Adam had gone, and her words were left hanging in the air.

"Why? Why? Why?... Damn the man!" she exclaimed in frustration. "Men can be so difficult." She returned to the kitchen and her coffee and checked the time. "Fifteen minutes… must be someone close by, but who?" She muttered some more about men being insufferable at times and dashed upstairs to get dressed. She decided she would attempt to follow him. He hadn't taken the car so must be on foot. Vanda hurriedly dressed, grabbed her mobile phone, and coat, and ran out of the house in pursuit of Adam. After all, if he was right, he could be putting himself in danger. Silly man. And, she didn't want anything to happen to him. She stared about her wildly… 'But which way did he go?' She shaded her eyes from the sun and scanned the vista. She couldn't see him. 'Is he headed to town on foot? No, surely not. He could have gone along the cliff path or onto the Brinkworth Road.' "Oh, bugger," she exclaimed as she made her way along the road that led to the cliff path. She hoped she was right.

ADAM HAD RUN TO THE cliff path and was now striding out on the track that led towards the lighthouse. Ted's beat up old vehicle was parked close to the cliff edge. 'Good, he is on duty.' Adam quickened his stride and moved to the base of the towering structure. He looked up. Ted was busy cleaning the reflectors as he did every day. His tatty duffle coat hung on a rail. Adam glanced at his watch. 'Good, he won't be long now.'

Adam turned back and quietly walked a little way down the cliff trail towards an overhang that harboured a rock on the cliff edge where he could sit without being seen. Adam stared out at the innocent sea, calm and serene, except by the rocks and a jagged pinnacle that rose up, where the water crashed ferociously, and spray flew up almost thirty feet in the air. The sky was a stunningly deep azure blue where seagulls circled and soared, calling to each other in the gentle breeze.

Adam found it hard to reconcile his feelings, a mixture of trepidation and anger, if he was right, about the man whom he had met who seemed so pleasant, and he was not sure what he would do. If he was wrong, then no harm would be done. However, the view was spectacular in front of him, and was so spectacular it served to calm him. It filled Adam with joy and something else. In his head he heard the tinkle of wind chimes, and the aroma of patchouli oil filled his senses. He was inexplicably certain now of what had seemed his wild assumption.

The ladder rungs of the lighthouse vibrated against the tall structure as the lighthouse keeper, wearing his new glasses, climbed down it towards the cliff top. He was carrying a large heavy flashlight, wearing his duffle coat that had one toggle missing. Adam turned and clambered off the rock and scrambled up the overhang onto the path. He rose to his full height and walked casually towards Ted Johnson who stopped in surprise when he saw and recognised him.

Ted's manner was friendly and his voice warm, "Oh, hello, Mr Barrie. Nice day, again."

Adam smiled noticing the missing toggle. Now, he was absolutely certain. "Yes, it is. Quite beautiful. I don't believe I will ever tire of this view. It's really breathtaking. You're a lucky man to work in these surroundings, even if it is a somewhat lonely existence."

"Oh, I don't mind my own company. I feel blessed and privileged to be employed here."

"I bet... And I have some good news."

Ted raised his eyebrows, "And what might that be? Not won the lottery, have you?" he said with a laugh.

"No, nothing like that. The news is for you."

"Really?" said Ted both surprised and interested. "Me?"

"Yes, your spectacles."

"What about them?"

"They've been found."

"Really? Just as I'd gone and had new ones made up. Sod's law," said Ted genially, pointing at the new pair he was wearing. "Where on earth did you find them? I looked everywhere."

"Oh, not me. I didn't find them. The police did."

"What?" Ted's face paled beneath his weather beaten tan.

"Yes," Adam spoke with certainty even though he was winging it, and didn't really know where they had been found, but something inside convinced him he was right. So he went on, "Right next to the body of Caroline Mitchell. So, what do you say to that, you bastard?"

"Then they can't be mine. Heavens, you can't think..." he trailed off.

"I don't think... I know. That missing toggle from your duffle coat. That was found, too."

"Not me and not from my coat."

"Well if that's not enough for you. They also have your DNA after you raped her." Adam squared up to the man and looked him right in the eyes.

Ted's calm expression turned to a grimace as he hurled his heavy flashlight at Adam who ducked and dodged out of the way. The lamp tumbled over the overhang and shattered against the rock.

Ted hurried to the ladder and began to climb it, but Adam pursued him and tried to catch the man's foot. For that, he received a vicious kick in the face. Determinedly, Adam recovered and rubbed his cheek before clambering onto the ladder, intent on following Ted, who had now reached the door, and was struggling to open it. Ted kicked out at him, again. This time, Adam caught hold of Ted's foot, grasped it tightly, and finding strength from somewhere, he wrenched it, and smashed it against the metal rungs. Ted winced in fury giving an angry roar and grabbed at the lighthouse door. He fumbled with his keys and kicked out with his other foot catching Adam on the chin. Adam's face and chin were now cut and bleeding. Raised red welts were starting to show up on his skin.

Ted tore open the door with such force that it swung back and hit him in the face, smashing his glasses and almost knocking him off the ladder. The lenses broke and cut into the skin around his eyes. His face poured with blood as he scrambled inside. He tried unsuccessfully to close the door against his pursuer and began to struggle up the spiral staircase, closely followed by Adam.

Ted swung out onto the catwalk and looked for a weapon, anything he could catch hold of, to defeat Adam, who with a surge of adrenalin had moved swiftly towards him. Ted grabbed his polishing cloth and threw it at Adam who flicked it off his chest. Ted snatched a brush and chucked that hard, too, which Adam managed to dodge, and it clattered behind him.

Ted's face was now a blood spattered mask of evil. There was a brief pause as the two men faced each other. Bellowing like a raging bull Ted rushed at Adam who neatly sidestepped him. Unable to stop and blinded by his own blood he plummeted over the rails and fell over two hundred feet screaming hysterically.

Adam peered over the parapet rails and looked down. Ted Johnson's body lay twisted on the rocks below. The deadly pinnacle of rock had pierced his body like a skewer. The salt water now crashed around his lifeless form as if to devour him.

Vanda, stood shaking on the path below, her phone in her hand. She had witnessed and because of her quick thinking she had filmed the whole episode. Sirens could be heard in the distance as two police cars raced towards the house. The dispatcher kept her on the phone until she confirmed they were in view, and she was able to curtail the call having described the whole incident as it happened, which was now recorded. Her face that was stricken in fear now flooded with relief as she saw that Adam was safe.

Adam made his way back down the spiral staircase and to the door. He climbed down the ladder and saw Vanda who rushed to him and hugged him tightly as two policemen came striding towards them. An ambulance travelled over the rough ground to the lighthouse and two paramedics jumped out.

"He's over there," said Adam indicating with his head where Ted Johnson had fallen. "I believe he must be dead. No one could have survived that fall." The paramedics rushed to gain access to the spot where Ted Johnson had met his death.

"Mr Barrie? Miss Sullivan?" said one of the policemen. "We need you to accompany us to the house where DCI Vance is waiting."

Adam and Vanda said nothing but followed the two coppers back to the house at Black Head Ridge.

Police swarmed over the cliff top by the lighthouse, on the catwalk, and ground below. A team of SOCOs had arrived and were examining the area thoroughly. Detective Ian Bray was interviewing Vanda and had the 999 call to the dispatcher relayed so he could hear everything she had said.

Adam was facing Vance in the kitchen who was remonstrating with him over his foolhardiness. "That was a very stupid thing to do."

Adam had the good grace to look shame-faced. But his eyes sparkled with elation. "He's the one who murdered Caroline. I'm sure of it and I think you'll find the toggle I found matches the ones on his duffle coat. He had one missing."

"That's as maybe. We need concrete proof."

"The toggle, Ted Johnson's glasses and his reaction to me, surely that's proof enough?"

"All circumstantial. We needed him alive for further questioning. If it was him and these disappearances are related there are two more victims out there. We need to find them before it's too late."

The previous elation in Adam's eyes diminished. "Sorry. I didn't realise."

"No. And then there is the more serious matter of his death at your hands."

"But I didn't kill him. He charged at me, and I sidestepped out of the way. He just hurtled over the rails."

"But you pursued him. You could have just left him or not challenged him at all. The whole incident will be thoroughly investigated. I understand Miss Sullivan filmed the whole episode whilst talking to the dispatcher?"

"I don't know, did she?"

"If you're exonerated for murder then it will be her you have to thank."

"You're not taking me in?"

"At the moment, no. But be prepared; as that could change. You may have acted bravely but it was a completely stupid thing to do. You can just hope and pray that those other young women will be found. You don't want those deaths added to your conscience."

Adam fell silent as he realised the enormity of his actions.

The remote shepherd's cottage further along the cliff was now enveloped in darkness. There was no light yet to ease Angie's discomfort. She knew it was on a timer and she hated the dark. She had been asleep but had awoken with a start as her restraints had bitten into her skin. Her wrists and neck were red and sore from where she had pulled against them. Her eyes adjusted to the gloom, and she could see the back of Lisa, still sitting, seemingly drugged and mute. She just wished she would speak, and she called out, "We need to get out of here before that nutcase comes back." She glanced up at the clock with its luminous dial on the sideboard and shuddered as its tick seemed really loud and was exaggerated in her head marking time. "He's late."

Then a small lamp in the room clicked on as it did at the same time every day. It wasn't an eye-twinging bright light, but she could see well enough. At least that was something.

Angie curled up as tightly as the restraints would allow. Tears began to fill her eyes and she let out a heart wrenching sob. She told herself sternly, 'I mustn't break down. I must be strong.' But it was no good. Once she had started to cry she couldn't stop. Eventually, the sobs subsided but she was refusing to give up. She had too much to live for. What did this kidnapper want? She couldn't work it out. She knew she needed to compose herself before he returned. She would not let him see her weakness. But where was he? Angie tried to put that thought from her mind. If he didn't come back, what then? She could die here and that didn't bear thinking about, she had a life and would not be a victim anymore.

Angie swallowed hard and bit back her cries. "Come on, Angie. Think!" she told herself sternly. Angie stared about her as she struggled to compose herself. Her eyes searched the room for something, anything that she could use to cut the restraints that chafed her wrists so painfully.

She knew the table was laid up with knives and forks, some other cutlery and glasses as if expecting guests. Lisa still held a knife and fork in her hands. If she could somehow get her to drop them, she might be able to retrieve them. Angie's feet were tied. She stretched out her feet in an attempt to kick the chair. She tried again. It was no good. The chair was frustratingly near if only she could stretch further. She pulled at her wrist restraints, but that put pressure on the rope around her neck almost choking her. However, she managed to stretch out across the floor so that she was horizontal. She tugged again, until she was at her limit and as far as her bonds allowed. Angie tried to kick the chair to get Lisa to drop the cutlery. "Fuck!" Her feet couldn't quite reach the chair.

She wasn't giving up. She stretched out again as far as she could go. By now, her wrists were bleeding. Angie twisted as she kicked out trying to jostle the chair. But she kept missing. It seemed impossible. She pulled back and wept in despair.

The face of the full moon glared balefully down on the house at Black Head

Ridge. Inside the mood wasn't much better. Vanda sat in the living room with Elsa on her lap, and the loving cat purred reassuringly as Vanda stroked and petted her. But Vanda's face looked pinched and pale as she struggled with her thoughts and feelings.

Adam sat silently, scarcely moving, apart from his chest rising to show he was breathing. He was morose and looked the epitome of misery. The tension between them was obvious as they sat in brooding silence. Finally, Adam spoke. His voice was so loud in the strained atmosphere that Vanda jumped, disturbing Elsa who laid her ears back and mewed plaintively.

"It's all my fault. If Ted was still alive we could have made him tell us where the others are. If I hadn't been so arrogant and God damned hot-headed... and now..."

Vanda said nothing. It was clear that much more had been said between them and Adam was unable to reconcile himself with what he had done.

Vanda rose placing Elsa carefully on the floor. She didn't look at Adam but walked to the door and murmured in a voice tight with emotion, "I'll see myself out." She closed the door quietly behind her and Adam thumped the arm of the chair in anger.

Vanda put on her coat, closing the front door firmly, and walked back to Cliff House with Elsa running after her, her tail straight up in the air. The strain showed in her face, and she tried hard to blink back the tears that filled her eyes. The lighthouse keeper's attack on Adam had shaken and shocked her. She knew she was being unreasonable, he had attacked Adam, and it was obviously self-defence but the fact that Adam could be so aggressive had frightened her. She hated violence in any form. After her original reaction of relief, the events continued to play like a video in her head and this disturbed her. What she had witnessed would live with her forever, or so she believed, and the unnerving twisting in her churning stomach just wouldn't go away.

Vanda felt that if it *had* been the lighthouse man stalking her she should feel better but somehow she felt uncertain. What if it had been someone completely different? In which case she could still be in danger. She didn't want to think about it. She reached her front door and felt for her keys in her pocket.

Vanda went to unlock it but when she inserted her key, the door opened. It wasn't locked. The door had been left on the latch. Vanda put one foot inside the door and called out, "Hello… who's there?" A door slammed upstairs, and Vanda stiffened.

She suddenly felt very unsafe and alone. However, she silenced the devil on her shoulder scaring her and said aloud, "I know there's someone here. I have called the police they will be here at any moment." Vanda closed the door and switched on all the lights. She picked up an elegant umbrella with a long pointed metal ferrule on its tip, like a spike. It would do as a weapon she thought, and she carefully crept up the stairs to where she heard the door slam.

Vanda crossed the landing and looked about her, something was missing. Three of Caroline's pictures were gone from their hangings, and she knew. Someone had broken into steal them. Were they still here? She didn't think so or they would have shown themselves by now and each room she examined was empty. The spare room's window was open and two of the pictures lay on the floor. She had obviously disturbed whoever it was. Vanda peered out of the window and could see the figure of a man disappearing down the fire escape and fleeing into the woods at the back of her house. He had what looked like a cloth wrapped picture tucked under his arm.

She sighed deeply, and firmly locked, and closed the window before checking the whole house, and ensuring all the rest of the doors and windows were securely locked. She wished Adam was there. Her mouth turned down and she bit her lip. She missed him already. Why had she fled in such an ungracious manner? She had seen him fight for his life and after her initial relief she then started questioning herself and her feelings. Damn that questioning inner voice that made her doubt herself.

Vanda knew she needed to report the incident, but it was late, and she figured she could just as soon call in the morning after a decent night's sleep. Besides, the cops were already tied up in searching Ted Johnson's house looking for evidence. No… the morning would be fine. She convinced herself of that and prepared for bed but left on the landing and hall lights.

The sunlight filtered through the blinds on Brinkworth's police station window. DCI Vance stood in front of his assembled team in his shirt sleeves. He looked exhausted as he ran his fingers through his hair. His tie was loosened, and it appeared that he and members of his team had been up all night. The frustration came out in his voice as he exclaimed, "We've got nothing. His house has been searched from top to bottom."

Detective Andrew Harding chipped in, "House of horrors more like. Never seen anything so spooky. Dead stuffed animals and birds everywhere. Inside the lighthouse was the same. Dead eyes watching." He shuddered as he remembered the experience.

Jacobs entered the squad room and joined the team. Vance looked up expectantly, "Well?"

Jacobs shook his head. "I talked to everyone we know that he came into contact with."

"And?"

"No one said anything bad about him. Thought he was pleasant enough but a bit of a recluse. Kept himself to himself, didn't mix much. Seemed harmless."

Harding jumped in, "The chemist said he bought enough chemicals and embalming fluids to preserve a sleuth of grizzlies."

"Sleuth?"

"That's the proper term."

"Well, we don't have grizzlies here, let alone a sleuth of them."

"No. I bet no one else has heard of it either. Could come in useful."

"Forget your quiz questions now, Harding. We need to get inside his mind. Think … what are we missing?"

"Was he indeed our man?" Jacobs asked.

"Looked like it. Why did he react like that to Barrie? If he was innocent he would have behaved differently," said Vance.

Harding looked up. "What if he had an accomplice?"

"Do we have any evidence of that?"

"Not yet," said Harding ruefully.

Vance said, "We have no evidence of anything. Nothing."

Jacobs added, "We have the film taken by Miss Sullivan."

"Thank goodness we do, or Adam Barrie would now be incarcerated for murder."

"Is he still facing charges, sir?"

"That I don't know, yet." His words were left hanging in the air.

Adam was alone in his bedroom in Black Head Ridge House. He hadn't seen Vanda since the morning and was now worried. He wasn't a fan of confrontation and yet she had said some pretty damning things. Did he really act like a madman? He knew he had frightened her, and he prayed he hadn't alienated her. Violence wasn't really in his nature. He turned to look at the clock, which read one fifteen. He studied the remains of a bottle of brandy and glass on his bedside table. "That won't do you any good, you idiot," he murmured.

So many thoughts crowded into his mind that he just couldn't sleep and all the brandy in the world couldn't numb the feelings he was going through. He turned over determinedly after he punched his pillow. He closed his eyes tightly willing sleep to come. But it wouldn't. He started trying some breathing exercises he'd read about in a magazine somewhere. He took a deep breath in through his nose for a count of three, held his breath for three and then let out through his mouth as slowly as he could. He did this three or four times. It seemed to be working and he relaxed a little and attempted to sleep.

As he settled he heard the wind chimes tinkling. Adam tried to ignore them and the strange fluttering that had manifested in his stomach. He tried a couple more of his breathing exercises, but his breath turned frosty in the air and the temperature dropped in his room. It was icy and he shivered with the cold. A spirit hand touched his shoulder. He was now wide awake and sat bolt upright.

At that very moment, he exclaimed, "That's it! Of course." Ted Johnson's voice echoed hollowly in his head, "I keep it well away from the house. Don't want to upset the neighbours." Adam flung back the covers, dashed out of bed and began to dress quickly. Out of habit he walked to the window as he buttoned his shirt.

He took a deep intake of breath and was almost mesmerised as there on the cliff path stood Caroline Mitchell in her white dress with a blue ribbon sash. Her hair blew in the wind. She appeared to be looking directly into his eyes. She beckoned to him. Whispered words could be heard on the breeze, "Find her, save her."

Adam broke from his stupor, put on his shoes and hurried from the house. He headed for the cliff path, where he had seen her. He stumbled on the cliff top, still a little unsteady on his feet from the brandy he'd consumed. The apparition of Caroline Mitchell seemed further away as she continued to beckon and call him. Adam sped towards her, but her image dissolved. He spun around anxiously searching for her. It was no use, she had gone.

"Caroline!" he shouted into the air. "Where are you? Caroline? Show me what to do. Where to go!"

Across in Cliff House, Vanda was unable to sleep. She had tried without success to still the chatter in her head. She was still reliving what she had witnessed and experiencing flashbacks of times with Adam and knew he was a good man at heart. She knew he had found Caroline's killer and that he was only defending himself. She had been too hard. So how could she make up with him?

Vanda tossed and turned before sighing heavily. She pushed back the covers and stepped out of bed yawning. Perhaps she would make a hot drink. That would settle her and then she might be able to sleep. Elsa rubbed herself around her legs purring. Vanda yawned, stretched and ambled to the window, where she stared out at the water. A movement caught her eye. Was it the intruder? Or...? She squinted her eyes and looked harder. It was Adam, she was sure of it. Why was he out there? At this hour in the morning? Was he all right? Vanda knew she needed to be certain. All angst forgotten she rapidly dressed, grabbed her phone that was on charge and rushed from the bedroom. Elsa jumped up on the bed and settled herself as Vanda flew from the room, down the stairs and out through the door. She searched the cliffs with her eyes and could just see Adam scrambling along the cliff path. He stopped and appeared to be listening and staring ahead. Vanda quickly followed but didn't attempt to catch up with him, yet a look of determination manifested on her face.

Adam stood stock-still and scoured the hillside willing his eyes to see the figure of Caroline. In the distance he spotted a movement. He concentrated as hard as he could and focused on seeing and hearing the young artist whose life was so cruelly taken.

Chanted breathy words carried on the wind and he heard, "Find her. Hurry, find her." The last 'her' was drawn out and vanished on the wind.

Adam steeled himself, as the shimmering apparition of Caroline Mitchell reformed and seemed closer. She beckoned to him, "Come." It was a whisper in his head.

"You want me to follow?"

Caroline turned and put her hands together as if in prayer and nodded before turning back and gliding forward.

Adam hurried along the deserted coast road. Still lightheaded from his consumption of brandy he began to breathe heavily as he speeded up trying to follow the direction of the apparition that had vanished once more. He stopped to catch his breath and shook his head in an effort to sober up. The cool night air was helping to clear his head and he strode on with more determination.

The now icy wind began to rise and swirl. It nipped at his face and nose. Adam paused and glanced behind him. Storm clouds were rolling across the horizon in the night sky and rapidly billowing towards him. Stars disappeared as the cumulous nimbus clouds devoured them in their steady march across the water to where Adam stood. He watched as a flash of jagged lightning lit up the sky behind him, which was followed by a rumble of thunder. Adam knew he had to keep moving and travelled on.

Another lightning strike lit up the glowering sky. It snaked down either side of the spirit of Caroline Mitchell who could now be seen again. She was standing further along the road and still beckoned to him.

The roar of the thunder seemed to bellow at him to get a move on. Caroline turned back and began to run around the bend in the road and vanished from sight. Adam quickened his pace and raced after her.

Vanda could see Adam, who was now running. She was getting closer and tried to shout above the rising storm, but her urgent words were lost in the rushing wind. "Adam! Adam, wait up!"

The menacing rain-loaded clouds drew closer. Vanda looked up at the wild sky. Her face was etched in fear, this storm had erupted so quickly, and she felt it wasn't natural. There was something very wrong about it.

Adam struggled determinedly along the road. He tripped on the uneven surface kicking some loose stones and went sprawling. He picked himself up as the first drops of rain began to fall. He'd twisted his ankle, but he doggedly limped on towards the bend in the road and finally turned the corner. There on the headland stood an isolated shepherd's cottage. Caroline hovered next to it, and she gestured for him to come mouthing, 'Hurry,' before she dissolved into the air, again.

Vanda had reached the end of the cliff path and ran onto the road as the driving rain began to fall. The storm raged violently around her. It was now overhead. She started to sprint after Adam trying frantically to catch up with him. The rain stung her face, and the ground became soggy squelching over her trainers. She was so glad she had put them on, rather than her shoes.

Caroline stood and waited outside the shepherd's cottage. Tears streamed down her face. Adam ran as fast as he could over the uneven and now sodden ground. He was soaking wet. As Adam nearly reached the dwelling Caroline simply disappeared into the air again. But where was she? Was this where he was meant to be? Had she moved on?

Adam stood in confusion uncertain what to do.

INSIDE THE COTTAGE, ANGIE WAS woken by the rain beating against the glass in the windows, which rattled with the ferocity of the wind. The storm appeared to be growing and the wild wind whistled around the cottage as if in a maelstrom. Her face was tearstained and red. She snivelled miserably. The dim light from the lamp that was on a timer allowed her to see around the room, but then a flash of dazzling sheet lightning followed by a splintering crash lit up the whole room. Caroline Mitchell materialised before her and stood there. Angie's eyes widened, her mouth dropped open in fright and she screamed in sheer terror.

Outside, Adam heard the terrified scream above the roar of the wind, and he hurried towards the cottage. He tried to peer in through the grimy windows, but the curtains were pulled, and he could see nothing.

Behind him came a shout that he just heard above the blustering wind. "Adam, wait!" He turned to see who had called him and saw Vanda scurrying towards him. He waited until she reached his side. They were both drenched to the skin.

Adam exclaimed in surprise, "Vanda?"

"What are you doing?"

"This must be it. Caroline has led me here. We have to get inside." They hurried to the door, which was firmly locked. He peered through the letter box but couldn't see anything. Adam scoured the land around him looking for something to batter the lock.

The raging storm had moved on inland and to their relief, it had now stopped raining. It had stopped as quickly as it had started. Vanda picked up a rock, "We could smash a window."

Adam nodded and shouted through the letter box, "If there's anyone in there, shield yourself, we're going to smash a window."

Vanda passed the rock to Adam and said, "We should call the cops."

"I don't have my mobile."

"I've got mine," she took it from her pocket.

"If you can get a signal."

Vanda walked away towards the road holding her phone up to the sky. She persisted until she found a signal and dialled. Her voice could be heard, as she spoke to the emergency services, ordering the police and an ambulance to come to the remote cottage on the headland off the Brinkworth Road.

Adam pulled his sleeve over his hand and held the rock. He hit one window hard. It cracked but didn't break. He limped back and finding strength from somewhere he hurled it super hard, and the glass shattered. Adam hurriedly limped to the window and yanked his sleeve over his hand once more. He picked up the rock, which had fallen outside the window and used it to knock out the remaining jagged shards of glass in the frame.

A cry for help came from inside. Adam filled with adrenalin clambered inside and fought against the thick curtaining. He hunted for a light switch feeling the wall beside him. He found it and turned it on. The room flooded with light. He stared at a bench covered in bottles of chemicals and medical instruments. It looked like a chemist's lab combined with an undertaker's embalming parlour. Adam shivered and limped to the door, opened it, and found himself in the hall. That, too, he flooded with light when he found the light switch. He called out, "Hello? Anyone here?"

An answering call came back at him, it was a woman's voice. "We're in here."

Firstly, he moved to the front door and unlocked and opened it before approaching another door that was bolted from the outside. He drew back all three bolts, top, middle, and bottom, opened the door cautiously, and stepped inside, where he switched on the main lights.

He saw Angie tied up on the floor and Lisa sitting at the table glassy eyed.

He took a closer look at Lisa and stepped back in shock. She had been stuffed and treated like one of Ted's animals. He struggled to stop the sickness that rose quickly to his throat.

Swallowing the sour taste he crouched down by Angie who was now sobbing in a mixture of fear and relief. He reassured her, "It's okay, you're safe now."

He searched around him for something to cut her bonds. He grabbed a sharp knife from the cheese board on the table and used it to saw at her restraints. Her wrists were cut and bleeding, her neck chafed and her ankles sore. "You're lucky you didn't choke with this rope around your neck. You're very lucky."

In the distance, sirens could be heard.

Vanda stood close to the road. She waved hard at the approaching police cars, which pulled off the road and onto the grass. Their headlights lit up the cottage, and their flashing lights strobed around the headland. The policeman in the first car wound down his window. Vanda peered in to explain and pointed at the cottage now brightly illuminated as if in the holiday season. The two cars drove towards the cottage and stopped.

Vanda ran towards the dilapidated building followed by the police. They used the red enforcer to batter the door in. On the third ram, the door gave way and splintered open. Vanda followed the police inside. She went through the hallway to the room used as a prison and saw Adam helping Angie, who looked gratefully at him, into a chair, where she dissolved into tears. Vanda crossed quickly and attempted to comfort her.

Vance, Harding and Jacobs searched the cottage and soon entered the room with the captives. They scanned the room and stared in shock at victim, Lisa Devereaux, now preserved forever.

Vance shouted, "Where's the damn ambulance? It should be here by now."

Harding murmured, "I'll check and see." He went back outside to his patrol car and radioed the dispatcher. He hurried back with the information. "Ambulance is on its way."

Angie finally found her voice and blurted out to Adam and the officers, "Thank you so much. If it hadn't been for you I might never have been found. I could have died here."

"But you didn't," soothed Adam.

"You're one lucky lady," interrupted Vance.

"The bloke's nuts. Kept saying he liked beautiful things around him. That I'd live forever as his companion. That nothing would corrupt my beauty not even age. It didn't make any sense." She gestured to Lisa, "He's drugged her, made her immobile and mute. She can't speak or anything."

"Nor will she," said Vance grimly. Angie looked puzzled but Vance didn't explain.

Another siren could be heard approaching. Harding hurried to the door and ushered in two paramedics who knelt down to examine Angie. Once sure she was safe to be moved, they helped her out to the waiting ambulance and aided her into the back where they placed a probe onto her finger to check her oxygen levels.

The paramedic stepped down from the ambulance and addressed Vance, who had emerged with Adam. "We'll take her to hospital and get her fully checked out. She has lacerations on her wrists, ankles and neck, and her oxygen levels are low. She's dehydrated and must be hungry."

Vance nodded. "What about the other one?"

"Nothing we can do about her. We'll send another ambulance out to collect her and take her to the morgue. Poor girl. It must be one sick bastard who did this." He returned to the ambulance and was about to close the back doors with the other paramedic attending to Angie who was explaining why Lisa was not in the ambulance with her. Angie's face registered with shock and horror.

"Oh my God. That's why he said I would live forever, and my beauty would never fade." Suddenly, she convulsed and just managed to get up and be sick outside the ambulance. "That could have been me," and she dissolved into tears. The paramedic gently helped her back and the other one closed the rear doors. He moved around to the driver's door, climbed in, and set off with lights flashing.

Inside the cottage, Vance looked around at his team, "Get this place closed up. It's a crime scene, now. You two come with me." He indicated Adam and Vanda. "I'm taking you both back to the station."

Vanda and Adam exchanged a glance wondering what was in store for them, and Vanda tucked her arm into Adam's as they walked. Adam looked down at Vanda. He instantly felt better and hoped this meant that she had forgiven him.

Back at the station, Vance sent Harding to do a follow up interview with Angie Hartman and sent Jacobs to notify her parents and fiancé that she had been found. He would undertake the more unpleasant task of informing Lisa Devereaux's family of her death. He turned to Vanda and Adam, "You two. In with me." He jerked his head to the first interview room. Vanda and Adam meekly followed him inside.

Once seated Vance spoke sharply. "Okay, you two. Tell me exactly what happened and how you knew where to find the abductees. You realise this doesn't look good for you."

Vanda glanced at Adam who swallowed hard and nodded. She eventually spoke, "We'll tell you but you're not going to believe us."

"Try me." He switched on the recorder.

Adam interrupted, "You better turn that off."

"Why?"

"I'll tell you and if you decide it can be recorded, then I will explain again. But I don't think you'll like it."

"All right. I'll play along." He switched off the recorder. "Now go ahead and explain." He picked up his notepad and pen to take notes.

Adam took a deep breath and launched into his narrative about exactly what had happened, after he had moved into the house at Black Head Ridge. Every now and then Vanda would chip in with an extra detail here and there. She affirmed Adam's description of the music, the tinkling wind chimes, the scent of Patchouli oil and mysterious white feathers. Vance's pen stopped working and he opened his drawer to get another. Sitting on top of his folder was a white lace handkerchief. The aroma of Patchouli filled the air, and he snatched it up to smell. Vanda and Adam exchanged a glance.

"That's the same hankie that appeared in my desk drawer at the house and that I picked up on the beach."

Vance was dumbstruck. He picked up a transparent evidence bag and placed the handkerchief inside and sealed it before he returned it to his drawer. He murmured, "That's impossible."

Adam continued with his story and Vance continued to be stunned as the tale unfolded. He had to admit he was gripped by the information provided. After they finished he sat back in his chair and twisted his mouth. "I don't know what to say. That's some story, you've told. Although, I don't know how much I can put in my report. Maybe I ought to lose this evidence, too." He opened his drawer and removed the evidence bag, which they could all see was empty. "It can't be," he said with a shiver. "Is it me or has the room become incredibly cold?"

"No, the temperature has dropped," said Vanda. She indicated the evidence bag, "Now do you believe us?"

"No one else will," replied Vance.

"Even though it's the truth," queried Vanda.

"Who'd believe me? I can hardly say you followed a ghost to find her. It's best left unsaid. I think you should say, after being caught in a storm when out walking, which is true, that you heard a scream and forced a way in as it was very suspicious and called us at the same time. It's the truth with just a few omissions."

"If you're happy with that?" muttered Adam.

"I am. Best not to say anymore. And no one mention that handkerchief. Come on, I'll give you both a lift home. I dare say Mr and Mrs Hartman will want to thank you both as will young Luke. Come on." They left the interview room and followed Vance to his car.

As they approached the vehicle Vanda took Adam's hand and squeezed it. He looked at her and gratefully returned the squeeze, before getting into the back of the car with her. She looked up at him with love and forgiveness. Adam's heart soared. She leaned her head on his shoulder and sighed softly. Adam put his arm around her protectively, somehow he knew all would be well.

"One thing I didn't report," said Vanda. Adam looked at her questioningly. "With everything that's happened I forgot to mention it. I was going to report it first thing."

"What's that?" asked Vance.

"My house was broken into last night and some of Caroline's work was stolen. I saw the thief escaping through the woods at the back of the house. I'm sure Philip Chapman is involved."

"I keep hearing that name," said Vance. "He broke his appointment with me, and I haven't bothered to chase him up. Seems I'd better look into him some more. You had better come in tomorrow and file a report. It's too late now. We all need some shut eye."

"I will," affirmed Vanda.

After they waved Vance goodbye they went into the house. There seemed to be an emptiness pervading the atmosphere, which Adam commented on, before entering the kitchen to make a hot drink before they went to bed. Vanda caught him by the arm, "Adam, I'm so sorry."

"No, I'm sorry," he insisted. "I couldn't help myself. Once I realised who was responsible I just saw red. I didn't think about the consequences or you."

"And I overreacted, I'm sorry. It's just…"

"Just?"

"I hate violence and confrontation of any kind. I had enough in my marriage. It was the main reason we broke up. I couldn't stand the threat of violence that always ran under my ex's actions and his controlling behaviour. I don't want to talk about it. You are nothing like him."

"But, I was so fixated on finding the truth I ignored everything else. I stupidly thought I could play the hero and find Caroline's killer."

"Which you did."

"Yes, but through my stupidity another girl almost died."

"But she didn't. She's alive and you saved her."

Adam's eyes filled with tears. Vanda snuggled into him, "Forget all about it now. Let's start afresh. What do you say?"

Adam's response was to crush her to him and kiss her tenderly. "And now, let's grab a hot shower and fall into bed. You must be exhausted I know I am."

Vanda tucked her arm in his and they mounted the stairs together.

Thirty minutes later they snuggled in bed together. Vanda sighed contentedly, "So, it's finally over."

"Don't say that. Remember what happened last time?"

"But we've found Caroline's body and her killer, and saved another victim."

"And poor Lisa Devereaux."

"That was horrible. Stuffing her to make his own extended family. The man was crazy."

"Yet, he seemed so genial."

"That's how he got away with it. Hiding in plain sight."

"Yes, nothing incriminating in his own home. No one knew about his other property."

"But everything is peaceful once more…"

Wind chimes began to tinkle. Adam put up his hand to silence Vanda. "No. It can't be…"

Vanda breathed in sharply. "There can't be another victim, surely?"

Adam climbed out of bed and walked to the window. He beckoned to Vanda to join him. "Quickly, look!" She slipped out of bed and joined him at his side, and stared out of the window, "I can't see anything."

"Over there." Adam pointed and took her hand, and as he did so, Vanda gasped.

"I can see her. I can actually see her." She dropped his hand and the vision vanished. She caught hold of his hand again and was astonished by what she saw.

Outside stood Caroline her hair blowing in the wind, wearing her white dress with a blue ribbon sash. She looked beautiful, relaxed and happy. She smiled at them and was surrounded by an ethereal halo of light. A swirling tunnel took shape behind her, like a vortex. There was a really bright light glowing at the end. Caroline blew them both a kiss and whispered, "Thank you." Her words carried on the breeze and filled their heads. She turned and started to walk down the tunnel, turned and gave a final wave before she disappeared into the light. The vortex closed up and the tunnel vanished.

Adam dropped Vanda's hand and placed his arm around her. Vanda's eyes were filled with tears, and she looked completely astounded. "I saw her... For the first time ... I saw her," she murmured in amazement. "But only when I touched you..." She shook her head in wonderment, "Then it really is over."

"It is now," and he kissed her gently on her forehead, took her hand and led her back to bed.

The next day, Vanda went in to see Vance while Adam waited outside for her. She went through all the details of the break-in, what was missing and what she had seen. Once the report was made and signed Vanda rummaged in her shopping bag and took out a thick file and laid it on Vance's desk. "In there you'll find everything I've got on him. It should be more than enough. I am about to do an exposé on him."

"And I have him coming in at eleven. This time, Harding and Jacobs are collecting him in a car. No wriggling out of this appointment, which is..." he glanced at his watch, "about now."

Vanda rose and shook hands with Vance. "You can keep the file. I have everything on a flash drive." There was a knock at the door and Jacobs entered with Chapman who looked more than surprised when he saw Vanda about to leave.

"Vanda?" exclaimed Chapman.

"Philip," she said guardedly. "I think you have everything, Inspector." She lifted her head up and went out to meet Adam.

They left the station and walked down the High Street. They had hardly gone a few yards when the first person stopped them. Mrs Blewitt smiled broadly and congratulated him, "It's a wonderful thing you've done, Mr Barrie. A killer off our streets and young Angie Hartman back home where she belongs." Adam beamed and Vanda smiled proudly.

They continued down the road and more people stopped him and congratulated him. Some insisted on shaking his hand, others patted his back. It seemed he was becoming something of a celebrity.

As they passed the newsagents, the billboard outside blared the headline: 'Angie Hartman found'. In smaller letters underneath: 'New local resident saves third abducted victim'.

They made their way into The Dog and Duck for a drink and a spot of lunch, where everyone wanted to buy Adam a drink. It was there that Detective Constable Jacobs found him. "Mr Barrie, Miss Sullivan, DCI Vance wanted you to know that thanks to your file, the county judge has issued a search warrant for Philip Chapman's properties, business and personal. He is in custody at the moment, although a smart lawyer could soon get him released and out on bail. When the search is completed we will need you to identify any stolen works."

"I'll be more than happy to do that. Thank you."

"Also, I have been advised to take you along to see Mr and Mrs Hartman. They wish to meet and thank you."

"Can we do this tomorrow?" asked Adam.

"Most certainly. Shall we say meet at the station at ten, tomorrow?"

"We'll be there," said Adam after getting the nod from Vanda.

Jacobs smiled agreeably and said, "Perfect. See you tomorrow then," and he left.

There was a babble of voices in the pub and Steve crossed to them bearing them each a drink. "On the house. I couldn't be more pleased that Caroline's killer was caught and to my mind he got his just desserts. Better he's dead than the taxpayers have the expense of a trial and have to keep him in prison for the rest of his life. He must have been nuts."

"He was definitely unhinged. Who goes around stuffing people?"

Adam shrugged and another person piped up, "So, how did you know? What made you suspect him?"

"It was just a hunch," said Adam colouring up.

"Yes, and a missing duffle coat toggle found at the scene of the crime," added Vanda.

"So, that's why the cops wanted to see our coats," said Steve. "Well, I never. I did wonder."

"Yeah, we were all suspecting each other. It wasn't a pleasant feeling," said John Grey.

"We all thought he was harmless," added Steve. "Shows how wrong you can be." Adam smiled and drained the last of his drink. "Want another?"

"No thanks, we'll finish our lunch and be off," said Vanda.

"Of course, of course. You do realise there are about six drinks put in for you?"

"And I am sure I will get to them," said Adam with a smile. "Just not now."

Steve chuckled, "I expect more will be added to the list. You could be drinking free for quite a while." He looked at Vanda more closely. "You know, you remind me of someone. Can't think who for the minute."

John Grey blurted out, "It's Caroline. Caroline Mitchell. Can't you see the resemblance?"

"Now that you come to mention it, yes... you do. Are you any relation?"

Vanda paused and then nodded. "Actually, she's my sister."

The pub erupted with questions, which Vanda did her best to answer.

Finally, Steve said, "Come on, gentlemen. Let them get on." He turned to them, "You are very welcome here any time. Caroline was a lovely young woman. She will be missed, and I am sorry for your loss."

Vanda's eyes had started to fill with tears and the two made their escape. Once outside, Vanda took some deep breaths and murmured, "Well, the truth is out now and I for one feel much better for it. Come on, let's get back. Elsa will be wanting her supper."

ADAM AND VANDA HAD LEFT the pub and begun to stroll back to the car park when Adam's phone went. "Hello?"

"Mr Barrie, Vance." Adam stopped in the street and put his phone on loudspeaker so Vanda could hear.

"Yes, Chief Inspector?"

"The Hartmans really would like to see you both."

"Yes, DC Jacobs has already told us. We're meeting him at ten tomorrow."

"Change of plans."

"Oh?"

"In the light of something Angie Hartman told me, it might be best if the police aren't present. You'll understand when you hear what she has to say."

"Okay," said Adam slowly.

"Can you pop across afterwards or tomorrow around eleven?"

Adam looked at Vanda who nodded. "I think we can manage that."

"Great. I'll text you the Hartmans' address and then if you could come into the station afterwards, I would appreciate it." Vanda raised her eyebrows. "It's to do with Chapman. I think you'll be interested." Vanda nodded.

"We'll be there," affirmed Adam and ended the call. They carried on towards the car park. "That was a turn up for the books."

"I hope it's something good and that creep hasn't wriggled out of anything. It sounded as if they had enough to put him away."

"We will see."

"We can but hope. Now, where do the Hartmans live?"

They looked at the text that had just come through and entered it in their Sat Nav. "Right. Now off we go."

They followed the directions to the outskirts of Brinkworth town and drove down a pleasant leafy avenue and turned off into a cul-de-sac in a smart suburb. The cultured female voice told them, "Your destination is ahead... You have arrived at your destination."

Vanda and Adam alighted at the roadside and locked their vehicle. They walked up a sweeping pea gravel drive to a large, detached house with three steps leading to a strong oak front door and brass lion head door knocker. It was flanked by two marble pillars. The elegant house had been rendered and painted white. It sported dark green wooden shutters around the windows. Above the door was a semi-circular window segmented with panes that resembled the rays of the sun.

Adam commented, "Must be a monied family. This house looks tasteful and stylish."

"I agree. Definitely a wealthy family."

Adam rang the bell and moments later, a woman opened the door in a dark uniform with a crisp white apron and ushered them inside. "Mr Barrie? Miss Sullivan?" They both nodded and exchanged a look that said, definitely money if they have a housekeeper. "You're expected. Step this way, the family are in the drawing room." They followed the housekeeper come maid, into an impressive hallway with a grand staircase flowing down like something from an old Fred Astaire musical. They walked down the corridor and entered another grand room, with high ceilings and a plaster cast ceiling rose, cornices and picture rail. The walls had carved wooden panels and wainscoting halfway up the walls. The room was bright and airy with dual aspect windows. From the centre hung a crystal glass chandelier that glinted with rainbow lights in the morning sun. Inside, was a large grand piano at one end, and Chesterfield sofas and wing-back chairs at the other, surrounding a magnificent marble fireplace, which had a fire burning although the day was hardly cold. There was other antique furniture including a writing bureau, coffee table, sideboard and decorative corner unit displaying photographs. Portraits of ancestors and family members adorned the walls as well as a family crest.

A man and woman rose to meet them as they were admitted. The woman was an older version of Angie, and the man was tall with military style bearing. They beamed at Adam and Vanda and shook hands. Angie and her fiancé, Luke sat on one of the Chesterfield sofas. They, too, stood up to greet them.

Mr Hartman turned to the housekeeper, "A pot of coffee will be in order, Emily and some of your fine fruit scones, I think. Thank you." Emily nodded agreeably and left the room. Mr Hartman continued. "Please sit down. We can't thank you enough."

Mrs Hartman interjected, "Angie's our only child. I don't know what we'd have done if..." She stopped, emotion clearly made it difficult for her to speak.

Luke added, "I never want to let her out of my sight again." Angie smiled up at him her face shining with love.

Mr Hartman returned to his seat and spoke again. "My wife and I would really like to do something for you, something to show our thanks."

"That won't be necessary," said Adam.

"Please, there must be something."

"I assure you, I am already well catered for by my grandfather. Save your money."

"In that case, Miss Sullivan?"

Vanda shook her head, "I have no need of any gift." She saw the disappointment in their eyes. "Neither of us need or want any reward. However..." she said as an idea occurred to her. "Why don't you set up a charity in Angie's name to help other victims and families who have been abducted, kidnapped and have suffered domestic violence? I'm sure that would be a very worthy cause. Think of the people you could help."

Adam nodded vigorously, "I think that's a great idea."

Mr Hartman looked at his wife and she, too, nodded and said, "Yes, why not? It's a small price to pay for giving us our daughter back. I dread to think what would have happened if you hadn't found her."

Mr Hartman added, "I can speak to my solicitor and sort something out. Maybe it's something you would like to be involved with? You don't have to answer now. Think about it. On another note, tell me, how did you manage to find her?"

Adam hesitated uncertain how much or what to say when Angie burst in, "There is something you can tell me. I have been puzzling over it... I don't know if I was hallucinating or what, but I swear that at one point when you came in to rescue me there was a woman. A woman in a white dress with a blue ribbon sash. She had long blonde hair... but she just vanished..."

Adam and Vanda exchanged a glance between them.

"What?" exclaimed Angie. Mr and Mrs Hartman, and Luke looked questioningly at Adam.

"It's a long story," said Adam.

"A very long story," added Vanda.

"We have time," said Mr Hartman. "Why don't you tell us?"

Adam and Vanda walked in to the police station and were ushered into DCI Vance's office. He looked up as they entered and smiled. "Please sit down."

They sat opposite him. "Firstly, you will be pleased to know that the Crown Prosecution Service is not going to take your case any further. You need no longer fear a knock at the door by the police coming to take you away."

"That's good news!" exclaimed Vanda.

"Yes. After they reviewed your statements and the footage of the film you took, Miss Sullivan, they could see clearly that Ted Johnson attacked Mr Barrie. No charges are to be brought against your personage."

"Thank you," said Adam clearly relieved. "But, you said this meeting was about Philip Chapman?"

"Yes... although we have a slew of evidence regarding Mr Chapman, much of it is hearsay and inadmissible in court."

"What?" said Vanda clearly shocked.

"Don't give up. We may still get him, yet."

"How can you do that?"

"We have a lead on the theft of the paintings stolen from Cliff Head House. We're hoping it will lead us directly to Chapman. At least then, we can get him on something."

"But that could take forever," said Vanda in dismay.

"Don't be disappointed. I interviewed someone from his gallery who let it slip that there were some paintings done to order that have not been recovered or found. This person also intimated that Chapman was worried because Caroline had told him, she kept a journal documenting everything. Do you have any idea where this could be?"

Vanda shook her head. "Sorry, no. Didn't you search the cottage?"

"We did, but we weren't looking for a journal. I wondered if you would take another look or at least try and think of where she might have hidden such an item."

Vanda nodded. "I'll do my best. Where is Chapman now?"

"We had to let him go. Don't worry. We have him under surveillance. He won't be any threat to you. If he does step out of line or contact you let me know immediately."

"Of course," she answered. "Although, I don't like the idea of him being out there. He knows some very unsavoury people. Are you sure I'll be okay?"

"And she'll have me to keep an eye on her. No one will hurt her while I'm around," said Adam.

"Just don't do anything foolhardy, Mr Barrie. You don't want any charges brought down on your head." Adam looked suitably chastened and agreed with a nod. "Also, and I don't know how you feel about this…"

"Go on…" prompted Adam.

"I wondered if you'd like to take up a position with the Force?"

"What sort of a position? I'm not cut out to be a copper."

"Not a member of the Force, but you clearly have some special talents. These of course would be kept quiet, but I feel we could use you in an advisory capacity on some cases."

"What like a consultant?"

"Yes, if you put it like that. How do you feel about helping us out every now and then, when we need it? You have strong instincts and a bit more."

"A kind of psychic advisor?"

"If you like, but we won't call it that."

"What will you call it?"

"A special investigative advisor and profiler. What do you say?"

Adam nodded. "I like the sound of that. I have been wondering what to do.

Renting out the cottage won't take up much of my time and I need some sort of focus in life. Doing nothing doesn't suit me…Yes, okay. Count me in."

"You don't have to think about it?"

"No, I'll just trust my instincts," said Adam and winked.

Vance laughed. "Very well. It's a deal." They rose and shook hands. "See if you can find that journal, Miss Sullivan."

"We will. In fact we'll go there now and make a start. Right, Adam?"

"Right," agreed Adam and the two left the office.

Vance watched them leave. He was sure he had done the right thing.

When they arrived back at Black Head Ridge House, Vanda said, "No time like the present. Let's get back into the cottage and have a look around." Adam collected the keys, and they went into the annexed cottage. "Feels strange coming in here. Although I know she's gone I can feel her everywhere."

"Well, she won't be able to help us this time," said Adam. "We will have to rely on ourselves. Where do we start?"

"Let's take a quick look in the kitchen. Caroline often wrote in her diary in the kitchen. If there's nothing there we can start at the top of the cottage and work our way down," said Vanda.

"Okay, kitchen first and then from the top of the house."

They walked into the kitchen and opened all the unit drawers and cupboards, and under the sink but there was nothing, except for kitchen equipment, cutlery and cleaning stuffs. On the counter top was a torch next to storage jars for coffee, tea and sugar. "Check the kitchen table drawers," murmured Vanda.

Adam opened one. There was a notebook, pens and pencils and a bunch of cable ties. "Wonder what she used these for?" mused Adam.

"She had an old easel that was broken and used to cable tie the legs to secure them," said Vanda. "Later she bought a new one, maybe she had these just in case it went wrong."

"Maybe," agreed Adam. "What's in the notebook?"

Vanda flicked through it. "Shopping lists, preliminary sketches and ideas. Nothing like we're looking for. It was just a thought."

"Okay, then let's get upstairs. I'll start in the bathroom. You tackle the spare room."

"What about Caroline's bedroom?"

"We'll do that together."

They went their separate ways and Adam examined the bathroom thoroughly checking the bathroom cabinet, behind the wood panelling across the side of the bath. He even checked the cistern as he had read that drug dealers sometimes hid things there. He looked, even though he believed a cistern would not be the right place to keep a journal or paintings. He lifted the bath mat and checked the floor underneath. There were no hidden cavities or places to hide anything. He called out to Vanda, "Any luck?"

She called back, "No. The spare room doesn't look as if it's ever been used. The cupboards are empty as is the wardrobe and chest of drawers. No false panels or anything. I've lifted the rugs and checked the floorboards - nothing."

"No, me neither," said Adam.

"Meet you in Caroline's room."

They both met on the landing and took a cursory look around there, but it was carpeted, and it didn't look as if any part of it had been disturbed. They walked into Caroline's room and a white feather floated down and landed on the bed. Vanda swapped a look with Adam. This time Adam heard his grandfather's voice in his head. "Keep searching. Vanda knows where to look."

"What is it?" asked Vanda.

"I just heard my grandfather's voice. He said that you will know where to look."

"Me?" she said surprised. "But why…? … Wait a minute. Of course." Vanda got down on her hands and knees and turned up the bedclothes and felt around under the bed frame. "There's something here. Wait. Have you got a light?"

Adam dashed down the stairs and picked up the torch left on the kitchen worktop. He hurried back, and held it out to her. "What is it?"

Vanda slid under the bed and stretched out her hand for the torch. She switched it on and looked at the slats on the base. There taped underneath was a long cardboard tube, which she carefully unstuck and passed out to Adam. She flashed the torch around and saw something else inside a plastic bag also taped to the underside of the bed. She picked at it carefully and untaped it. Grasping it tightly she rolled out from underneath. She was covered in dust and fluff and attempted to brush herself down.

"You need to sack your cleaner."

"What?"

"She doesn't clean under the bed."

Adam grinned and indicated what she was holding, "Well?" said Adam earnestly.

"I totally forgot. Whenever Caroline wanted to hide something she would stick it to the underside of the bed. No one would care to look there. When she smoked, she would Sellotape packets of cigarettes and matches, underneath her bed, out of sight of Mum and Dad. I completely forgot. She would also hide her diary there, one of those with a lock, to stop anyone reading it. Not that it was a secure lock. It was her secret place." Vanda undid the plastic wrapping. "Oh my God, this is it. Her journal," she said triumphantly. "What's in the tube?"

Adam carefully undid the cardboard tube's lid and shook out three rolled up canvases. He unrolled them and gasped. "If I didn't know better, I'd swear that these were by Monet. Look!"

"This must be what Vance is looking for." She opened the exercise book, labelled journal and flicked through it. "Everything is here. Dates, jobs, names, works in the style of Renoir, Monet, and more. This is brilliant. Vance will have enough to put Chapman away for a long time." Vanda looked delighted. "Oh, Adam! We've got him!"

Adam put his fingers to his lips. He put the paintings and tube on the bed, and signalled to Vanda to replace the journal as he tiptoed to the door. Someone was downstairs. Vanda hurriedly scrambled back under the bed with the exercise book and after emerging, again covered in dust, brushed herself down. She hurriedly rolled up the canvases and tried to place them in the tube while Adam was calling Vance to tell him of their discoveries, and he spoke in hushed tones.

Vanda couldn't get the canvases back inside the tube and was forced to roll them up again. There was another creak on the stairs and they both froze. Vanda tiptoed to the door and peeped out to see a man in a balaclava creeping up the stairs wielding a gun. She mouthed at Adam, "There's a man with a gun."

Adam just about caught what she said and whispered, interrupting Vance, "Vance, there's someone in the cottage. He's got a gun. You need to get out here, now."

Adam set his mobile to record and placed his phone on the dresser to run.

Vanda didn't know what to do. Her eyes were panicked. Adam gestured for her to hide somewhere and pointed to the wardrobe. Vanda shook her head. It was too obvious. She stooped down and rolled back under the bed leaving Adam to struggle with rolling up the canvases. He picked up the tube and had started to put them inside when the door inched open and a voice spoke, "I'll take those if you don't mind."

The man in the balaclava pushed the door open further and pointed the gun at Adam's chest. "And where's your lady friend, Vanda Sullivan?" Adam shrugged. "Well, I saw her come in here and I didn't see her leave."

"That's because she went out of the kitchen door to the greenhouse and shed outside," said Adam eyeing the man carefully.

The man snorted derisively. "I doubt that's true."

"Do you mind not pointing that thing at me. It's making me nervous."

"Where is she?" He moved to the wardrobe and flung open the door. He leaned back and tapped the wooden panel with his other hand still keeping the handgun trained on Adam. He waved the firearm at him. "I asked you to put the canvases back in the tube. Do it!" he ordered.

Adam fiddled with the paintings and the container. "You're giving me the jitters, please…" said Adam.

"I'll do more than that in a minute. Hurry up!"

"If you lower your gun, I'll be quicker."

The intruder didn't falter. "You must think I'm stupid. I know your rep. The gun stays. Now move it."

Adam pretended to fumble and dropped the tube and canvases. He was playing for time. His eyes darted to the gunman's feet. Could he floor the man if he tackled him, without getting shot? Or was that reckless? A bullet might hit Vanda under the bed. Adam struggled with his emotions, but Vance's words rang in his ears after Ted Johnson's death. "That was a stupid thing to do…"

Adam rose slowly clutching the tube and canvases. He made another attempt to roll them up and place them in the cardboard cylinder. This time he succeeded.

"Now, put the lid on it." Adam did as asked. "Pass it across." The invader snatched it from him. "Now, where's the journal?"

"Journal?" said Adam pretending to look confused.

"Don't play games," said the masked man viciously. "The journal kept by Caroline Mitchell. It has to be here. Where is it?"

"I don't know," said Adam defensively. He knew he had to keep the man talking to give Vance time to get to the cottage. He tried to stall him. "Vanda and I have been searching for paintings and other items that might have belonged to Caroline. That is what we've found so far. But we've only just started."

The man hesitated, "Where is Vanda?"

"I've already told you. She went outside to the greenhouse and shed."

"Call her. Tell her to come in."

"What?"

"Go to the kitchen door and give her a shout. Call her." He waved the gun at Adam gesturing him to the door.

Adam looked flustered and edged forward slowly. The man stepped behind him and shoved the gun in his back forcing him downstairs. Adam determined to take his time. He daren't attack him, yet.

Vanda was still cringing under the bed. She had heard the whole interchange between Adam and the man, whose voice she didn't recognise. As soon as they had cleared the room, she rolled out from under the bed. She lightly dusted herself down, once more, crept to the doorway, and peeped out, careful to remain hidden. She could see the gunman forcing Adam down the stairs and was in a panic. She had to do something, but what?

Vanda looked around her, she needed something she could use as a weapon; something to disarm him or knock him out without endangering Adam. On the bedside table was a bedside lamp that appeared to have a weighty stone base.

She crossed to it and picked it up. It was heavy. She unplugged it and wrapped the electric cable around it and removed the lampshade. She moved stealthily to the door and peered out. She could just see the man and Adam reaching the foot of the stairs.

Vanda waited until they had entered the kitchen and then she sneaked out carrying the lamp. She manoeuvred herself carefully down the stairs staying close to the bannister to avoid any creaks or squeaks. She reached the kitchen doorway and could see Adam pretending to fumble with the door. The man yelled at him, "For Christ's sake hurry up!"

Adam retorted, "You're making me nervous, and the door is stiff." The intruder closed in on Adam and shoved him aside. Adam saw Vanda, out of the corner of his eye. His eyes widened as she sidled up behind the man and clouted him hard on the back of his head. The gun went off and he dropped to his knees. She hit him again, and he lost his firearm. Adam stooped down and kicked the revolver away and pushed the man face down on the floor. He sat on his back and ripped off the balaclava. It was no one he recognised. He pulled the man's arms behind his back and called to Vanda, "Get a couple of cable ties from the kitchen drawer."

Vanda scrabbled about in the table drawer and pulled out a handful. She passed one to Adam, who secured the criminal's hands. She passed him another and he tied the dazed man's ankles together.

It was to this chaotic scene that Vance arrived.

"Here's one of the crooks," said Vanda. "And we have the paintings." She pointed to the cardboard tube now on the floor, picked it up and passed it to Vance. He opened up the tube, unrolled the paintings and looked up in surprise.

"And the journal," added Adam. "All the evidence you'll need."

Vance indicated the man on the floor. "Who is he?"

"Haven't a clue," said Adam. "But, you can see for yourself, exactly what happened."

Vance raised an eyebrow. "Won't be a tick."

Adam left the kitchen and ran up the stairs. He returned moments later with his phone, and the journal in its polythene wrapper.

"What's this?" asked Vance.

"On my phone is most of the whole sorry episode. Look." He passed his phone to Vance who pressed play and watched everything unfold in front of him.

Vanda then explained what had happened after Adam was forced from the room. She then told him what had occurred before the filming began.

Adam passed Vance the journal, which Vance examined. He gave a low whistle and smiled. "This is exactly what we need." He turned to Jacobs who had followed him in and pointed at the miscreant, "Get him on his feet." Jacobs hoisted him up.

Vance stared at the man. "Name?" The man said nothing. "You might want to think a bit harder. I'll ask you again, name?"

"No comment."

"No matter, once we get your prints and mugshots, we'll know." He addressed Harding standing in the doorway, "Search him."

Harding stepped forward and patted the man down. He removed a mobile phone and wallet, which contained his driving licence. Harding opened it up. "Says here, Murray Fletcher."

Vance's face flooded with recognition at the name. "Arrest him and take him downtown. I'll follow on shortly with Harding. I need a word with these two. Wait for me outside." Vance waited until the room had cleared. "What were you thinking? Tackling a dangerous man with a gun?"

"Would you rather we got shot?" said Vanda.

"No, of course not."

"Then what? You can see he broke in and threatened Adam. We did what we had to. It was him or us. I have no doubt he would have shot us. Thanks to us, you now have your evidence against Philip Chapman. He can't wriggle out of this."

"No, he can't. I'll need you both to come down to the station and make a full statement. And although I hate to say it, you are right."

"Oh?" said Adam. "You knew the name, didn't you? Murray Fletcher."

"Yes," admitted Vance. "He's been on Interpol's wanted list for two murders that we know of and much more. You have had a lucky escape."

"Do you think you can get him to talk? He must be involved with Chapman," said Adam.

"Oh, he's involved all right, not as an art expert but as a hitman to get rid of you both, I expect. I just hope we can keep this quiet until I've arrested Chapman. We don't want him sending someone else after you."

Vanda and Adam swapped glances looking shocked.

Adam felt an enveloping warmth as if his mother had wrapped her arms around him and he gasped.

"Is everything all right?" asked Vance.

Adam nodded. "I think so."

He heard his mother's voice, "Don't worry, Adam. Everything will be fine, you'll see."

THE SEA MIST BROUGHT A sheeting drove of drizzle that encompassed the whole of Black Head Ridge. It was a gloomy day with no sign of the sun to brighten things up. Adam stood at his window and stared at the now fog limited view, which he hoped would change to reveal the spectacular view he so loved.

He was itching to get back out on the water and had purchased a motor boat with a cabin and onboard accommodation for two. He wanted to surprise Vanda with a little trip around the coast, but she had been incredibly busy with work since the arrest of Philip Chapman, and with arranging Caroline's funeral; and as Adam had said, she needed time to relax and recharge her batteries in order to plan an exhibition of her work.

Just as he was thinking about her, she breezed into the sitting room beaming delightedly. "It's finished!" She waved a few papers at him. "Read it. Tell me what you think."

"This is it?"

"Yes, my exposé on that scoundrel Philip Chapman. I want you to read it first before I pass it on to Vance."

"Vance?"

"Yes, he will let me know when I can take it to press. We don't want to risk the trial being prejudiced by my article. That would never do."

"No," agreed Adam. "Not after everything we've been through. Tell you what, I'll read this, and you can make us a coffee, if that's okay?"

"Of course, but don't get used to it. It's share and share alike in this relationship. The chores, the cooking, the lot!"

Adam laughed. "Are you suggesting I am not a modern man?"

"No, I know you are. Just want to keep you on your toes. I'll let you read it in peace and then I'll bring in the coffee and a hot croissant."

Vanda passed him the article and left the room, while Adam settled down to read Vanda's words. He muttered a few sounds of agreement as he avidly devoured the piece. He called out to the kitchen, "I'll have that coffee now."

Moments later Vanda returned with a tray of croissants and freshly brewed coffee. She looked at him expectantly. "Well?"

"It's brilliant!"

"You really think so?" she asked, flushing with pleasure.

"Really! It's a perfect exposé. With all that you've discovered, and the evidence Vance has, he should go down for a very long time."

"We were so lucky to find those paintings and her journal. They could have stayed taped under her bed forever."

"No. Not until that bed was turfed out. By which time it would have been too late. Those pictures and her journal held the crucial evidence. But I am surprised the police didn't look under her bed."

"They probably did but wouldn't have seen them taped the way they were. Caroline hid things that way for years. Just wish I'd remembered sooner."

"Now you can concentrate fully on sorting out the arrangements for her memorial and exhibition. We've not got long."

"We're almost there, not a lot more to do and with your help we should get quite a bit of publicity."

"I am on it. Local paper, local radio and adverts in a couple of Nationals and shops. It's all in hand. We may even get some television coverage. Steve has put posters in the pub and Jake is putting flyers through everyone's post boxes. The turnout should be great."

"Hmm. Now you said you had a surprise for me," said Vanda in a wheedling tone.

"Yes, but not today the weather is no good."

"Oh, tell me, please…"

Adam laughed. "I can never resist you. Okay. I'll tell," and he explained about the boat and what he had planned.

Vanda had just sat on Adam's lap and wrapped her arms around his neck, when the phone rang. "Just when things were getting interesting," she murmured.

Adam shooed her off and went to the landline. "Adam Barrie."

"Adam, Rick Vance here."

"Yes?"

"I believe I have need of your special talent."

"Yes?"

"Drop by the station when you're next in Brinkworth."

"Will do."

"What was that all about?" asked Vanda questioningly. "You're looking all mysterious."

"Vance wants me to drop by. He needs my help."

"Oh?"

"That's all I know."

Adam and Vanda had gathered themselves together and arrived in Brinkworth and parked. They caught sight of several people they knew who acknowledged them with a smile and a wave. As they passed the newsagent, the blaring headline on the billboard outside read: 'Body found in trunk of local dignitary'.

"I wonder if that's got something to do with it?" mused Vanda.

"Only one way to find out," said Adam and they headed for the local police station.

Vance received them with a broad smile and shook hands. Vanda passed her article to Vance, "For your approval. And you'll let me know when I can safely go to print?"

Vance nodded. "Of course. He is currently on remand at Exeter prison. His preliminary hearing is in two weeks and then we have to wait for a trial date. Who knows when that will be. The system is cluttered with a backlog of cases waiting to be tried. I am hoping that this one, because of its seriousness, might rise up the list. I will let you know."

"Please. I am also hoping to cover the trial for one of the major tabloids."

Vance turned to Adam, "We also have something to discuss."

"Yes," said Adam. "I'm thinking it may be something to do with the headline we saw on the billboard."

"You'd be thinking right. You had better sit down and I'll explain."

Adam looked at Vanda, "You go on, Vanda. I know you have to see John about the exhibition and check the hall for all the exhibits. I'll come along there after I've finished here." She acknowledged with a smile and left the office.

Vance leaned forward in his seat and eyed Adam. "This is strictly confidential, and you are not allowed to talk about it with anyone. Understood?"

"And Vanda?"

"Anyone and that includes Vanda."

"That may be difficult."

Vance sighed and looked uncomfortable. "In that case, only if you absolutely have to, but no further, no one else."

Adam concurred. "I can live with that. So, what is this all about?"

"On the outskirts of Brinkworth on the coast road an abandoned car has been parked in a layby for the best part of a week."

"Go on."

"No one took much notice until a tourist parked behind the vehicle to take some photographs of the scenery. He noticed a foul smell coming from the vehicle. There was no one in there and no one around, so curiosity got the better of him. The car was unlocked with the keys inside. He opened the door and took the keys, but the smell made him gag and he was violently sick. He plucked up courage and went to the rear and unlocked the boot. Curled up in there, was the body of a young girl."

"Who?"

"That's it. We don't know. No one has been reported missing. There was no identification on her corpse or in the car. Preliminary examinations approximate her time of death as eight days ago."

"Has the car been identified?"

"False number plate, vin number filed off and no trace of who it belongs to. It looks like something taken from a scrap yard and dumped here. It doesn't even fire up."

"What about the girl?"

"The M.E. reckons she is between fifteen and eighteen years old. Nothing conclusive."

"What do you want from me?"

"Help. Anything that you can sense, anything at all. We are stuck."

"How did she die?"

"She was stabbed through the heart. We are waiting for toxicology screen to come back. They can take four weeks."

"Where is she?"

"Brinkworth General."

"Can I see her?"

Vance nodded. "We can go now, if you like?"

Adam nodded. "Yes. I'll just let Vanda know… Tell her to go home without me, if you can run me back?"

Vance acquiesced. "Of course. Come on. Let's get going."

Brinkworth General was situated on the top of a hill overlooking the town. It was surrounded by pleasant grounds with well clipped lawns and trees and had a small lake with wooden benches surrounding it where people could sit and watch the ducks and other water birds that inhabited the place. There were three car parks, one for staff, one for visitors, and an overflow one for anyone who needed to park.

Vance parked as close to the hospital entrance as he could and the two alighted. They entered the foyer with its reception, information board, café, and small shop. They crossed to the lifts and travelled down to the basement and walked along the corridor to the mortuary.

Adam shivered.

Vance glanced across at him. "What is it?"

"It's the stench of death."

"I don't smell anything."

"That and a succession of lost souls wandering through the passageways, who don't know where they are."

Vance looked around him, nervously. "How do you live with that?"

"You get used to it. But I've never been a fan of hospitals for this reason. I don't see dead people everywhere in the normal scheme of things."

"I'm glad to hear it," said Vance.

They eventually reached Pathology and the morgue. Vance showed his credentials and they entered. An orderly took them through to a refrigerated room and pulled out a metal drawer on runners containing the cadaver, which because of its decomposed state was in a body bag.

The orderly unzipped the top revealing the victim's face, which was purple in colour; her ears and the tip of her nose were turning black. Adam shuddered. Vance interjected, "The M.E. told us that the victim may have been in a kneeling position or fallen forward hence the discoloration." Adam stretched out his hand and touched the bag surrounding the girl. He paused for a moment and then pulled his hand back. "Have you seen enough?" Adam nodded. He had turned quite pale. Vance alerted the orderly who zipped the body up and closed the drawer.

Vance took Adam gently by the arm and steered him out of the refrigerated room and back out into the corridor. "You're shaking."

"It was cold in there."

"It's more than that. You felt something, didn't you?"

Adam nodded. "Let's get out of here, go to a café, or somewhere... Anywhere..."

Vance and Adam made their way outside, where Adam took in a lungful of fresh air. He breathed in deeply a few more times before joining Vance in the car, and they travelled back towards the town.

"You might as well take me home. We can have a coffee there. There will be no one to hear our discussion or listen in."

Vance turned off the main road towards Black Head Ridge. Adam was silent on the journey home. Vance didn't interrupt Adam's thinking and he waited until they were in the kitchen at Black Head Ridge House, seated at the kitchen table, with a cup of coffee each.

"Well?" queried Vance.

"It was not a pleasant experience."

"I don't suppose it was. What did you learn?"

"It's bizarre. She is just a school girl. I had the impression of her attending a boarding school. There was a uniform, a kilt worn with a white blouse and plain green tie."

"Like a man's tie?"

"Yes."

"That's something we can research, schools are currently on holiday. We can look up the uniform as you've described."

"It's an all girls' school."

"That should make it easier."

"Woodland surrounds the school and there was some kind of event happening at night in the woods, where the girls were dressed in… how can I describe it? Like a long white chemise and they wore headdresses and masks. There was one adult there with them."

"Some sort of club?"

"Possibly."

"What else?"

"I had a feeling that she had remained at the school for the holidays with a number of other students."

"So, if her parents were away they wouldn't know she was missing?"

"I suppose not, no…"

"Anything else?"

"Was there anything else with her body?"

Vance frowned. "How do you mean?"

"Any item of anything: clothing, jewellery, phone?"

"Why?"

"I feel that if I have something of hers it may help me to connect with her."

"Well, there was no phone, would that there was. It would make things a damn sight easier. Her clothes are with Forensics being checked for fibres etc. But…"

"But…"

"But she was wearing a pair of earrings."

"Do you have them?"

"I can get them."

"Were they of wolves?"

"How did you know?"

"I didn't. It was just a guess, a feeling. Can you get them for me?"

"I can. Will tomorrow be soon enough?"

Adam nodded. "Do that and I may be able to tell you more."

"Well, you have given us something to research and look out for. It's a start. Thank you."

Adam's mind was racing. He hadn't liked his encounter in the morgue and the child had an aura of innocence tainted by corruption from an evil entity that she had been unable to escape from. Adam decided he would do a little research of his own.

Once he got back to Black Head Ridge House he absconded to the study and fired up his laptop. He did a search for boarding schools in the area. There weren't many, but one caught his eye, 'Gilbert Bray Boarding school for young ladies'. It was located inland about twenty-five miles away. He clicked on it and was taken to the school's website with its extensive grounds and games' facilities. The large stone fronted building resembled a manor house more than a school and backed onto an expanse of ancient woodland and looked very impressive.

Adam ran through school year pictures, and he then focused on the page depicting staff members with photographs and studied each one carefully. He stopped at one, a master with thick dark wavy hair and piercingly penetrating blue eyes. He didn't know why, but the photograph unnerved him, and yet he was drawn to the man at the same time. He read the small bio under the teacher's photo and learned that he taught Chemistry, Biology and General Studies. He ran an after school club for games and recreational pastimes and was Head of Year Nine with his own tutor group of thirteen-year-olds. His name was Leonard Shaitan. Something prickled in the back of Adam's mind. Something about the name. He determined he would look it up.

Vanda strolled in and stepped behind Adam placing her hands on his shoulders and peered over his shoulder. "So what's this?" she queried.

Adam explained what had happened with Vance. Vanda was enthralled. She drew up a chair from the side of the room and sat alongside him. "So what's this that you are looking at?" Adam enlightened her and Vanda clapped her hands, "Now this is something I could get my teeth into. I feel another scoop coming on. Let me know what I can do to help?"

"I will. But, firstly, you need to finalise the details of the memorial and exhibition. We've not got long."

THE CLOYING MIST THAT HAD slithered across the sea and encompassed Black Head Ridge had begun to dissolve. The sun was fighting for a space in the wrap-around clouds to push its way through and warm up the land. Adam opened up the door of the big house and strolled to his car. He sat in the driver's seat, opened his window and drummed his fingers on the steering wheel as he waited for Vanda to cross from Cliff House and join him.

He spotted her emerging from her front door and gave her a toot and a wave out of the driver's side window. She smiled gaily and waved back and hurried across the cliff top towards him.

Adam caught his breath as he saw the developing sun catch the threads of gold in her hair and gasped. She really was quite beautiful. He felt an overwhelming surge of pleasure that she was his girl. He was unashamedly proud of her and her unique talents.

Vanda finally reached his car and clambered in. She twisted back in her seat for her seat belt and leaned back with a sigh. "Right, let's go. Do you know the way?"

"I've set the satnav. We should be okay." Adam moved away towards the cliff road that led to the routes out of Brinkworth.

"Better get our story straight if we're challenged."

Adam nodded as he started the car. "So we are doing a recce for your sister's little girl. What's her name?"

"My sister is Caroline, and her daughter is Poppy."

"Surname?"

"Palmer."

"Where do they live?" queried Adam.

"They're moving from Chester to the South West and we are looking at all the schools in the area."

"Why not a day school?"

"Her husband works on the rigs and is away a lot. Poppy is quite headstrong, and they felt she needed a firmer hand with regards to discipline, hence looking at boarding schools."

Adam interjected, "But, she's very bright. Her wild child behaviour has arisen through boredom and not being stretched enough. We need her to be someone talented who would be an acquisition to the school, not someone completely off the wall."

They continued on the highlighted route until they felt they had filled in all the details of their fabricated niece. They changed their names and made up their family history, sticking as closely as possible to what they knew.

"This is fun," said Vanda. "Like playing make believe."

"Well, we are," said Adam with a grin.

They continued on their journey chatting and adding bits to their story until they arrived at the Gilbert Bray Boarding school for young ladies. Vanda had a mini voice activated recorder in her jacket. She patted her pocket. "As soon as we arrive, I'll turn it on and then we'll be good to go. It's proved invaluable for me in the past."

Adam drove up the sweeping gravel drive and parked in front of the impressive mansion style building with its Gothic wings and towers. "It looks like something from Harry Potter," said Vanda.

Adam stared in awe at the stone building with seven wings, that they could see, and a single tower that stretched up into the sky. Each wing had pinnacles at their apex that resembled a cross. There were pointed arches, stained glass windows, flying buttresses, ribbed vaults and spires. There was an elaborate entry portal surrounded by glossy, green ivy that rambled thickly around the entrance.

There were grotesque gargoyles, decorated water spouts, that projected from the roof to carry water away from the roof and walls. Adam frowned, he recognised a female gargoyle that was different from the rest. More research, he thought.

They alighted and walked towards the entrance as three young girls burst out from the building and ran past them giggling. They dashed around the side of the building and disappeared from view. Adam felt a chill settle on his shoulders as they passed. He shivered.

Vanda eyed him curiously, "You feel something, don't you?"

Adam nodded. "Yes. There is a pervading evil about this building, like Dracula's castle."

"And there's something else?"

"Yes, those girls."

"The ones that passed us?"

"Yes, there was… oh, I don't know. A feeling that chilled me. All was not as it seemed." Vanda looked quizzically at him. "I know it sounds crazy, but I felt there was something with them. Something other worldly."

"Now you're giving me the heebie-jeebies."

"Right. We'll both take a deep breath. Are you prepared for this? Ready?"

"Ready." She turned on her mini-recorder.

The two mounted the well hewn stone steps and entered the school foyer. They gazed around them at the splendid archways and vaulted ceiling before studying a sign, which read 'Reception this way' together with an arrow.

They followed the arrow and came to an office with a large oak wooden reception desk. Sat behind it was a woman that looked as if she'd escaped from the eighteenth century with her elaborately coiled and plaited hair on top that then hung down in tresses onto her shoulders. She wore a dress, with flamboyant leg of mutton sleeves, that nipped in tightly at the waist with a white frilled trim to the bodice and full skirt. With her pale porcelain complexion she resembled someone from another era.

Adam coughed and she glanced up from her computer and blushed. "Oh, excuse me," she said girlishly. "You must think I look really odd." Adam just managed a weak smile. "I am to model for the art club in a couple of hours. They have been studying the period in class and neoclassicism movement, where artists embraced the ideals of ancient Greece and Rome, seeking to inspire their works with harmony, rationality and order in the pursuit of what is beautiful and tasteful." She turned a deeper shade of pink and gave an embarrassed smile. "Sorry, I don't mean to give you a lecture just to explain why I am dressed like this. The school wasn't expecting any visitors. There's nothing in the book."

"No, it is I who should apologise arriving unannounced," said Adam returning her smile. "We came to request a brochure for the school for our niece whose family are moving to the area."

"Yes," added Vanda. "We hoped to be able to take a look around the school, too. If it's not too much trouble?" Vanda asked sweetly.

"Um… I will have to ask permission. It is most unusual. We don't normally have visitors in the holidays."

"Sorry, I didn't realise… we did see some girls earlier…"

"Boarders who were unable to get home for one reason or another." She rose from her seat and went to the large metal filing cabinet in the corner of the office and pulled out a drawer and selected an information pack on the school. She glided to the desk. "This is all the information you will need, including fees. If you'd like to wait, I'll see if there's someone available to show you around?"

"That would be wonderful," said Vanda with a gushing smile.

"Then if you'd like to take a seat in the foyer. I will send someone to you."

"Thank you. That would be most kind," said Adam.

"And appreciated," added Vanda.

Grasping the information pack they retreated to the foyer and sat on an oak settle to wait. They spoke in hushed tones as their voices were likely to carry and echo in the stone building.

"Are you feeling anything?" whispered Vanda.

"Dread," answered Adam, "and foreboding. Something is very wrong here."

They were interrupted by a sixth former, a leggy eighteen-year-old brunette. She smiled sweetly, "I am told, you want a tour of the school and accommodation blocks?" They nodded. "I'm Michelle. You could say I'm your tour guide." She smiled again. "If you'd like to follow me… Mr… er…?"

"Oh, sorry. I'm Adam Carver and this is…"

"Julia," said Vanda. "Julia Cummings. I'm Adam's fiancée." She twiddled the dress ring on her ring finger.

Michelle studied the two of them and said, "Well, Mr Carver and Miss Cummings. You had better follow me. This way."

The sixth form student marched off confidently her head held aloft, and she strode down the corridor. Adam and Vanda hurried after her.

Michelle did indeed act like a tour guide, she showed them the first, second and third year student block in the West Wing where English, Maths, History, Geography, Languages, and R.E. were taught. She showed them the older pupils' quarters. All was looking good.

On they went to the Art studios, Music rooms, Gym and Science block. Adam and Vanda agreed that the facilities were excellent. They were suitably impressed with the dormitories, bathrooms, the recreation areas, and canteen and agreed that the surroundings were remarkable. Including a chicken coop with hens running freely, scratching and pecking at small insects and looking for worms.

It was when they reached the science block that Adam was overcome with an unnerving feeling of dread. Young girls' voices echoed inside his brain, chanting intermingled with screams. Adam shuddered. Vanda looked at him concerned, "Are you all right?"

The student, Michelle studied Adam and said, "You don't look too well. You seem a little woozy. Would you like a drink of water?"

Adam nodded and steadied himself. He sat on one of the wooden stools at a science bench and as he did he received a vision of flames and a large bonfire that crackled and smoked.

Michelle rinsed out a measuring glass beaker, ran the tap for really cold water and filled it. She passed it to Adam and their hands touched. He received a flash of images of girls in white robes wearing animal masks similar to the visions he received at the morgue, when he viewed the girl's body.

Michelle jumped back almost knocking the water from Adam's hand. "What was that?" she said alarmed.

"Static electricity," said Vanda. "I saw the blue sparks. I get a lot of that."

"Oh, he must be highly charged," said Michelle.

"Certainly is," murmured Vanda. She turned to Adam. "Feeling better?"

Adam nodded. "Don't know what happened there."

"I do. You've had no breakfast, drove all the way here, without a break. We need to get you something to eat. Sorry, Michelle. You've done a wonderful job. I need to get Adam to the local pub. He'll feel better once he's eaten."

Michelle smiled limply, "Of course. I'll show you out."

"Please do. It's quite a maze here. However do you find your way around?" said Vanda.

"Oh, you get used to it and of course, you stick to your blocks according to your year except when doing Art, Music or Gym."

"What about IT, Drama, Domestic Science, and CDT?"

"They are all included in after school clubs."

"I see. Good idea. What other clubs do they have?"

Michelle pursed her lips. "Photography, debating, car maintenance and so on. You'll find all the information in your pack" She smiled primly, "By the way what's your niece called?"

Adam and Vanda looked at each other and went to speak at the same time. Vanda laughed, and continued, "It's Poppy. Perhaps look out for her if she's accepted."

"I will," said Michelle too brightly. "Ah, here we are. Back in the foyer. Will you be all right from here?"

Adam replied, "Of course. Thank you for your time."

"Pleasure. I may see you again, then?"

Adam nodded. "You may." He turned and went through the stout oak door, quickly followed by Vanda.

Once outside he gulped a lungful of fresh air and sighed deeply. He almost sprinted to the car but restrained himself feeling eyes watching him. He opened the door and sat in the driver's seat.

"Well?" asked Vanda.

"I'll explain later. Now we need to look as if we're leaving…"

"You mean we're not?"

"I want to take a look at the woods behind the school. Check the map. I'll start the car and we'll go. Have a look and see if there's any access to the woods other than through the grounds."

"Why?"

"I think something happened there that could be linked to our young girl." Adam started the car, and they pulled out from their parking space and began to progress down the sweeping drive. As he drove, he explained what he had felt in the science lab.

"So you believe there is something going on in the school?"

"Yes. Let's find somewhere to eat, we can look through the literature, check the map and see if we can enter the woods after dark."

Adam and Vanda drove away from the school and kept a lookout for a pub. They found one just a mile from the school, 'The Jolly Waggoner'. Its sign swung lazily and creaked on its hinges in the growing wind. They parked up and went inside to find a table. There were a couple of drinkers at the bar and three tables occupied. They found one near the fireplace that was stacked with logs on both sides. A fire burnt merrily in the grate giving out quite a lot of heat, which was needed as the day was quite cold.

Adam went to the bar to order drinks. The barman was a big bluff fellow with a thick dark beard. "What can I get you?"

"A dry white wine and soda and something non-alcoholic like Beavertown Lazer Crush Alcohol Free IPA, please."

"Don't think I know that one. Don't get much call for it around here. Let me see." He picked up a drinks' menu and passed it to Adam. "Got a couple of low alcohol beers…"

Adam scrutinised the menu and shook his head. "I'm driving, can't take the risk. I'll have a soda and lime and your food menu please."

The barman gave him two menus. "Not seen you round here before. On holiday?"

"No, we live further down the coast."

"Day out?" questioned the barman.

"Not quite. Doing a favour for a relative. We came to check out the Gilbert Bray boarding school for young ladies."

"Oh? And what did you find?"

"Not sure really. Seems a decent enough place. Why?"

"If I were you, I'd think twice about sending any child there."

"Why's that?"

The barman dropped his voice conspiratorially. "Strange goings on. The last three years. Weird things happened there. If you want to know any more ask Kenneth here." He jerked his head at one of the drinkers at the bar as he poured their drinks.

Adam took the menus and passed one to Vanda, before collecting his drinks and delivering them to the table. "You choose something for me and let me know. I just want a word with that chap over there." He inclined his head towards the man known as Kenneth.

"Here, take my recorder, I've set it to go." She surreptitiously passed it to him, and he secreted it in his pocket.

Kenneth was a lean-faced man with receding auburn hair. He had freckles and a dimple in his chin. He looked pleasant enough. Adam crossed to him, "Can I get you a drink, sir?"

Kenneth studied Adam and muttered, "Don't mind if I do. Pint of IPA please," which Adam duly ordered. "And the name's Kenneth. Don't stand on ceremony here."

"Kenneth." The two men eyed each other. "The landlord here reckons you might have some information that will be useful to me."

"Oh yeah? About what?"

"Gilbert Bray Boarding School."

Kenneth shuddered, "Not thinking of sending anyone there, are you?"

Adam hesitated, "Not me personally. Just doing a recce for my fiancé's sister."

"Tell her to find another school."

"Why?"

Kenneth was just about to launch into something when the door to the pub opened.

Kenneth looked around, and spotted the newcomer. "Not here. You have your meal and I'll come to your table." Kenneth turned back to his drink.

Adam crossed back to Vanda and stole a look at the person who had entered. He was of medium build, athletic looking, with a full mane of thick flaxen hair. He had a handsome face, one would say striking, with large blue grey eyes. He had an aura about him, a superficial glow but Adam noticed something else. There was a dark shadow that appeared to be on his back, which suddenly dissipated into the air.

The man stared at Kenneth who took no notice, but just gazed into his drink. He then began to study Adam and watched him as he crossed to Vanda.

"Well, have you decided?"

"Mm. I think I'll go for good old fish and chips. Can't go wrong."

"Great. That'll do for me, too." He walked to the bar and ordered, and paid before returning to his seat.

Vanda whispered, "What was that all about?"

"I'm not sure, but we'll wait until we can hear what he has to say. Here, take this back." He returned the recorder to Vanda who placed it back in her jacket pocket. The move didn't go unnoticed by the flaxen haired man, who narrowed his eyes and then fixed his gaze on Kenneth, watching him.

ADAM AND VANDA HAD FINISHED their fish and chips, and both agreed it was excellent. They sipped their drinks and looked warily about them. Ever since the entry of the flaxen haired man there was a tense uncomfortable atmosphere that wasn't present before. Adam watched and waited. The young man glanced at his watch, finished his drink and left whistling cheerfully. As soon as he had gone the mood changed and lightened. However, once outside he stopped outside the window and peered in to watch, keeping himself hidden.

Kenneth strolled across carrying a shot of whiskey. He pulled up a chair as Adam said he'd get them all another drink. He was still on lime and soda.

"Another pint, Kenneth?

"Another one of these, please."

Adam returned and placed a second shot in front of Kenneth, adding, "So, can we talk now?"

"Couldn't speak before. The man who came in…"

"Yes?"

"Russell Draper, teaches Art there. He's a weird one, very pally with Leonard Shaitan. Thick as thieves those two and not to be trusted."

"Why? And how do you know all this?" queried Adam.

"I used to be groundsman over at the school. It was a lovely job. I kept the sports field up to smack, and all the grounds. Did it for twelve years, would still be doing it except for the events that happened when Leonard Shaitan came to work there. That's when it all started."

"What exactly?" asked Vanda.

"It all started with rumours and strange sounds."

"Sounds?" questioned Adam.

"Like wolves howling at night. Shapes seen wandering the corridors and…" he dropped his voice considerably so that Vanda and Adam had to lean forward to catch what he was saying. "Then the deaths."

"Deaths?"

"Oh, they tried to hush it up. Never made the nationals, just the local press and the stories fizzled out. There were no investigations or anything. They said it was suicide, but I know different. Something scared those girls to death. Terrified them. School said they'd taken their own lives. Little Carol Ashton was found hanging from a tree in the woods behind the school. They said she'd done it herself. I don't believe it."

"But why?"

"They made excuses she was depressed and homesick. Said because her parents were divorcing she couldn't cope… Oh, it *looked* like suicide. But it wasn't. They said birds had got at her body, pecked her eyes out. But it was more than that."

Vanda looked away shocked. Adam pressed him, "Go on."

"Carol's friend, Patti Smith, she ran away. They found her in the woods and brought her to the infirmary."

"Did we see that?" asked Adam.

Vanda shook her head, "No."

"I wonder why? Sorry, Kenneth, continue please."

"She went in the infirmary and wouldn't talk or nothing. Just stared blankly ahead and when one of the teachers went to see her, she screamed and screamed, and ended up having some sort of fit. Kid choked and died. They said it was an accidental death. And then there were the chickens."

"Why? What happened with the chickens?" asked Vanda.

"Something or someone snaffled them. Let them out of the henhouse after dark. A fox got some, at least I think it was a fox. But one of them was found upside down staked to a tree, all the blood drained out of it. School said it was an ugly, cruel prank that had gone wrong and blamed it on local children." Kenneth stopped and downed his shot of whiskey.

"Why did you leave?"

"They tried to shift the blame onto me, said I wasn't doing my job properly. I'd been there for twelve years with never a problem. The school was a happy place, and I loved the kids. All of a sudden we had dramatic changes." He paused. "Then after the two deaths, and the affair with the chickens, we had a couple of runaways."

Adam became more alert. "Runaways?"

"Yes. Two of them. Friends they were. Two little uns. There was a search. Neither of them were found. Still no sign of them."

"So why did you leave?"

"I didn't want to. They said I was poking about too much in things that didn't concern me and after the chicken fiasco told me my services were no longer required. They gave me severance pay, which was a reasonable amount as long as I didn't bring a case for unfair dismissal, so I took the money. I'm working as groundsman at another school now, same type of job and much better. No weird goings on there."

"That's quite a story, Kenneth," said Vanda. "One that convinces me that my niece should not attend Gilbert Bray. Thank you so much."

"My pleasure. You mark my words, something will come out about that place in the future. It's bound to."

"And for all your help, let me get you another whiskey."

"Thanks very much. I'll not say no."

"As a matter of interest, who were the two runaways and what did they look like?"

Kenneth screwed up his face as he thought... "Lass called Margaret Lake and her friend, Lucy Ward. This was about two years ago. First years they were, state schools' year seven. Sorry, can't tell you much more."

"No, I understand, thank you. I'll get your scotch." Adam rose and went to the bar.

Vanda turned to Kenneth. "You've been most helpful, thank you."

"There's also the question of some of the staff." Adam returned and passed Kenneth his scotch, which he took gratefully. "The chap who was in here, Russell Draper..."

"You were saying..." prompted Vanda.

"The staff were a pretty good bunch and then Mr Shaitan arrived. As I said, that's when things changed. Oh, not immediately but once he found his feet. The girls adored him, struck by his good looks, same with Draper and the men became big buddies. He was really popular, but I had misgivings and a feeling about him."

Kenneth paused and Adam prompted, "Always trust your instincts, never deny a feeling. I don't."

Kenneth cleared his throat nervously. "He worried me. Too good to be true. He took a special interest in some of the girls, that to me, seemed totally unhealthy." Vanda and Adam exchanged a look. "I've no proof of anything. Like I said, I didn't trust him." There was a lull in the conversation.

Adam smiled. "We definitely won't be recommending that school. The search will have to go on."

"If we need to talk to you again, is there any way to contact you?" asked Vanda.

"I'm in here lunchtimes, Tuesday and Thursday and always of a Saturday night. If not Mick," he jerked his head at the barman, "he'll know where I am. But why would you need to do that? I've told you what I know."

"Let's just say, there's obviously some kind of mystery here and you have sparked my interest in it. I'd like to do a bit of digging. If what you say is right, the community should know about it," argued Vanda.

Kenneth's demeanour became anxious. "I don't want my name dragged into anything. I've said more than I should already."

"Rest assured, no one will do that. After all, I may find nothing, then no harm is done. But, if I do, then people have a right to know. Our children need to be safe."

"Who are you people?"

"As I said," interrupted Adam. "We came here as a favour for a relative, but I am also a private investigator, and my fiancée is an investigative journalist."

"Yes," added Vanda. "If there is something untoward going on here, we will find out what it is, and it could be a big scoop for me."

Kenneth sniffed, "You won't mention my name?"

"Not unless you wanted me to." Kenneth grunted and nodded. "Remember we might not discover anything or indeed we could find that these incidents were indeed just as they have said."

"Hmm. I doubt that. There is something going on there and it's evil."

"Kenneth, can we ask you something?" said Vanda. Kenneth looked up from his drink and raised his eyebrows. "Please don't mention what we do to anybody. Just keep that fact to yourself."

"I'm not likely to. I don't want a barrel of trouble landing on my head."

"Then we have an understanding?" said Adam. Kenneth nodded and they shook hands. Russell Draper saw the exchange and slunk away.

"So," said Vanda with a grin as they set off in the car, "you're a private investigator now, are you?"

"I had to say something that would warrant the questions. Anyway, it's not far from the truth. I am a consultant for the cops."

"What now?"

"Let's take a look in those woods and then get back."

They made their way back towards the school and skirted around the back road and parked just out of sight in the trees. Adam grabbed a torch, and they were making their way through the trees, when Adam stopped.

"What?"

"It was here. Some sort of ritual look at that tree." Adam shone the light on the bark of a spreading oak, which revealed bloodstains. "Possibly chicken's blood but just in case... have you got a tissue?" Adam took a penknife from his pocket and scraped some of the residue into a tissue that Vanda gave him, and further examination of the clearing found other places of splatter and Adam took samples of that, too. "We'll get these to Vance in the morning and now we'd best get back."

The rest of the journey back to Black Head Ridge was interesting as they played back the tape, while they travelled. "What do you think?" asked Adam after they switched it off. "Did you hear it?"

"What?"

"In places, that background white noise."

"I didn't notice. Well, there was some distortion. But nothing major."

"There was no noticeable noise as we walked around but it was predominant when those girls ran past and with that receptionist in costume. And again, when that chap walked into the pub."

"There's definitely a story here. Something unsavoury is going on. You felt it, didn't you?"

Adam nodded. "I did." He paused. "You'll think I'm crazy…"

"No I won't. What is it? Tell me."

"I will have to listen again, but I am sure I heard voices in there."

"In the white noise?"

"Yes."

Vanda went silent for a moment before announcing, "It's happening again. Isn't it?"

"We better get back to Vance and report."

"Not now, surely?"

"No. Tomorrow morning will be soon enough. Besides, I want to do a little research. See what else I can find."

"I've got chills," Vanda said rubbing her arms and shivering. "Oh, Lord, here we go again."

Once at home, Adam fired up his computer. He searched the internet for the name Leonard, apart from the accepted meaning of 'lion strength' another definition caught his eye. Leonard, it seemed, was a demon or spirit, grandmaster of sabbaths, chief of the subaltern demons and inspector general of sorcery, black magic and witchcraft. Adam leaned back in his seat and turned his attention to the name Shaitan. This, too, had an unnerving definition.

Shaitan was an evil spirit in Islam inviting humans to sin by whispering in their hearts. Adam frowned, things seemed to be adding up. He called out to Vanda, "Come and see what I've found."

Vanda rose from her iPad where she was researching something else. She shuddered. "Do you think the names are important?"

"I do. It's almost like hiding in plain sight. And what's more that's how cults get started. Look at the power David Koresh wielded. He told his followers, where and what to eat, what to do and even what to think. He was a charismatic man, which sounds very much like Leonard Shaitan and that chap who came into the pub."

"Russell Draper?"

"That's the one."

"You better come and see what I've found out so far," said Vanda. "I've been delving into the archives of the local newspapers. Got much more to do but you may find this interesting."

The headline read, '*Tragedy at Gilbert Bray Boarding School*'. Adam read it avidly. The report seemed to verify what Kenneth had said. It stated the child had been extremely depressed over her parents' divorce and schoolfriends had insisted that she had withdrawn into herself and didn't want company or to involve herself with any school activities and when she was told she would have to remain in school through the half term holiday, she just snapped.

"Makes sense, I suppose. See if you can find anything else about the other children."

Vanda nodded. "I'll get back on to it." She returned to her iPad and continued trawling through more reports, while Adam researched various animal cults. He scoured Wikipedia and newspaper archives for anything regarding wolves but could find very little of value. He sighed heavily and closed his laptop.

Vanda alerted him, "I've found something. It's not much. Just a few lines about the runaways, but there are pictures."

"Print them off. They could be useful."

"Will do. I'll see what else I can find."

The telephone interrupted them, it was John Grey. "Vanda?"

"Yes?"

"Everything has been set up. Just needs you to give final approval. Can you get down to the exhibition hall?"

"Of course." Vanda waved at Adam. "We were just about to leave."

"Great. See you in about thirty minutes?"

"Absolutely." She closed the call and alerted Adam. "With all the excitement of this school case, I totally forgot I have to check out the exhibition before tomorrow. Are you coming?"

Adam closed his laptop. "You bet. Let's go." He grabbed his jacket and keys, and they left the house. Conversation en route to the hall was limited, they were both thinking about the mystery at the school and although excited that Caroline would at last receive recognition for her work, they were more excited about solving another mystery.

Adam murmured, "Hope Steve has managed to get all the champagne I ordered delivered and kept chilled on site."

"I'm sure he won't let you down. And I need to check with the caterers that everything is on point."

Adam nodded. "Give them a call, while I park up. Who was doing the decorations?"

"John was getting balloons and tables, a podium for the presentation and I have a number of village girls booked for serving drinks. Everything should be in hand."

Adam smiled, "Then let's get your examination of the hall over and done with. Tomorrow will be here soon enough. I need to get this to Vance." He pointed to a plastic bag with the tissues containing pieces of the stained bark.

Adam faced Vance and told him what they had discovered and passed him the suspect blood trace evidence.

"I'll do what I can. Don't hold out too much hope but we'll see what it will reveal. I don't expect it will be back until after the weekend. Now, tell me about the exhibition. I hope to see you there."

Adam shook hands with the detective and received an image of Vance careering off road and plunging through a wooded area. But the image was fleeting. Vance noticed the strange sensation and the look on Adam's face. "What is it?"

"I'm not sure. I just need you to be careful when driving."

"You can't leave it at that," complained Vance.

"It's not clear. I just had an image of you leaving the road and ploughing into a wooded area. Not how, when or where. It was very quick."

"Nevertheless, I'll be careful. Thank you. If you get anything else, let me know." Adam nodded. "Now tell me about the exhibition I know it's not long before the big day."

The day did, indeed, arrive sooner than expected. The exhibition hall looked impressive displaying portraits and seascapes in both pastels and oil paint. The walls were adorned with Caroline's art, which flowed through the different phases and styles of her work.

There had been a huge turn-out of people from Brinkworth who had come to pay their respects to Caroline. Other guests of different gender and ages, from across the country had descended on the small town, which had gained some notoriety after the bizarre deaths of Caroline and Lisa Devereaux and the end of taxidermist, Ted Johnson. People were curious to see the work of the artist now gaining popularity and interested in the people helping the police who were instrumental in solving the case.

Champagne flowed with each person arriving being given a glass on entry. Art critics met old friends and freely discussed the pictures on display. Vanda and Adam sat at a table with a ledger recording sales. They looked on in delight at the buzz of chatter and praise that seemed to be heaped on the artist's work.

Photographers and reporters were there to capture the atmosphere and scene. John signalled to Vanda that the time was now, and the entrance doors were closed. Everyone fell quiet as Vanda stepped up to the podium to address the assembled guests.

"It gives me great pleasure to welcome you all to the Caroline Mitchell exhibition. Her life was tragically cut short when her talent was just beginning to be recognised. If you are interested in any of the pictures on display then please speak to my friend and colleague Adam Barrie sitting over there." She indicated where Adam was sitting. "There is only one thing left to do. Please raise your glasses in honour of my sister. To Caroline Mitchell."

Vanda lifted her glass as did all the other guests who chorused, "Caroline Mitchell."

The outside door opened carefully, and Vanda stared curiously. Her eyes widened as she recognised Russell Draper entering the hall. He took a glass of champagne from a tray and stood at the back of the hall and watched.

Vanda stepped down from the podium and looked around the room. Russell Draper was in deep conversation with someone appraising one of Caroline's portraits of Victor Channing. She crossed to Adam and leaned across the desk, "Did you see?"

"What?"

"Russell Draper. He came in the back door when I was talking, took a glass of champagne and now he's talking to someone in front of one of your grandfather's portraits."

Adam craned his neck to see. "This isn't good."

"No, it isn't and if he discovers our real names…" she trailed off.

Adam tried to placate her, "He teaches Art at the school, maybe he's just interested in a new artist's work. A coincidence?"

"I don't believe in coincidences and nor do you…" she said fiercely.

"No, we had better be careful. I'll keep an eye out."

Vanda moved away to the storeroom to check on supplies of champagne before returning to mingle with dignitaries and guests and Adam watched Russell Draper.

The evening progressed well. Several of Caroline's pictures were sold and deposits put on others to reserve them. The exhibition had been a resounding success. Adam had observed Russell Draper who had been chatting with Geoff Merryweather who ran the hardware store. Draper had gone around the exhibition and left shortly afterwards. He hadn't, Adam didn't think, spoken to anyone else. Adam caught Geoff as he was about to leave.

"Hi, Geoff." Geoff turned as he was donning his coat.

"Adam?"

"Geoff, I noticed you were in intense conversation with an Art teacher, Russell Draper?"

"Was that his name?"

"Yes. I recognised him. What did he want?"

"Not a lot. He talked about Caroline's art. He was interested in how the exhibition came about and what had happened to her."

"What did you tell him?"

"I told him the story. Why? Have I done something wrong?"

"No, no. Just curious. He's not been to the area before?"

"Apparently not. He was keen to learn that Caroline had a sister."

"Did you point Vanda out?"

"I was going to but couldn't see her in the room then. It was after that he left. Seemed personable enough but…"

"But?"

"I don't know. I can't explain it, but I just couldn't warm to the man."

Adam thanked Geoff and went to find Vanda. He relayed what Geoff had said. "He must have connected you to Caroline."

"Possibly. We can but hope, he didn't," replied Vanda.

"He's only got to look up the stories in the press. He'll know all about us then," said Adam looking concerned.

"Can't be helped. We can still investigate but will just have to be careful," murmured Vanda.

"Hmm," said Adam doubtfully. "I feel we must tread very carefully. I don't like it."

"And we have a wedding to attend. So, what's next?"

"A wedding?"

"Yes. I forgot to say. The invitation came this morning."

"Whose wedding?"

"Angie and Luke. In the light of what happened, they've brought it forward and added us both to the guest list."

"That was quick."

"You can't blame them. Luke thought he'd never see her again."

"That will be great. I'll have to get something decent to wear."

"Me, too," murmured Vanda.

"Okay. Let's finish up here and get home."

"John is finishing clearing up tomorrow. He's made a start and packed most away already. There's not a lot left to do," said Vanda.

"Good. Then let's go. I have all the figures here," he patted the ledger and picked it up. They grabbed their coats and left the hall.

Adam glanced around the car park, he was feeling uncomfortable.

"What?" asked Vanda. "What is it?"

"I don't know. Something doesn't feel right." Just then the lights flooding the car park fizzed, popped and went out, plunging the area into the dark. Adam took Vanda by the arm, "Quickly let's go."

They unlocked their vehicle with a chirrup and sat inside. Adam's hand shook as he started the car. "Going to take a detour."

"Why?"

"Just to be sure."

"Adam you're scaring me."

"Bear with me. We'll drive into the centre of Brinkworth and check in at the Arundell Arms."

"Why?"

"We can spend the night there."

"What about Elsa?"

"She'll be fine. You left her plenty of food. She'll have to have a late breakfast."

"But we don't have any toiletries or change of clothes," Vanda protested.

"They will have toiletries at the hotel, I'm sure. I just want to be certain... I don't want to lead Russell Draper to our respective homes. I'm being careful, that's all."

"You think he'll follow us?" said Vanda aghast.

Adam nodded. "I think that might be on the cards." He set the car in motion and turned towards Brinkworth constantly checking in his mirror for following lights. As they drew nearer the road leading to town he ignored the turning to Black Head Ridge and ploughed on towards Brinkworth. As he did so, he noticed the headlights of a vehicle come up behind them and veer off sharply in the direction of Black Head Ridge. Another car proceeded behind him at a safe distance and into Brinkworth.

"Now when we get out, act as normally as possible. Look carefree and happy," he ordered.

"Got it," said Vanda.

They parked up and entered the hotel and made their way to Reception. The girl behind the desk looked up surprised. "Mr Barrie?"

"Do you have a double room available tonight?"

"We're pretty full with visitors who attended the exhibition, let me check." The girl whose name plate read 'Avril' perused the booking in register. "You're lucky, we have one double on floor three. Is it for one night?"

"Please. We'll take it and do you have any toiletries I can purchase? We came in a bit of a hurry and left our bags behind."

"Certainly," said Avril with a smile. "There's shampoo, conditioner and soap provided in the room, and I keep travel toothbrushes and paste here at the counter for just £2.50 each. Will they suffice?"

"Perfect," purred Vanda. "Do we pay now?"

"I can add them to your bill." She smiled again. "How would you like to pay?"

"Mastercard debit," said Adam flourishing his card. Payment was taken, card keys made and passed across. They crossed to the lifts and Adam glanced in the lounge bar where some of the guests from the exhibition were enjoying a drink. "Fancy a nightcap?" asked Adam.

Vanda nodded and they moved into the bar where they were greeted by a number of friendly faces. They ordered a couple of brandies and retreated to a table in a booth with glass panels and were able to watch the others in the bar unnoticed.

"What now?" asked Vanda.

"We sit and wait. Keep your eyes open."

They sat and chinked glasses as if celebrating and sipped their brandies quietly. Moments later two more people entered the bar. One was Michelle the girl who had shown them around the school. Vanda and Adam both dropped their heads and turned away. The other was Leonard Shaitan. There was no sign of Russell Draper.

"Well, well," murmured Adam. "Think we ought to slip away asap."

"But not immediately. We will be spotted."

"True. Best move ourselves so we are facing away from them. I can look in the glass reflection and see when it's safe to do that." They manoeuvred themselves into a position that obscured their identity and waited.

"I'll watch and on my signal, you get up and return to the room. You should be safe."

"What about you?"

"You're more easily recognisable than me. Just go when I say." Vanda didn't argue, but nodded and drained her brandy. Adam watched the man and student and saw them head towards the back of the room. He whispered urgently, "Now."

Vanda slipped out from the booth and made her way to the lifts unobserved as Adam watched the two select a table at the back of the room, which gave them a good view of everyone in the bar and he silently cursed. At least Vanda was out of the way.

Time ticked on and people began leaving the bar. Adam took a chance and slipped out between a group of five people still raving enthusiastically about the exhibition. He walked with them to the lift and as they waited he engineered himself to the stairs and disappeared up them instead of using the elevator.

Vanda was waiting anxiously in their room. "I was just about to phone downstairs. Is everything okay. Were you seen?"

"I don't think so. But then again, you never know. Shaitan doesn't know us, only Michelle. I just hope she was looking the other way when I slipped out."

"So what now?"

"Well the room is paid for. We can either stay or we can sneak away. What do you think?" Adam smiled playfully.

"How can you be so calm about everything?"

"I'm not. Just trying not to panic and do the best for us."

"I don't feel comfortable."

"Your wish is my command. We'll sneak away. But we will do it carefully and quietly."

They waited until a sufficient amount of time had passed and they had heard people in the corridor talking and doors opening and closing. Adam peeped out and gestured to Vanda who slipped out behind him. Instead of taking the elevator they took the stairs and on entering the lobby took the back door entrance to the car park and went to find their vehicle.

Vanda heaved a sigh of relief once she was in the passenger seat. Adam took off the handbrake and allowed the car to roll down the slope towards the road without switching on his lights until he was in the street. He kept flicking his eyes to his rear view mirror to keep an eye out for any other cars.

"Are we safe?" queried Vanda.

"I think so. But keep a look out just in case."

They travelled out of Brinkworth with no unusual sighting of threatening vehicles or anyone following them. Once they turned onto the road leading to Black Head Ridge they both heaved a sigh of relief and relaxed.

Adam parked and they both stepped inside Black Head Ridge House and Adam stopped.

"What is it?" asked Vanda suddenly alert. "You feel something, don't you?"

"I'm not sure. I thought I heard a wolf howling."

"A wolf? What does that mean?"

"I don't know. I honestly don't know," said Adam shaking his head. "I have to see Vance tomorrow and let him know what we have."

"And leave it to him. I don't like where this is all leading." Adam made a non-committal grunt, so Vanda continued, "I mean it, Adam. We have to learn from our previous mistakes. Give him the info and let the police deal with it."

There was a pause and Adam finally nodded. "I'll see Vance tomorrow."

ADAM EXPLAINED HIS FINDINGS AND intuitive feelings to Vance the best way he could. Vance rubbed his chin thoughtfully, rose, walked to the window, and looked out at the street, and the clear blue innocent looking sky. His reply was measured.

"Adam you have done more than I asked, much more and from what you have told me, this could be a dangerous game. I don't want you to investigate anymore. It sounds as if whoever has taken this young girl's life is on to you. You could be bringing more trouble on your head and Vanda's. Leave the rest to us."

"But, I can help. I want to help."

"But Vanda doesn't want you to, does she?" Adam shook his head. "I thought so... Now we know the school, we can go in and see what we can find. I'd prefer it if you weren't involved."

"But we are involved. You asked for my help, remember? My special talents you said."

"I know. And I am not saying that it's permanent. You *have* been of great help. Please leave it with us. I will call you when I need you."

Adam pursed his lips and swallowed the retort that rose to his lips. He tempered his words. "What if something else occurs to me or comes to me?"

"Then by all means speak to me. I just don't want you jumping in with both feet. We know how impulsive you can be. If what you have said is true then we are dealing with a very delicate situation involving children. We still have to find the name of the child and contact her family."

A name whispered in Adam's brain. He heard it quite clearly, "Her name is Melanie. Melanie Parker."

"How do you know?" said Vance sharply.

"I don't. I just heard it in my head, just now."

Vance sighed. "Look, it will be difficult enough. Just let us get on with the job. If you think of anything else, let me know. I feel strongly you need to take a break. And that's my intuition talking. I'll bring you back in, if I need to."

Adam was forced to accept what Vance said although it was clear he didn't like it. He finally agreed. "All right. But I don't believe it will be long before you need me again."

"That's as maybe. We'll see and thank you." He extended his hand to Adam, which Adam took, and they shook hands. "Good. I'm glad we're in agreement." As they made contact Adam shivered and Vance ever alert asked, "What? What is it?"

"I'm not sure. I just had an impression…"

"Of what?"

"Be careful around any dogs. Take precautions."

"I don't know what you mean."

"It was fleeting… but I saw you facing something that looked like a wolf, a German Shepherd type animal. Be careful. Maybe take a dog handler with you. Take a catch pole, you know, a control pole, you might need it."

Vance paused. "Thank you. I will."

Adam nodded and left the office.

The next few weeks passed uneventfully. He didn't contact Vance and Vance didn't contact him. But Adam was restless. This restlessness increased when he started receiving images and hearing voices. They didn't all make sense as he tried to explain to Vanda. "It's weird. I don't know if I am seeing flashbacks or something that's coming."

"What? Is it anything you can give Vance?"

"I don't know. I'd like to try and make sense of it first."

"It's Angie and Luke's wedding this weekend. Can you put this all aside until afterwards? At least let us have a decent time there."

"You talk as if I can control this. I can't," said Adam ruefully.

"I know. I'm sorry. It's just…"

"Just?"

"I think you're rubbing off on me. I've been feeling things, too."

"You've never said. What? What are you sensing?"

"Nothing specific; just a feeling of unease, like something is going to happen."

"Don't witch it!"

"Witch it?"

"Something my mother used to say. She believed words had power and saying things out loud could make them happen."

"I wish I'd met your mother."

"You'd have loved her. She had a great voice."

"So you said."

"It's often my mother's voice I hear." Adam sighed. "Okay. I'll try and curb things until the wedding is over, but I can't guarantee it. You understand?"

Vanda nodded. "I know." She smiled and added, "Now come here and let's talk outfits. We need to look our best on Saturday." She beckoned with her finger and put her arms around his neck as he reached her. He nuzzled into her hair, and she stiffened as a vision transmitted itself to her. "You must have seen it?"

Adam nodded. "What did you see?"

"It was Vance facing a snarling dog."

"I've had it before. I have warned him. I hope he's listened."

"Why do you think I see things when I touch you?"

"I don't know. Perhaps, because we have a connection and so sometimes I can communicate it to you when we touch. It's strange inexplicable phenomena and there are no rules. There again, it doesn't always happen."

"No. Seems like the spirits are being selective."

"Maybe. So, we'll just have to wait and see. Now, let's talk wedding fever. It seems to have overtaken everything else."

The day was perfect. It was like something from a romantic movie. The birds were singing, the sky was blue, and the invited guests were all smiling. Church bells rang joyously, and wedding guests stood outside the church in their finery, waiting for the bride and groom to emerge after photographs in the church.

Vanda and Adam chatted happily with those that they knew. A ripple went around the crowd as the photographer hurried out ahead of the bride and groom snapping pictures as they emerged from the sandstone arched entrance.

Angie and Luke appeared looking a picture of delight as they were showered with rice-paper confetti. The photographer organised the family and wedding groups and shot traditional poses before allowing the happy couple to escape to the wedding car that would take them to the reception.

Angie stopped on the kerb and turned away from those gathered behind her and she tossed her bridal bouquet into the air that was caught by a stunned Steve, the barman from The Dog and Duck. He fumbled with the flowers and flipped them from his hands. The flowers landed at Vanda's feet. Bemused she picked them up and tried to return them to Steve who protested, "Oh no, not for me. I don't intend to get wed for a long time. I don't even have a girlfriend."

A young woman who had been eyeing Steve smiled shyly and stepped forward. She spoke to Vanda, "I'll take them if you don't want them. It's a sign of good fortune. Besides, they're beautiful."

Vanda passed the flowers to the guest. "Here, take them. Good luck."

Steve who had watched the interchange moved to the woman's side and they began to talk. Adam smiled knowingly and nodded at Vanda. They had begun to make their way towards the car when a police car rolled up outside the church.

Vance alighted and alerted Adam, "Adam! A word."

Adam and Vanda stopped, and Vance hurried across. His voice was hushed but he spoke with urgency, "Adam, we've got another." Vanda and Adam exchanged looks. "That groundsman you talked to…"

"Kenneth?"

"That's the one."

"What about him?"

"He's dead."

"What? How?" exclaimed Vanda interrupting.

"That's the mystery. That's why I need your help, again."

AUTHOR THANKS

MANY THANKS FOR READING THE first of the *Adam Barrie paranormal investigations*. If you have a little time, I would appreciate a review. I really value my readers' thoughts about a book. It often helps me craft future stories. They are vital for indie authors like me.

You are welcome to contact me at elizabethrevill@protonmail.com or visit the website: www.elizabethrevill.com

****

I have free stories for you as well, all I'd like in exchange is your email address and you can unsubscribe at any time.

The first is called *Dead or Alive* just follow the link.

I'd like to keep in touch. Either via the newsletter, I'll send out once a month, or you can join my Facebook page: Elizabeth Revill. If you join either, there will be notifications of new stories, releases of covers and the occasional giveaway and special deals just for you. There will also be an opportunity to join my *Advanced Reader Team*.

ACKNOWLEDGEMENTS

I would also like to thank my commissioning editor and mentor Sarah Luddington and her team at Mirador. Sarah is a tower of strength to me; my terrific proof reader Jeff Jones who works very hard to get everything right. My son, Ben Fielder who helps me with all my newsletters and my husband Andrew Spear who encourages me to write and supports me.

OTHER TITLES BY ELIZABETH REVILL

DCI Allison Thrillers:

Killing me Softly

Prayer for the Dying

God Only Knows

Would I Lie To You?

Windows For The Dead

Dead Eyes Opened

Mother's Not Dead

Llewellyn Family Saga:

Whispers on the Wind

Shadows on the Moon

Rainbows in the Clouds

Thunder in the Sun

The Adam Barrie Paranormal Investigations:

The House at Black Head Ridge

Against the Tide

Turn of the Tide

The Electra Conspiracy Part 1
The Electra Conspiracy Part 2

Stand Alone Novels:
Sanjukta and the Box of Souls
The Forsaken And The Damned
Web of Fear
The Dreamtime of the Artful Dodger with Norman Eshley

Children's book
And an illustrated children's book *The Secret of Gidon*

www.ingramcontent.com/pod-product-compliance
Lightning Source LLC
Chambersburg PA
CBHW031224260626
47169CB00007B/2177